THE SUN & THE MOON
THE HILL & THE WELL

MICHAEL SMITH

Published in 1997 by House of Isis Publications
PO Box 64
Stourport on Severn, Worcestershire. DY13 OYR

Copyright © Michael Smith 1997
All Rights Reserved

ISBN: 0 9530469 0 7

Produced in Great Britain by:
'E' Tech
Tel: (01299) 879219

Special Thanks:

To James Boyle for the countless hours he spent reading and amending the manuscript, Lawrence Lynch for help with the final edit, and David Taylor for his appreciated help and advice; including the preparation of art-work for the front cover.

Special warm thanks to Jackie; for her teaching and guidance in those early days.

Acknowledgements:

In alphabetical order, thanks to: James Boyle, Brian Ellison, Simon Fraser-Clark, James Griffiths, Paul Griffiths, Tracey Irvine, Lawrence Lynch, Sue Newlands, the other Mike Smith, Dave Taylor, Trudie, Ian Waldron, Chris Whale & Chris Wright.

To Trudie, Daniella & Hollie.
For all they have endured.

May the magic that flows betwixt us, do so forever more.

Contents

Preface vii

The Awakening ix

1   Three Swords 1
2   First Stirrings 8
3   Initial Contact 12
4   The Magic Of Baydon 24
5   The Lady In White 27
6   The Significance Of 1947 40
7   The Holy Qabalah 49
8   The Serpent And 1947 54
9   New Beginnings 62
10   The Hilltop Meditations 68
11   The Plot Thickens 80
12   In The Sanctuary Of The Well 89
13   St Kenelm's Church 95
14   The Legend Of St Kenelm 101
15   The Crone 112
16   The Winter Solstice 119
17   The Golden Arrow Of Sabrina 127
18   Saturn, Old Father Time 139
19   The Temple Of The Sun 146
20   The Rollright Stones 155
21   Meon Hill 163
22   The Hill & The Well 168
23   The Puzzle Of Sabrina 172
24   Final Preparations 177
25   The Guardian 180
26   Healing The Land 191

Notes/Bibliography 201

Postscript 207

Index 210

Preface

The collection of events portrayed within the pages of *The Sun & The Moon, The Hill & The Well*, occurred between the spring of 1993, and 1st May 1994, forming the backdrop to a series of affairs which are in every sense true. The material presented within this text, has been written largely from a personal belief point of view, having been amassed from a comprehensive and detailed collection of original notes and micro cassette recordings. The work itself, contains a cross-section of ideas inspired from a collective combination of emotional feelings, intuitive dreams, local legends, psychic material, and the never ending quest for truth. My objectives, were to carefully collate, synthesise, and finally supplement this data, with information cited from selected sources - credited where appropriate, in order to provide an explanation to the perplexing enigma of *The Sun & The Moon, The Hill & The Well*.

In a time where many believe that science, history and religion, seemingly fail to provide us with answers to the countless unsolved enigmas which continue to surround us, more and more people find themselves turning towards the esoteric/magical arts, in order to procure insight into these often perplexing aspects of our lives. This was exactly the avenue that I chose to adopt when faced with the Baydon/Kenelm scenario. The countless visualisations and investigations, which occurred during the above period, produced a consortium of subjective results; information which included a host of what can only be termed as apparent psychic information. This material, I can assure you, the reader, has been faithfully recorded within the pages of *The Sun & The Moon, The Hill & The Well*, written as it *actually* occurred.

With regards to the collection of conversations accounted within the text, these have been substantially condensed, and where convenient, checked by each individual, subsequently facilitating the task of recording them.

Whilst writing this work, it was never my intention to attempt verification of anything from either a scientific or theological standpoint. Moreover, I do feel that certain aspects of this material will help elucidate Baydon Hill - a Midlands based prehistoric hill-fort, and consequently, offer new sentiment in relation to the holy well situated in St Kenelm's Church, Romsley, Clent; hidden deep within the picturesque countryside of the Heart of England.

At no point during the preparation of this manuscript, has there been any attempt to embellish any of the acquired data, in order to align it with personal theories held during that period of my life. Lastly, and most importantly, the one thing that I do ask of you, the reader, is that before you arrive at your conclusions, you consider this work with a clear, open mind.

Author's Note
Out of respect for the custodian of the land, and in the interests of maintaining the sanctity of the hill featured centrally in this account, the true identity of this sacred site has been withheld. For the purpose of this story, the hill has been prefixed 'Baydon'. Associated locations have also been renamed accordingly. This does not however, in any way, negate the truth of this account.

Mike Smith
May Eve 1997

Prologue

The Awakening

Monday, 10th May, 1993. Heavy rain lashed relentlessly against the walls and windows of the 19th century town house. Darkness encroached, and still the howling winds battered the old willow tree, as it cowered beneath the thunderous elemental force that ravaged the rear gardens. A flash of burning light flooded the semi-darkened room; overpowering the shimmering candles, slashing through the whirling mists of pungent incense.

Within their mind's eye, the ring of pulsating white light surreptitiously constrained the four shrouded figures. Safe they were; secure and protected, amidst the vast current of brilliance that ebbed amongst them. Focusing their thoughts, the travellers stepped forward, each entering the sphere of the eternal; that great abyss that gathered before them. Darkness prevailed within the realm of shadows. This time their voyage had truly begun. This time the spirit of life was free.

From beyond the domain of darkness, a figure emerged; an entity of both space and time; a being of blinding light. The anomalous form, dressed in simple white cloth and bearing the sword and shield of a warrior, approached the travellers. It was time to lead them beyond the perimeter of dreams. It was the time of their awakening.

Before them, lying proudly amidst a cloud-laden skyline, stood a single majestic hill; a green and grassy precipice, a holy site, where once an abundant forest had reigned. Led by their guide, the travellers found themselves positioned conveniently around the base of the hill. Dense hedgerows encircled the grounds of the sacred site, barring their immediate entrance; defending an eternity of enigmatic truths.

Why had they been drawn to such a place, the travellers

inquired. What's more, what were they likely to gain from such a visit?

The prophet of light appeared before them, sword raised uppermost.

"This is the land of our fathers," the anomalous form announced in a deep sonorous tone.

"As herald, it is my duty to protect the gateway of the threshold."

An overwhelming sense of silence prevailed. The travellers patiently awaited further communication. The candles flickered to and fro, casting ghostly images, invigorated amidst the dense veil of acrid incense that saturated the darkened room.

Inevitably the silence broke.

"Only the pure of heart can possess the keys to the gateway," the entity proclaimed. "Others have come before you, yet all have failed. Believe only with a pure heart, and you will find your true destiny - that narrow pathway which leads us all on towards the eternal."

A thunderous force struck the house, filling the room with brilliant white light. The windows burst open, leaving the curtains billowing, as the gale force gust of wind extinguished the candles that crudely lit the room.

Solemn moments passed as the house settled back to normality, as did the perception of the travellers. The images faded into memory.

The hill awoke....[1]

Chapter 1
Three Swords

Tuesday, 6th July, 1993. A single golden ray of sunshine, burst unexpectedly through the picturesque window of the sitting room. Sitting back, sinking into the delightful comforts of the soft cushioned armchair, I watched as a myriad dust particles danced freely, to and fro, illuminated by the miracle of dazzling light.

Outside, the gentle perfumes of wild flowers growing frantically in the garden, wafted secretly, silently, in through the lead paned glass of the crooked bay window; filling the room, encompassing it, invigorating it amidst that all too familiar scent and sense of the onset of another prosaic British summer. Out beyond the confines of the sitting room, yet well within the boundaries of the overgrown garden, the soporific sound of a bumble-bee could be heard, humming aimlessly, undisturbed, hidden deep amongst the wild flowers which encircled this historic country house. Hanging from the oak beamed ceiling, a sea shell mobile gently jingled, as the soft, warm summer breeze, furtively took its quorum of pearly shells, and pleasantly made its presence felt.

Gradually, almost intuitively, I became aware of an overwhelming sensation; a feeling suggesting that the cottage was crying out in pleasure, as its ancient withering timbers, creaked and cracked amidst the gentle early morning warmth of the new born summer sun. This was a truly wonderful place, a peaceful place, such a happy place I thought, as I slowly cast my welcoming eyes around the beam-clad walls of our 17th century Cornish holiday cottage.

Returning my attention to the inspiring view of the gardens, I could hear the relaxing chorus of singing coastal birds, as they filled the cloudless, clear blue morning sky. It was 5.00am. I

The Sun & The Moon, The Hill & The Well

closed my eyes. It was time to continue with my morning meditation. I was finally at peace.

Opening my tiresome eyes, I looked up. The hypnotic sound of the small wall mounted pendulum clock, registered 7.30am. Sadly, this idyllic scenario had all but ended for another day, as our tranquil cottage burst into life, succoured amidst the frenetic hustle and bustle of Daniella and Hollie, our two little girls.

The refreshing aroma of home ground coffee infused the morning air, as my wife Trudie, called out to the girls, settling them, and hurrying them along with their breakfasts. The prospect of our forthcoming family adventure to the quaint historic coastal village, Tintagel, had no doubt excited them.

We had been informed that Tintagel, or Trevena, to coin its original name, was a pleasant, petite community, positioned overlooking the Atlantic Ocean, and situated equidistant between Camelford and Port-Issac, Northern Cornwall. What's more, Tintagel was situated approximately one hour from Perranporth; the coastal village in which we were staying.

According to popular belief, Tintagel is considered to be an important key placement in relation to certain aspects of the alleged Arthurian Romances. Within local legend, we were soon to discover that the mythical King Arthur was said to have been both conceived and born within the confines of Tintagel castle. Tradition testifies that the castle, built on the remains of an earlier monastic settlement, was the romantic setting of King Uther Pendragon's deception of Ygerna, the wife of Gorlois, Earl of Cornwall. The legend attests that Uther Pendragon called upon the magical assistance of Merlin, his wizard, requesting access in to the coastal fortress by assuming the guise of Ygerna's husband. Once inside the castle, it is said that Uther Pendragon impregnated Ygerna.[1]

The legend resumes, stating that Ygerna gave birth to a boy child, who, under the guidance and protection of Merlin, grew into a virtuous warrior, and became known to all as the chimerical King Arthur.

The focal point of the village is the castle ruins, which stand proud on a resplendent arrangement of rugged barren cliffs, and overlook and enhance the power of the Atlantic Ocean. Common

Three Swords

belief implies that the ancient ruins appear bathed in a countenance of enigmatic legend and timeless romance. In fact, it is customary for the ghosts of Arthur and his Knights in shining armour, to be seen drifting soundlessly, eerily, amongst the desolate remnants of this most distinguished Cornish castle. Beneath the crumbling cliff-top structure, lies a legendary cavern, a hideaway where it is purported that on certain days, that the ghost of Merlin - or Myrddin, to use the Welsh form of his name, can be seen walking silently, secretly, magically amidst the thundering surf which breaks across the threshold of what the locals have aptly titled, Merlin's Cave.[2]

Local Historians believe that the castle remains are those of a royal Castle, a structure built by Reginald of Cornwall during 1141, and with further developments being implemented by Richard, the son of Henry III, sometime during the late 13th and 14th centuries.

Tintagel, as we were soon to discover, was a thriving cottage industry; a village brimming to capacity with a host of Arthurian related craft shops, bookshops, public houses, and even Arthurian titled car parks. This unfortunate evidence compelled me to conclude that the legend of King Arthur had been completely exploited. Nevertheless, amidst the vast wealth of historical culture emanating from within the village, there were three buildings with which we felt an immediate affinity.

Firstly, there was the Old Post Office, a mid 14th century structure situated amongst the heart of the high street. Research revealed that the village had seemingly grown up around this early building, presumably having been a manor house in those bygone days.

Second on our proposed visiting list, was St Materiana's Church, a Christian shrine positioned slightly west of Tintagel Head, and accessed via a single coastal road which led across from the perimeter of the village. Our information suggested that St Materiana's Church, was a Norman structure, which dated back to the later part of the 5th century.[3]

Our final place of interest had to be King Arthur's Great Hall of Chivalry, a vast neo-gothic building, where, during 1988, and under seemingly mysterious circumstances, a ceremonial short sword was uncovered. In many respects, the discovery of the

3

The Sun & The Moon, The Hill & The Well

weapon had been the catalyst that had instigated our subsequent visit to Tintagel.[4]

King Arthur's Great Hall, was built by Frederick Thomas Glasscock, who, in 1928 and upon his retirement, had decided to open a specialist shop in the village, focusing primarily upon reviving the geomythical memory of King Arthur and his associated legends, in particular, those relating to Tintagel's past.

On its completion in 1933, King Arthur's Great Hall exhibited a superb and fascinating collection of some of the world's finest stained glass windows - seventy-three detailed scenes in total, each depicting various aspects of the legendary quest for the Holy Grail and the symbolism of Chivalry.[5]

It seemed only too right that the village should be classified as a natural centre from which the Arthurian current should radiate. The castle and Arthur's Great Hall, suitably personified his birthplace, acting as a kind of focal point into which the thoughts and beliefs of all people could turn, and thereby enabling King Arthur's ideals to become a living force once again.[6]

Closing the cottage door behind me, I opened the side door of our Fiesta and got into the car. Trudie and the girls were already sitting in the rear seats, with Chris Whale, a close family friend who had joined us on our summer vacation, sitting up-front. A light, refreshing, summer breeze brushed effortlessly around my face. I gazed outwardly towards the rolling breaker waves that crashed against the nearby shoreline. Sitting there with the early morning summer breeze blowing gently in through the open door of the car, I felt myself begin to drift off.

Thought provoking images, triggered by a semblance of how the sea looked that day, filled my elated consciousness. Commodious feelings of being perceptibly led along an avenue of unadulterated light, slowly descended upon me. The reflection of the sun cast a glistening image of pure gold across the multifaceted mirror like surface of the sea that day. Reality returned.

The engine roared into life as we began the forty-mile coastal journey that was to lead us to Tintagel. Chris indicated, and we left the main Newquay road, heading north along the assiduous A30. With the summer sun reflecting across her face, Trudie

Three Swords

reached forward from the rear of the car and offered us both an eclair. We'll soon be there, I thought, as I eagerly unwrapped the chocolate eclair and popped it into my mouth. Changing gear, Chris eased off the accelerator and entered the busy A39.

For a comparatively small coastal village, Tintagel appeared relatively busy as we slowly drove through it, fruitlessly seeking somewhere to park. As Chris carefully manoeuvred the car along the bustling high street, he finally exclaimed that at last he had located a car park displaying vacant space. Sadly though, this, like so many other places in Tintagel, was complete with its unfortunate Arthurian pre-fix.

With the vehicle successfully parked, we ambled out of the car. A keen local parking attendant, suddenly descended upon us, requesting the customary toll necessary for our short stay upon King Arthur's Car Park. Reluctantly, we paid the tariff, wondering if such a high levy had ever been bestowed upon the legendary Arthur, or for that matter, any of his trusty followers?

Our first port of call was King Arthur's Book Shop. The small window display at the front end of the main shop, was just as I had come to expect; filled to the brim with every conceivable Arthurian artefact. We walked in through the front of the shop, pausing briefly to listen to the calm and relaxing sounds of new-age music, as it lightly filled the summer air.

Leaving the peaceful surroundings of the shop behind, we headed up along the busy high street. Never before had I experienced anything quite like this, I concluded. Everything was either King Arthur this, King Arthur that, or simply King Arthur the other! Even the usual collection of pubs and restaurants, which adorned the busy main street, were there, trying to tempt an easily pleased tourist with its enticing selection of Arthurian oddments. I looked towards Trudie - she knew exactly what I was thinking. Lovingly, I took hold of her arm and we continued our stroll. Chris looked at his watch, it was late afternoon and time for us to begin heading towards the car. I turned towards Chris, it was obvious that he was anxious for us to beat the rush hour traffic.

Walking along the high street, the girls decided that they each wanted a plastic sword, something to commemorate their short visit to the antiquated village. Daniella called out. She was the first to notice the curious looking craft shop positioned directly to

The Sun & The Moon, The Hill & The Well

our right.

"Daddy! Daddy!" she cried out.

"Daddy look! That shop has got lots of big swords in its window. Do you think we could both have one, please?"

Smiling, Trudie turned around. Like myself, she realised that we would have to take a brief look inside, otherwise, we would never hear the end of it! Peering in through its main front window, and hoping to recognise what Daniella had obviously seen, to my total surprise lay a fine selection of broadswords, each crafted in the Arthurian tradition, and presented with a list of fanciful names, comprising of Excalibur, Lancelot and Merlin.

My attention turned towards the two girls. Poor Daniella had sincerely believed that the swords displayed in the shop window, were toys, playthings made of plastic. I laughed to myself, overcome by a strong inner feeling proposing that I would simply have to buy one. Looking at Trudie, I suddenly realised that she too had experienced a similar inclination. After ten minutes of intense deliberation, we made the somewhat rash decision of purchasing all three, thereby giving us the complete and collectable triad of Excalibur, Lancelot, and Merlin. Chris watched dumbfounded, he simply failed to believe what was happening; two seemingly level headed people - with no obvious interest in medieval weaponry, about to 'blow' a vast proportion of their holiday savings on a collection of well-crafted, but seemingly useless artefacts. I had to admit though, that we too were struck by the spontaneity of our actions.

Leaving the confines of the craft shop behind, we scrupulously carried our extravagant purchases along the crowded high street, heading in the direction of the car park. Sauntering along, Hollie noticed the enticing collection of brightly coloured plastic swords hanging up outside King Arthur's Book Shop. She smiled, prompting me to buy them each a plastic sword.

Having carefully packed away our new acquisitions, Chris remarked that as we were obviously interested in the Arthurian Legends - of which we were not at that time, then had we realised that back home in the heart of the industrial West Midlands, an apparent connection with the mythical story of King Arthur had recently been made. It appeared from the conversation, that seated within the sleepy Worcestershire village of Woodleigh, situated

Three Swords

some five miles out of our hometown Kidderminster. An Iron Age hill-fort namely Baydon Hill, had, over recent years, become the focal point of public interest. Chris informed us that the alleged history of the hill, did appear in some peculiar way, to be evidently connected with the mythical legends of King Arthur. Concluding, Chris mentioned that as we were both so obviously unaware of the where-a-bouts and mythical history of Baydon Hill, despite its rather close proximity. Then surely, on one of our free Sunday afternoons, we should take a relaxing stroll over it, in order for us to formulate our own conclusions as to the validity of this enchanting local tale.

Dreamily I looked towards Tintagel Head. Once again my thoughts filled with the magical images of Arthur, Merlin, and the Knights of the round table. But nevertheless, unbeknown to us, it would appear that Tintagel had somehow acted as a kind of nodal point, and was destined to shape the course of events throughout the forthcoming twelve months. Chris started the car and we reluctantly left King Arthur's Car Park.

Chapter 2

First Stirrings

Sunday, 10th October, 1993. Dipping a digestive biscuit into my piping hot cup of tea, I looked affectionately across the kitchen towards Trudie. Prevalent, vivid memories of our former summer vacation, slowly began to intoxicate my consciousness. Arduous as it had been to concur, we were unfortunately, once more well and truly entrenched amidst the customary cycle of day to day family life. With her hands covered in pastry, Trudie called out. The screaming of the telephone shattered the serenity.

"Mike, could you get that please?"

Images of our Cornish summer holiday, flickered and faded. Acknowledging her, I walked through the lounge and on into the dining room. Sam, our four month old border collie, accompanied me, barking and yapping all the way.

Lifting up the receiver, I was somewhat surprised to hear the distinct Black Country accent of our old friend, Chris Whale.

"Mike," he said in his rather excited style, "I haven't heard from either you or Trudie for quite a while, so I thought that it was about time that I gave you a quick bell."

I replied, offering him my humble apologies and explaining just how busy we had both been of late. He laughed.

"Well listen here, do you remember the visit to Tintagel? You know, the time when you purchased those swords?"

I certainly had not forgotten such a memorable occasion, I thought.

"Do you remember me mentioning about a visit to that hill?" said Chris, "You know - the one associated with King Arthur."

"Baydon Hill?" I queried.

"Yeah," he announced. "Well, as the weather seems fairly okay, maybe we should go and treat ourselves to that promised walk."

8

First Stirrings

I pondered the possibility of an afternoon adventure, informing Chris that I would just go and check with Trudie and the girls, to see if they were all keen on the idea.

Calling across to Trudie, who incidentally was still busy in the kitchen, I checked whether the prospect of a brisk, effervescent walk to the top of Baydon Hill appealed to her. It certainly did. The final arrangements were made, and it was agreed that Chris would arrive at the house at around half past two that afternoon.

Replacing the hand set, I casually walked back into the kitchen after informing the girls of our planned afternoon adventure.

Having finished lunch, Trudie politely reminded me of the time. It was 2.30pm, and Chris would be here anytime. Running through into the dining room, Daniella assumed the position of group look out. There she stood, patiently looking out of the window, eagerly awaiting the arrival of our lift. As Chris pulled up in his blue Ford Fiesta, Daniella dutifully informed us. Hurriedly, the four of us began putting on our boots and winter coats, preparing ourselves for the possibility of inclement weather. We left the house and clambered into Chris's car, and within minutes, the short journey from Kidderminster had begun, heading out towards Woodleigh, home to Baydon Hill.

Reaching Marsham Lane[1] situated off the A492[2] heading out towards Hasbury Grove, Chris slowed down and pulled up at the base of the hill-fort. Apprehensively, I looked up. The prospect of an arduous walk up onto the summit of the ancient hill, certainly appeared daunting.

The brick built folly standing dictatorial upon the antiquated hilltop, was one of the first landmarks of any particular interest, designated to divert our attention. I gazed up at the hill, as the folly cast an elongated shadow in the soft autumn sunshine, an image which stretched across the fields below. Positioned as I was, I was able to liken this semblance to that of an immense medieval lance, a symbolic needle held high above the windswept grassy slopes which encircled the prosaic monument.

I stepped out of the car and felt the cool autumn air brush effortlessly across my face. An analogy was formed, a parallel linking these new feelings with those experienced prior to our

The Sun & The Moon, The Hill & The Well

memorable visit to Tintagel, earlier that year. I continued staring out towards the desolate hill, an uncanny feeling began to stir, a subtle affinity maybe? But whatever it was, I felt as though I was initiating some kind of link with the hill, becoming part of its shrouded destiny. Furthermore, for some unknown reason, I began to sense that over subsequent weeks, the hill was to become a significant place for me, a place which I was to visit frequently, and a place where I felt I belonged.

The strenuous walk up to the summit of Baydon Hill, was certainly a tiring one. Persistent rain over the past few days had over saturated the already moist earth, making the task of reaching the peak, seem almost an impossibility.

Daniella and Hollie, walking just a few feet ahead, squealed with joy as the water clogged grass sent cold clumps of thick mud, squelching over the sides of their red wellington boots. Desperately trying to avoid a large pool of murky water, I realised that at last, we had finally reached the pinnacle of the hill.

Positioned directly before us stood the crumbling Georgian folly. It looked so unusual, so alien, so totally out of place. Scattered randomly around the crumbling foundations of the 18th century building, and lying half hidden amongst the dense undergrowth which covered the ancient hill, lay a large selection of bricks, blocks and other debris, which, over recent years, had become dislodged from the main edifice and consequently lay dispersed within the fenced off perimeter of the hill.

Investigating the monument, we noticed a collection of warning signs, perspicacious reminders of the dangers presently inherent within the crumbling Georgian folly. I found it hard to understand the possible reasons as to why such an impressive structure, had seemingly been allowed to fall into such a state of disrepair.

Slowly my concentration began to wane. Positioned alongside the folly, it appeared that the hill-fort played host to yet another startling, dare I say, eccentric looking building. Calling across to Trudie and Chris, I drew their attention to this secondary structure.

With the girls running up ahead, the three of us began the slow walk through the moist uncut grass, heading towards the confines of the curious looking brick built edifice. Turning

First Stirrings

around, I decided to take one final look at the folly, believing that with the afternoon sunshine shining directly behind it, I might be able to take at least one decent photograph of it in all its glory. Positioning the 35mm camera, I wound on the film and gently squeezed the shutter release.

"Mike!" Trudie called out. I quickly turned towards her; she had already felt the first few drops of the imminent rain. Collecting Daniella and Hollie, the five of us made a hasty descent of the hill, heading towards the protection and comforts of the car. We clambered inside the vehicle without a moment to spare, and the autumn downpour finally began. Listening to the hypnotic sounds of falling rain hitting the roof of the car, I agreed that it certainly had been an interesting afternoon. Eventually, Chris fired up the engine and we pulled away from Marsham Lane, leaving behind the magic and enigmatic mysteries of Baydon Hill.

Chapter 3
Initial Contact

Tuesday, 12th October, 1993. The bitter cold October winds howled angrily, as I looked out into the darkened garden from behind the safety of the lounge window. It was 7.30pm, and the fierce gales to which we had been subjected throughout the course of the past week, had risen to an unsavoury peak. Within the garden, the wailing winds were tossing around an array of leaves, twigs, and other debris, which had lay strewn upon the lawn, and was hurling them against the rear of the house with a vengeance. Suddenly, a loud violent cracking sound caught my attention. The dogs both jumped up with a start, obviously disturbed by the disposition of wintry sounds existent within the confines of the garden.

Deciding to investigate the matter, I switched on my hand torch and cautiously began the walk down the darkened pathway that traversed the length of the garden. I found it difficult to focus my eyes in so little light. The howling winds appeared to taunt me, scream out at me, lurch at me from within the nightmarish images of the surrounding trees. As the glare from the torch illuminated each contorted branch that moved aside the screeching winds, I began to realise the full impact that the storm had heralded across the entire garden. Devastation prevailed, but even so, I still needed to know what the source of the strange explosive noise had been. Armed only with my torch, I continued my search; scouring the contents of the rear garden.

Something stood before me. The beam cast from the torch outlined a peculiar alien like form. With a start, I instantly established what the source of the unpleasant noise had been. It was the old weeping willow, the tree that had ruled the far end of the garden for as long as I could recall. There it lay in the half-

Initial Contact

light, split in two, groaning to the cacophonic accompaniment of the cruel wailing winds, its dismal, deathly remains, spread violently across the sodden uncut grass. It had borne the full brunt of the storm that night, and sadly, was to be no more.

It had been extremely difficult, trying to settle and reassure the girls at bedtime that evening. Somehow, they both seemed evidently concerned at the prospect of the gale-force winds somehow inducing nightmares. Trudie, talking quietly to the girls, agreed to read them one final chapter of Beauty and the Beast. They loved that story so much, I concluded, listening to Trudie relaying the final chapter to them. I just hoped that those last few pages would encourage them to drift off to sleep.

Since our relaxing walk over Baydon Hill, earlier that week, I had become distinctly aware of the undeniable, and increasing difficulty I was experiencing, in concentrating and focusing my energies upon the mundane events which governed my life. After talking this through with Trudie, I was somewhat surprised to discover that she had also been experiencing similar problems. What was going on? We both were in need of answers, and it was time for us to find out.

With the children both fast asleep, we quickly agreed upon the belief, that perhaps our best course of action would possibly lie in the completion of a brief meditational exercise, a visualisation using Baydon Hill as a kind of focal point for the operation. We had arrived at this conclusion, as this had been the only place of any particular interest of which we had both visited during the course of the previous few days. Consequently, it appeared that for some reason or another, the hill was intrinsically linked with the peculiarities that we were currently experiencing. So, by conducting this meditational procedure, we believed that we might elucidate some of the many haunting thoughts to which we had both been subjected throughout the duration of the previous few days.

The relentless winds were still wailing outside as Trudie drew the lounge curtains and sat down in readiness to begin. Three lightly perfumed candles, sitting upon the pine fire surround, sent ghostly images dancing around the heavily textured, artex ceiling. Around us, the subtle smell of incense gently filled the darkened room. The stage was set and we were ready to begin.

The Sun & The Moon, The Hill & The Well

The operation that we had selected, originated with a slow and gentle descent into a state of complete and total relaxation. Once in this primary state, our objective was to then introduce a commonly termed practice, a procedure known collectively as creative visualisation. Basically, this technique is a form of meditation involving the use of stimuli in order to achieve dream like experiences. A commonly used formula utilised by many in this field, is to simply imagine that an individual, or group, are undergoing some form of mental magical journey; a pilgrimage of self discovery; an expedition to investigate the uncharted regions of ones own personal psyche. This approach frequently results in periods of personal breakthroughs, many of which, both Trudie and myself had encountered during the past. The stimulus that we had chosen for the forthcoming exercise, involved the use of a mental recollection of the enjoyable walk across Baydon Hill, undertaken earlier that week. With the ticking of the clock slowly fading away, reality made way for dream.

Darkness surrounded me, as I tried to walk inconspicuously past the dense thicket of trees which stood before me. Looking out towards the silhouette of the monolith, I began to realise just how different everything looked. Vivid, chivalrous images of the legendary King Arthur flashed radiantly across my mind's eye. Yet these I knew to be illusions; vague representations prompted by my own conscious expectations. I began to feel myself drifting into a deeper state of relaxation. A falling sensation overwhelmed my body as I gently slipped into a state of undiminished calm. Those erroneous Arthurian illusions seemed to quickly recede, leaving me totally alone on top of the antiquated hill.

Within my mind, a cognisant thought began to form. Something suggested I should turn around. I knew that there was something out there. I could perceive it. I could feel something calling out to me. I tried to focus my eyes onto the anomalous apparition that was lurking within the dense blackness. Whatever, or whoever it was, had seemingly emanated from within the immediate domain of the trees. Moving slowly towards the thicket of obscured trees, I became aware of an orange sphere of vibrant light, hovering four to five feet above ground level. Cautiously, I approached the entity, half expecting it to vanish before my eyes.

Initial Contact

Unsure whether it was real or just mere fantasy, I continued staring upon it. The sphere of resonant light remained perfectly still, changing in colour periodically, between hues of golden yellow and a deep rich orange.

For five minutes the amorphous object positioned itself before me, inducing me to feel that somehow, it had been trying to transmit some kind of cryptic message. Slowly the anomaly began losing vigour; visibly fading away.

Walking slowly towards the folly, I perceived what appeared to be a mixed collection of concentric wheels of dark reddish-grey and white light, hovering just above ground level, and looking like an impenetrable mist that surrounded the base of the secondary hill upon which the monolith had been placed. I watched in awe, as the ethereal circles of light rose up from the ground and positioned themselves level with the apex of the folly. Eight tentacles of light emanated from the epicentre of the circle, radiating out across the open landscape. I felt that this anomaly, in one sense, indicated the past presence of some form of religious energy centre.[1]

I opened my eyes to find the lounge plunged into blackness. The candles had long since expired, and an eerie sensation transgressed the room. Turning my attention to Trudie, I saw that she was still in a deep and sedate phase of relaxation. Picking up the pencil and pad which had been left ready to record our thoughts, I wrote out a detailed account of my encounter, concluding with the hypothesis, that at some stage during the history of the hill, Baydon Hill must have played host to some form of prehistoric energy matrix, therefore making it an important pre-Christian religious site.

Trudie opened her eyes. She picked up the dictaphone and began to record the results of her own meditation, speaking softly into to the portable tape recorder which she clasped tightly in her hand. She described the feeling of an irresistible magnetic field, a sensation from which she had found it increasingly difficult to break free. Trudie explained that this energy field, had seemingly emanated from within close proximity to the crumbling Georgian folly.

Upon receipt of this inaugural information, it became obvious

The Sun & The Moon, The Hill & The Well

that a series of further meditations would have to occur, a practice which we hoped, would shed some light on the growing accretion of data that we had already acquired. What our intentions were regarding this exuberant data, at this stage, seemed somewhat insignificant. However, it appeared to me, that perhaps our best course of action would be to merely sit back and wait to see whether we were to be privy to any further contact.

Distant thoughts of our Cornish holiday flashed vividly across my mind. The three mounted broadswords, affixed to the rear wall of the lounge, caught my attention. I couldn't help but smile, as I realised that had we not purchased the swords that hot summers day, then who knows, perhaps we would never have had cause to visit Baydon Hill, and therefore, would not have availed ourselves of the current data. Talking aloud, I realised just how absurd it all sounded. It appeared that successive late nights were beginning to take their toll.

Friday, 15th October, 1993. Friday evening marked the end of a rather prolonged and very busy week at work. It was great to be back home, I thought, as I walked through into the lounge and opened a chilled can of Banks's. Sitting down to relax, I began to contemplate the varied events of the previous week. What's more, I was certainly pleased that the bout of inclement weather had finally relented. But in the wake of the storm lay an immense trail of devastation; a pathway which could easily be paralleled in many respects, to those experienced during the memorable storms of '87.

Earlier that evening, Trudie had suggested that perhaps we should consider conducting the second of our proposed Baydon meditations. It had been the best part of a week since our initial visit there; nevertheless, those obsessive memories still invaded our every waking thought. I must admit though, it certainly seemed odd that we should still be encountering the impress of our recent visit to the hill, as to my knowledge, there appeared to be no logical reason for this occurrence.

Looking at my watch, I realised that it had been a good hour since the girls had retired to bed. All was quiet. Secretly hoping that by this stage they were both fast asleep, Trudie crept upstairs to ensure all was well, leaving me to set the scene for our

Initial Contact

proposed visualisation.

Placing the porcelain charcoal burner precariously on top of the fireplace, I walked over to the hi-fi unit and switched on the C.D. player. Wafts of incense gradually infused the air, as the hypnotic sounds of Tangerine Dream gently filled the room. Lucy, our eight-year-old black Labrador, caught one sniff of the aromatic incense and promptly made an exit for the kitchen! Although she had experienced countless similar situations with us over the years, it appeared that this one was just a little too much. Carefully, I positioned a couple of candles alongside the smouldering incense. Igniting them, I sat down in preparation, ready to initiate the meditation.

Darkness encroached, as a single point of white light appeared between us. Growing in size, the magical sphere slowly engulfed us, bathing us in a protective sphere of divine light. The circle was cast.

Walking out across familiar sunny slopes, Trudie realised that she was standing on top of Baydon Hill. Around her, the strong, enchanting fragrance of spring, gently filled the air. The graceful sounds of countless birds echoed around the slopes of the ancient hill. Suddenly, her life appeared brighter, more wholesome. The haunted darkness, which encompassed agonising memories of a childhood lost in time, quickly faded within the boundaries of this surreal world. Here was a world of uncharted trust; a kingdom that was as impeccable as snow. Here was a realm where Trudie could be alone, detached, and finally at peace. Here was her conduit of desire.

But no sooner had she orientated herself to these familiar surroundings, than she found herself placed within an alien environment, a region that she had never seen or visited before.

Positioned before her lay two fairly large pools of murky green water. A shallow grassy hollow housed the larger of the two, being positioned in such a way that it appeared to be on a much lower ground level than that of the first. From within the larger pool, Trudie perceived an accumulation of rings and ripples of light, each radiating out from the centre of the body of water.

Intuitively, she began to move her consciousness across the vision that had formed within her mind's eye. Positioned

The Sun & The Moon, The Hill & The Well

alongside the larger pool, was what could only be described as a medieval stylised Sun-face. It was a well formed and yet relatively plain looking face, but complete with a wide beaming smile and an overwhelming sense of timelessness. Trudie frantically tried to preserve this image whilst concentrating upon its eccentric qualities. She needed to know more. It was imperative to understand what it meant. Yet she knew that it was important to her, and fully recognised that this image could herald important clues. Reluctantly, she eventually broke contact with her ocular imagery. Its dream-like representations began to fade away. Darkness reigned once more.[2]

Opening her eyes, Trudie began to recall the experiences of her visual encounter. She picked up the pocket dictaphone and began to narrate her thoughts onto tape. But little did she realise the consequences which these images would herald. Trudie had unknowingly touched upon a matter that was to be of paramount importance, later within in the quest. Furthermore, these, like so many other intuitive thoughts collected during that period, were to be initially overlooked.

Listening with intense interest to what she had to say, allowed me the time to reflect upon the vivid images of my own encounter. Gradually, her soft distant voice slowly faded.

The rolling mists began to clear. Hundreds of bluebells covered the ground that lay before me. The onset of spring was finally here. Having been led to within close proximity of the Georgian folly, I found myself formulating a hypothesis. I began to realise that this was one of a selection of sites that had been, or was somehow, still connected on a perspicacious level with other locations of some such similar nature.

A vivid sequence of colourful images flooded my thoughts, as I became aware of an important festival occurring here upon the hill. Knowingly, I realised that the concept projected by these images, seemed to insinuate that it was a May Day celebration; a time of merriment in which the whole of Baydon Hill had been used as a beacon site. But what did it all mean?

Within my mind's eye, I tried to locate the enigmatic sphere of orange light, that anomalous feeling which had endeavoured to

Initial Contact

communicate with me during my initial visit to the hill. I was alone. It was no-where to be found. Allowing my thoughts to wander, I began to sense a voice calling out to me, a growing inner feeling welling up inside. Something was trying to make me aware of a problem, a localised instability.

Reality returned, and I found Trudie sitting quietly, patiently awaiting my return. However, no sooner had she realised that my eyes were in fact open, than she suddenly began to relate a sequence of events pertaining to her own visual experience, yet its curious contents captivated my attention.

Since meeting Trudie, I have always respected her intuitive thoughts, knowing full well that she, like myself, remains quite sceptical about the quality of information that we apparently perceive. Trudie, like countless other people, including myself, requires a convincing amount of hard fact, or proof, before accepting carte blanche anything which could be construed as out of the ordinary. This belief, we both firmly agree, heralded a healthy approach towards the type of new age perspective to which we were playing host.

The material with which Trudie now presented me, was certainly no exception to our age-old rule. She simply believed that the information was probably nothing more than pure fantasy. Unquestionably, the media presumed that all psychic or intuitive information could surely hold no tangible basis, nothing could really be ascertained from this kind of controversial material; or could it?

So what was different in this particular case? Could it be that there really was some kind of interaction occurring between Baydon Hill and our two minds? What's more, it was blatantly obvious that a lot more research would be needed before we could produce reliable answers to each specific experience. Only the test of time would tell.

Sitting quietly, contemplating the possibilities that our link with Baydon might produce, I realised just how naive we had been, believing that an elementary exercise would rid us of the troublesome thoughts that we were encountering. Instead, it transpired that what we had actually accomplished, was to simply accelerate the conspicuous involvement that we were experiencing, regarding the ancient site in question. Staring at Trudie, I realised that her new information had caused me even more confusion. I couldn't stop speculating on these events. Could it be that she really was onto something? I simply couldn't be sure.

A silver shower of moonlight penetrated the darkness, illuminating the lounge with its ethereal glow. I sat cross-legged in the half-moonlight, pondering Trudie's deliberations. Was I so wrong to believe that there really could be some deep significance in the succession of events that we had been encountering? Would it be wise to assume that perhaps there really was some kind of external intelligence interacting with our minds? However, I concluded that once again, I really did not know. Naturally, everything pointed to the fact that we were imagining far too much; merely constructing something out of nothing. But a momentary juxtaposition of the situation, revealed that we were really facing a collection of circumstances, which painted a somewhat different similitude. These, and countless other suppositions, needed immediate answers, explanations that could set our troubled minds to rest, once and for all.

During the course of subsequent visualisations, more information was perceived; the most significant result being, that some item apparently connected with the folly was about to reveal itself. In a peculiar way, I guess that it was correct to imply that it seemed as if we were embarking upon the start of a mystical adventure! Instantly, unrestrained images of the mythical Jason and his lengthy quest for the Golden Fleece, flooded my elated thoughts. But casting these allusions aside momentarily, if something was actually occurring, then what were its objectives, and why did it appear that we were personifying a part in its inherent outcome?

After much deliberation, we made the joint decision that for the time being at least, situation permitting, we would act merely as a compilation point for the increasing array of information, and proceeding further, only if and when we deemed it necessary. To be perfectly honest, I doubt very much whether either of us truly believed that there could be any truth in the notion that external intelligences were lurking behind our bizarre visualisations. But nevertheless, that belief was soon to be transformed by the results

Initial Contact

which were to be procured over the forthcoming weeks. A change was set to occur, a metamorphosis that would have a deep and profound effect upon us both.

Before we advance further forward with the developing issues put forth in this account, it is worth designating a little time to consider the association and embodiment of psychic information. I felt that by including a brief resume' of the many recurrent examples that this grey, or evidently borderland aspect of what I have come to summarise as 'contemporary experimental science' exhibited, then hopefully, we might perceive its accuracy in certain instances.

Today, as we hurtle towards the millennium, an increasing number of level headed individuals, are finally beginning to accept that the human race, on average, uses only a modest proportion of the immeasurable possibilities that our brain has to offer. This situation leads us to the obvious conclusion that our understanding of the human mind is woefully inadequate. Time and time again, we can cite countless occasions in which the human mind has demonstrated idiosyncrasies, peculiarities that seemingly contravene any conceivable, logical explanation; many of which have been, and continue to be recorded, each in the vague hope that one-day, further more detailed investigations will rightly occur.

For example, our ancestral archives embody numerous illustrations indicative of these 'alien-like qualities'. But in the past, those anomalous characteristics, would have been deemed as being of esoteric or supernatural origin. Today, however, we see a different picture forming, in that the scientific and extraneous study of psychic phenomena, comes to us under the colourful guise of parapsychology.

By studying the physiology of the human brain, we discover that it is divided into two halves, the right and left sides respectively. These areas are known as hemispheres, each gathering information in exactly the same way, but processing it in two entirely different ways. Medical science informs us, that the left-hand hemisphere of the brain, is the region responsible for the intricate process of logical thinking, including analysis, mathematics, languages, verbal skills, and science. Attributed to the right hand province, is the wide and varied field of the arts;

including music, inventiveness, imagination and fantasy.

Through the use and subsequent development of the right hand hemisphere, we are able to perceive intuitively, a host of events that to many, may well appear chimerical, or existent purely within the mind's eye. Here, we discover that by honing our intuition, and in so doing, opening up direct channels to our subconscious mind, we will often consummate greater insight, encouraging us to recall events that may well be real, despite being previously unknown to us.

Within the growing field of parapsychology, one distinctive area appears to dominate the rest. This particular dominion, has been given the curious title psychometry, a term whose definition literally means, the divination of information relating to an object from contact with it. This delineation can be substantially expanded upon, to include the belief that in certain situations, psychometry lends itself to a tenet where an individual or group can successfully interact and gain knowledge - otherwise unknown to them, about an object, person, or place, simply by mental attunement and concentration alone. Throughout history, this ambiguous subject has often been linked with various concepts pertaining to inspiration and intuition.

My own interpretation and application of psychometry, has often yielded incontestable results too numerous to mention within the confines of this text, yet have included a host of place, person and object psychometry. Of a further note, it is also worth mentioning that over recent years, the interaction of psychics and dowsers around archaeological excavations, has often aided in the discovery of previously unknown relevant information, factual data concerning the past history of the site in question.[3]

One event which curiously springs to mind, is the alleged tale of a past curator of a notable Egyptian gallery. The story suggests that certain insights into the complex religious history of ancient Egypt, were obtained from information insinuated by a six-year-old schoolgirl. Apparently, whilst visiting the gallery, it is said that she encountered a short fall on one of the many rows of steps which lead into the exhibition hall. The anecdote asserts that the girl sustained no serious injuries, but that upon her entrance into the Egyptian gallery, she suddenly believed that she could communicate with the ancient statues that reside therein. From all

Initial Contact

accounts, and assuming that there is an element of truth in the tale, it would appear that the information that she received, helped formulate the essence to many breakthroughs within the field of the curator's work. Furthermore, the young girl in question is said to have never previously displayed these somewhat magical qualities. Shortly after the incident, the young girl arrived at the uncanny conclusion that she had at one time lived the troublesome life of a peasant girl, residing in ancient Egypt.

This fascinating account reaches its conclusion, as we consider the work of the curator. At present, he is said to be one of only a handful of people who appear to have shed this much insight into the complex workings of ancient Egypt.

Perhaps most people will naturally attribute this account to the boundaries of pure coincidence. But likewise, this could be perceived as a brilliant demonstration of object psychometry. So it would appear that once an initial belief in psychometry has been procured, then the results which are obtained thereafter, frequently go far beyond the boundaries of logical, normal day to day coincidence.

Chapter 4
The Magic Of Baydon

Business within the shop was well and truly on the increase, and the usual pre-Christmas rush had finally begun. Sitting down at my cluttered desk, swallowing a mouthful of lukewarm tea, I suddenly realised just how engrossed I had become, contemplating and evaluating my research in respect of Baydon Hill. So much so, that I had almost forgotten about the ever encroaching pleonastic festive season.

Casually glancing up at the wall mounted clock, I took note of the time. It was exactly twelve thirty. The shop had quietened down considerably over the past forty minutes, allowing me enough time to consume a mouthful of cheese and onion sandwich, and then contemplate the many thoughts that surrounded me.

Once again the growing saga of Baydon Hill took precedence. Nevertheless, it was obvious that for our experiments to gain any validity, the most significant element to date concerned the need for us to learn something of the history of the hill, the accepted antiquity of Baydon Hill and its associated area. The local library seemed the most obvious and likely port of call in my efforts to elucidate the situation. With regards to the hill, the only fact that we possessed, was that locally, it was perceived that some correlation between the geomythical history of King Arthur and Baydon, had somehow come into existence. Clearly, we needed to be in possession of something more than mere magical myth. We were in need of pure fact, actuality that could validate the contents of our bizarre experiments. As far as I was concerned, without this data, our efforts could be judged as nothing more than mere fantasy.

The information that we required, arrived unexpectedly via a

The Magic Of Baydon

close friend. He had become aware of our rather sudden and keen interest in Baydon Hill, and after reading a specially commissioned article concerning the site, contacted us and kindly forwarded a copy of the article for our perusal.[1]

The report which he kindly donated, had appeared in a local earth mysteries magazine, and had attempted to outline both the hill and its immediate surroundings. The report proved to be a fascinating thesis, and answered many of our preliminary questions. The document, written by a local lady, Joyce Newley,[2] demonstrated her overwhelming passion for the ancient hill, and portrayed her empathic affinity with the surroundings of the site. The contents of the report were superb, emphasising the somewhat elusive history of Baydon, along with a selection of the more commonly known allegories of which it had been associated. This illustrious information couldn't have arrived at a better time, I concluded, as I re-viewed the contents of the report. It was just what we needed.

Baydon Hill and its Iron Age fort, is situated on the borderland of the West Midlands and Hereford and Worcester, and can be dated back to an epoch well within the Mesolithic period.

The fort, commanding a position of great strength at the north-west end of the Clent Hills, lies geologically upon a triple fault-line; standing upon the borderland between the Severn and the Trent valley.

Within the ramparts of the hill-fort, lie 28 ancient yew trees. These trees it would seem, have been dated, with the oldest example originating from the conjectural time of the proposed Arthurian Romances. Extensive archaeological and historical research by local historian/archaeologist, Graham Georgiadis[3], leaves us with the notion that Baydon Hill *could* in fact be the proposed site of King Arthur's Battle, Mons Badonicus. Georgiadis also suggests in his research, the distinct possibility that the hill could also be the reputed burial site of the legendary Arthur.

On the northern slopes of the hill, are placed a proliferation of mounds, which many believe include ancient burial sites. At present, this tentative information requires verification. It is also of notable interest, that a beacon site is positioned within the fields to the north-east, where it is suggested that Celtic field systems exist.

The arrival of the 1700s heralded the construction of many follies within the Woodleigh estates, with the most impressive of these structures being the Palace of Minos. This temple structure represents a remarkable, yet miniature version of the Athens based Hephaestion, and personifies an elegant example of classical architecture - Doric in nature.[4] The present oratory, is courteously dedicated to Hephaestus, the alleged son of Zeus, blacksmith to the gods, and husband of Aphrodite.

Indigenous history attests that the hill can be successfully dated to around 250 BC, the period generally perceived as the time when the Celts first began building their forts. Without doubt, Baydon Hill would have retained special interest for the Celts, since its defences were well fortified, this being due to the natural terrain upon which it was constructed. Popular belief suggests that these fort-building warriors were of the tribe of Cornovil.

There is also plenty of evidence, to suggest that Baydon Hill was occupied by the Druids, and could have conceivably acted as a Druid burial ground. In support of this theory, is the undeniable fact that the yew tree heavily populates the hill; a tree which for time immemorial has been sacred to the practice of Druidism. It is interesting to note however, that a comparable grove of yew trees, situated deep within Norbury Woods, Mickleton, is collectively known as Druids Grove.

Chapter 5
The Lady In White

November was upon us and the nights were drawing in fast. The weather in Kidderminster had already started to fluctuate quite considerably, enough at least for us to have already experienced the first autumn frost, as it played havoc dancing around the remaining plants that still embellished our overgrown garden. Once more it was time to prepare ourselves, resigning to the fact that the onset of another winter season had arrived.

The flourishing collection of affairs relating to what we, by that stage, had termed as the Baydon scenario, appeared to be continually on the increase. A dim glimmer of light shone perplexingly amongst the darkness which infringed upon those formative ideals, odd inklings and fragments of information, steadily began to disburden themselves on our ever developing portrayal of the hill, creating a veritable cornucopia of topics for discussion throughout those ever darkening, cold wintry nights. Logic testified that a series of subsequent meditations were destined to transpire. Trudie proposed an enticing concept. She believed that we should conduct a sequence of late night meditations, the prime consideration being, that they should actually occur on the summit of Baydon Hill.

As the wintry nights successively drew in, I perceived that things were about to change. Our beliefs suggested that the growing portfolio of material, would soon take on a fresh direction towards its inevitable destiny.

10am, Tuesday, 2nd November. Simon, a customer and close friend called into the shop. We had grown to know each other fairly well over the two-year period since we had met. I suppose the thing that first intrigued me about Simon, was his interesting demeanour, a poise that elevated him well above the average clientele who patronised the shop. It quickly emerged that he was a research scientist, a glaciologist to be precise, deeply involved in the rather complex and fascinating study of the geological actions of ice. As the two of us conversed that day, I suddenly realised that we shared, amongst other analogous interests, an avid fascination towards paranormal phenomena. Never before had we discussed such borderland topics. Things appeared distinctly different that Tuesday morning as we deliberated on our rather subjective conceptions of the paranormal.

Simon zipped up his ski-jacket in readiness to leave. Something was occurring between the pair of us. It was as though a succession of peculiar synchronicities were falling into place. He paused momentarily, before informing me of an event that was taking place in central London, a conference which he assured me, would be of mutual interest.

The seminar to which Simon had referred, was a Psychic Questing Conference. A congress due to be staged during the weekend of the 6th and 7th of November. He informed me that the event was dedicated exclusively to the curious practice of psychic questing. In fact it was to be the fifth Psychic Questing Conference to date; it being an annual event directed specifically towards enhancement of the general awareness and understanding of the incredible feats performed by psychics.

Author, Andrew Collins, when defining psychic questing, states that questing is where the psychic is taken out of the stereotypical seance room and into the open landscape. Visionary experiences, powerful mystical dreams, supernatural encounters, the retrieval of concealed artefacts, and other, more clandestine activities, blend together to form this fast-growing occupation.[1] Psychic questing, has often been successful in unravelling and explaining many hitherto enigmatic historical anomalies, and has often participated in successfully counter-balancing certain malpractice's relating to the black arts.[2]

It was Andrew Collins and fellow psychical researcher, Graham Phillips, who, in the late '70's, decided to revolutionise peoples attitudes towards psychic abilities. Instead of striving to prove the existence of paranormal abilities, as had been the case during the past hundred years, Collins and Phillips took the lateral

The Lady In White

step of accepting its existence. With this alternative approach, and the exciting results which transpired, it emerged that unbeknown to them, they had initiated the modern revival in psychic questing.[3]

It seems likely that throughout recorded history, supernatural quests have existed in one form or another. For example, during 1425, the popular anecdote of Joan of Arc, appears to appropriately embody such practices. It is said that Joan, during frequent visits to her local church, often experienced anomalous visions. These intuitive prophecies were perceived in the form of clairaudiance; a term widely used to indicate the apparent presence of some form of external voice, as heard by a psychic or visionary.

As a result of these bizarre visions, Joan of Arc came to the conclusion that God had instructed her to help save France from the invading English. The anomalous voices which had infiltrated her consciousness, also informed her that the sword she was to use for this task, was to be discovered hidden behind the altar at the chapel of Fierbois, dedicated to St Catherine.[4]

As an analogy to this tale, we could do well by considering the case of Joseph Smith, the founder of the Mormon faith. We hear that in 1880, Joseph Smith, who was by then a well-established dowser, made contact with the Angelic Entities Mormon and Moroni. Smith, it appears, was instructed by astral entities to retrieve a collection of golden texts; documents which he would discover hidden upon the highest hill-top. The enigmatic texts, summarised the homeric past of the Nephites; the first civilisation who had reputedly colonised ancient Northern America. Strangely, the mysterious scripts which he was later to find, claimed direct descent from the archaic Hebrews.

Smith was contacted again, once he had located the enigmatic texts, where he was instructed not to retrieve the sacred documents until a period of four years had elapsed. At such time, he was to redeem the texts wearing a breastplate constructed under angelic direction, which, he was informed, would act as a means of protection.

Classical mythology purports that on numerous occasions, great and powerful warriors were reputedly led by external intelligences - the gods, in order to reveal concealed weapons of immense power. Examples of the questing phenomena are even evident amidst early Christian Tradition. Here, we discover numerous accounts of devout pilgrims being guided under the premise of a vision, a sort of devotional calling, enabling them to uncover holy relics that often included prized saintly remains.[5]

On a contemporary level, authors, Andrew Collins and researcher Graham Phillips, were, during the fading months of 1979, guided under the apparent supervision of an external intelligence to a secluded Worcestershire pool. Once there, and under the protective cover of darkness. Collins and Phillips mysteriously recovered a ceremonial short sword, which featured the personal monogram of Mary Queen of Scots. The recovery of the sword, subsequently led to the paranormal retrieval of a mystical jewel - a green talismanic stone, which allegedly dated back to the enigmatic time of the Egyptian pharaohs.[6]

It would appear therefore, that the current revival in psychic questing could in one sense, be considered as a form of urban shamanism, with the questing conference acting as an annual celebration of this revival.

This was exactly what I had been looking for, I concluded, a weekend conference dedicated to the art and practice of psychic phenomena. I had to be there. So, with the pending convention in mind, I contacted an old friend, Ian Waldron, who, likewise, shared a deep and enthusiastic interest in the mysteries.

Saturday, 6th November, 1993. It was an early start for Ian and myself that cold Saturday morning. The Taxi had been pre-booked, leaving Kidderminster at 6am sharp, thereby allowing us to make the necessary connection with the seven o'clock, Birmingham to Euston inter-city train.

Arriving at New Street Station, we boarded the busy inter-city train, and settled ourselves for the proposed two-hour journey into the industrious British Capital. Within minutes, I found myself drifting off into a deep and relaxed state of sleep. It appeared that the early morning start had obviously caught up with me.

I felt cold and totally alone as I walked aimlessly around the summit of Baydon Hill; my head filled with haunting recollections of our first visit. There were so many questions that sought

The Lady In White

answers, so many potential possibilities. I needed to know more, I wanted to know more, I fought desperately to keep my eyes open, but it was no use...[7]

The conference room was packed to capacity when we arrived. It was so good to be amongst similar minded people, I thought, taking out the micro-cassette recorder and switching it into record mode. Hastily checking through the contents of the busy programme, we settled ourselves down for what promised to be an interesting, and equally thought provoking event.

Essex man, Richard Ward, gave the first address of the day. Nervously Richard began his lecture, outlining a recent quest which he had undertaken, spurred on by the apparent psychic retrieval of a strange artefact found hidden inside a stone circle on the Isle of Purbeck. Upon retrieval of the artefact, Richard realised that the apparent purpose of his quest, was to initiate a series of cleansing meditations at various ritualistic sites, which covered the open landscape. It was his belief, that these particular locations had seemingly become entangled in a conglomeration of dubious magical activities.

Rolling images of Baydon Hill raced gracefully through my consciousness, as the softly spoken words of Richard Ward drifted gently off into the distance.

Blue skies ensnared me as I approached the sacred precipice. A thick spiralling mist surrounded the base of the monolith as I looked up into the clear blue morning sky. From within the band of mist, eight tentacles of light stretched out across the open landscape...

The thunderous sound of clapping awoke me. I opened my eyes to catch Richard Ward leaving the stage. Once again my thoughts drifted towards Baydon, as a series of crystal clear images formed before me. What the hell was going on? I cursed. Why on earth should images of Baydon Hill invade my thoughts today? Why today?

After a short and well earned coffee break, it was time once again for the lectures to re-commence. John Horrigan was next on the bill, providing us with an interesting and entertaining lecture,

The Sun & The Moon, The Hill & The Well

based principally around the ill-conceived interactions with supposed guardian intelligences. These intelligences John explained, were thought forms believed by many to inhabit the web of ancient power sites, which are said to cover Britain. He focused his address primarily; on the disastrous results which can often occur when individuals or groups encounter such entities, quoting countless examples from his own growing list of experiences.

One o'clock signalled the end of the morning lectures. This gave Ian and myself the necessary chance to locate and check-in to the Ruskin Hotel, the lodge which we had booked for our overnight stay. 1.45pm arrived, and we headed towards the conference hall. Andrew Collins, the event organiser, was next on the platform, and talking to a capacity crowd. He delivered an enticing lecture that afternoon, dealing essentially with the nature and relevance of what he has come to term as 'black questing', an expression used to denote the psychic cleansing of ritual sites following alleged suspect activities, including the somewhat controversial issue of paranormal artefact retrieval.

We left the conference theatre, making our way slowly towards the Ruskin Hotel. It had certainly been a long and tiring day, and we were both looking forward to a good nights sleep. Sitting on the edge of the bed, I realised that the combination of an early start and the days events, were slowly beginning to take their toll. I found it increasingly more difficult to simply keep my eyes open. So, after a quick shower and a swift glass of orange juice, I decided that an early night would be my best course of action. Laying my head down on the soft crisp white pillow, my thoughts immediately drifted back towards Trudie and the girls.

I closed my tired eyes as the constant drone of busy traffic gently faded into the background; leading me away into the secret realm of dreams.

A dense, silver grey mist slowly began to engulf me. I felt overcome by a heightened perception, a sensation that gently passed throughout my entire quintessence.

Was I asleep and experiencing some kind of vivid dream? I wondered. Cautiously, I opened my eyes and slowly focused them on my watch. It registered 12.39am.

Looking around, I began to sense that something, or someone,

The Lady In White

had entered the room. I could still feel its electrical presence around me. Within seconds, I realised that whatever it was, had appeared to be situated only a few inches away from my face. I tried hard to focus my tired eyes upon the darkness that encompassed me, yet failed to perceive anything of any consequence.

Laying my head on the soft warm pillow, my heart began to pound intensively. Nervously I closed my eyes and attempted to fall asleep. Instantly, the transfiguration of a woman blinded my thoughts, she had been trying to communicate with me, and was in some way or another connected with the personification of water.

I awoke, recalling how I had seen the entity moving gracefully across the darkened room, bathed in a veil of silver white light. I sat upright in bed, and recalled how she had positioned herself close to my face, causing me to awaken. I focused my weary eyes, realising that it would appear that I had in fact caught a brief fleeting image of an angelic form; an entity of light which had instantly faded away.

Prior to my awakening, I recalled becoming aware of a soft breeze brushing lightly across my face. That was it! I thought, the window was obviously open. I jumped up out of the bed and dashed towards the window. It was securely closed. But nevertheless, I knew I had felt a breeze brushing up against my face, and it was most certainly not my imagination. So what was it? Reaching into my hold-all, my fingers nervously caught hold of a pen and some paper. I had to write down a journal of the strange encounter. I knew that it was important.

It took a good twenty minutes to write out an accurate account of the feelings that I had experienced. But as I put pen to paper, I still found it virtually impossible to fully come to terms with the encounter that I had evidently experienced. Feeling tired and uneasy, I gently closed my eyes and fell foul to the ever-tightening grip of sleep. A cloak of eternal blackness gripped me tightly amidst the warmth of its darkened wings. I was at rest once more, relaxed and on the threshold of infinity; at peace with the eternal sandman.

Sunday, 7th November, 1993. Sensitising and cautiously focusing

The Sun & The Moon, The Hill & The Well

my eyes to the alien surroundings of the hotel room into which I had awoken, I slowly began to recollect the peculiar events of the previous night. I became fully aware of a vivid memory prompting and flashing throughout the strata of my consciousness, and then recalling the contents of the unusual dream; remembering how peculiar it had been. The dream-like experience had left a series of impressions with me that were so strong, so unlike the kind of dream to which I had become accustomed, that, to my way of thinking, indicated the authenticity of the encounter.

Reaching out, stretching my fingers over the right hand side of the single bed, I picked up the note pad that I had used to record the experiences referring to the uncanny dream. I began reading through the pages of scribbled text, hoping to find a logical explanation to the occurrences of the previous night. Something felt distinctly odd about the situation, but, whichever way I considered it, I had no option other than to resort to the fact that there was no suitable explanation. Whatever it was that I had experienced, I had obviously failed to realise its potential significance.

Crunching on a slice of slightly burnt toast, I decided to recount my experience to Ian. Who knows, I thought, perhaps he had encountered a similar experience? Ian poured out two cups of coffee as I briefly broached the subject. However, it was obvious from his bewildered expression that he had been oblivious to the strange visitation that I had experienced.

Leaving the amenities and ardour of the Ruskin Hotel behind, we made our way into Museum Street. The second day of the questing conference, was to be centred principally on a guided tour of both the Egyptian and Greek rooms housed within the British Museum. By all accounts, it promised to be a real treat.

Ian looked at his watch. The lectures were not due to start for well over an hour. With time on our hands, we decided to visit the wonderful Egyptian shop that we had stumbled upon during our search for the Ruskin Hotel. Entering through the quaint doorway of the corner shop, I recalled countless images of the many Cornish craft shops which Trudie and I had visited during our summer trip to Tintagel. I smiled. No doubt she would have loved this place, I thought, allowing my eyes to peruse the vast array of

The Lady In White

Egyptian memorabilia that was out on display.

The centre of the shop housed a rather enticing selection of glass display cases, each playing host to some different aspect of the Egyptian pantheon. Looking into one of the smaller display cases, I caught sight of two miniature figurines; the notorious god Thoth in his baboon form, and Amoun Ra, the Egyptian Solar God. I simply knew that I would have to buy them. Ian drew my attention to the fact that it was two o'clock, and time to make our way towards the Museum.

Large groups of people were waiting on the Museum forecourt, when we finally arrived. With the initial introductions out of the way, we were all informed that the proposed lectures were destined to assume the rather curious form of a magical guided tour, an adventure which comprised of a lavish combination of address and guided visualisation.

The organisers had arranged for us all to congregate inside the Egyptian Galleries; standing amidst the eerie selection of ancient statues that adorned the walls of the British Museum. Enthusiastically, the group stood amongst the huge stone statues of the Egyptian Goddess Sekhmet, silently awaiting the start of the meditation. The event co-ordinators had advised the group, that should we witness anything which we believed to be of importance during the meditations, then we were to make a mental note of any such occurrences. The group slowly calmed themselves. It had been decided that we were to undertake a series of loosely guided visualisations, each centring on the three granite statues of the Goddess Sekhmet.

A serene sense of calm radiated from within, as the minutes passed and the supine words of the meditation reverberated softly, peacefully, evocatively in and around the tranquillity that prevailed within the Egyptian Gallery. The occasional extraneous collection of mumbled words, uttered by a passing guide, broke the silence, voices ricocheting back and forth across the mirror-like surfaces, present on the collection of ancient statues.

Closing my eyes and allowing myself to gently enter a sedate state of relaxation, I inevitably became engulfed amidst the spell created by the hypnotic pulse and the soothing rhythm of the spoken visualisation. A sudden rush of adrenaline raced frantically around my body as an immense cone of light slowly encircled me.

The Sun & The Moon, The Hill & The Well

Suddenly, I was plunged into total darkness, impenetrable blackness that swallowed the essence of life itself. Mentally, I struggled to hold on to my consciousness; staying contrite, preparing myself in readiness for the forthcoming adventure. I wanted to open my eyes. I needed to open my eyes. I wanted...

An intense raging fire penetrated the depths of my consciousness. Feeling it s purifying power upon my body, I struggled to resist. But it was useless, the benevolent force had overwhelmed me, and I inevitably lost consciousness.

In due time, I realised that the spiritual fire worked like a cosmic key; a sort of channel that could open up and reveal the hidden initiation that would lead me towards the many mysteries of the Goddess Sekhmet. I cried out in pain as I willed the radiant image of the goddess to configure herself over me, thereby creating a kind of ubiquitous funeral mask.

Residing within the centre of the iridescent void, was a likeness of myself, a semblance of my inner self; an icon of the real me. Somehow, I must have projected a portion of my vital life force into this living form of the goddess, I concluded. Images of immense power flashed vividly throughout my overwhelmed mind. Before me stood Sekhmet. I looked directly into her eyes and watched in horror, as a thousand universes crumbled beneath the apocalyptic might of her spoken name. She began to move. An intense white heat radiated towards me, as the power and eminence of her piercing eyes made contact with mine.

Tight within her raised right hand, she held forth a shimmering white Anch, the Egyptian symbol of everlasting life. Calling out to her, I volunteered my name. She smiled in recognition, holding aloft the divine key of life. Silently, I reached out to take hold of it as a stream of golden letters were released from some secret quarter lying deep within her torso. 1947! 1947! 1947! Went the message. The year is 1947! The year is 1947! The message concluded, repeating itself over and over while a series of monochrome images formed and accompanied this seemingly meaningless communication. What on earth did it mean?

After what felt like an eternity, the image of the goddess slowly began to dissolve. Her message was complete and her time was no more. A scattering of background noises emanating from

The Lady In White

within the museum, suddenly invaded my thoughts. Contact was broken. I was back amongst the living.

I must admit though, that I was a little surprised upon opening my eyes to find that the visualisation was only just drawing to a close. For a moment, I seriously thought that I might have been the only member of the group still standing in front of the three stone statues of Sekhmet. However, it was time to move on.

Slowly, the group made its way out of the Egyptian rooms and headed towards the Greek galleries. The second of the proposed meditations, was scheduled to occur amongst the commodious range of Greek temple furnishings that resided within the British Museum.

As the remaining members of the party eventually entered the exhibition room, the process of relaxation was instigated. I began by invoking my traditional deep breathing technique, a procedure that I had carefully refined, and a technique which had often yielded excellent results.

Andrew Collins, the event co-ordinator, proceeded with the meditation. He informed us, that by using the various artefacts adorning the walls and floors of the Greek gallery, using them as mental prompts, we were to visually climb up an imaginary mountain. Once astride this illusory precipice, the basic directive was for us to try and make contact with any anomalous intelligences which we believed might have accompanied us on our astral journey.

The group finally settled themselves, as the mesmeric resonance of the spoken meditation induced an ever-increasing state of sentience.

A tremendous hill stood before me. A green and grassy precipice, on top of which stood a traditional Greek temple. A reassuring voice propelled from within, intuitively informed me that I must climb the hill. I had to approach the shrine; it held no dangers for me.

I began the long and arduous climb that was to position me adjacent to the holy oratory. Having reached the uppermost point, I stood perfectly still, perusing the immense plateau that lay before me. Across the prairie, looking towards the Temple, I could see a huge golden crucible placed within the decorous confines of

The Sun & The Moon, The Hill & The Well

the holy structure. The burning midday sun reflected off the golden dome, casting fingers of light, which radiated across the plateau. Within the huge crucible, a fire raged uncontrollably. I could feel its warmth, its mesmerising passion. But I knew that I must enter the temple.

A bizarre sensation began to rush across my torso as I entered the sacred building. I hesitated, taking note of the alien feelings which encircled me.

Cautiously, I began to walk towards the crucible. The tingling sensation which I had experienced just moments earlier, suddenly became much stronger. A low-pitched humming noise began to slowly emanate from within the ground. Four raging winds suddenly rose up from within the depths of the holy temple, wailing violently, screeching from each of its cardinal points. I looked up. The temple stood before me.

Forcefully, the malevolent winds began to form an immense circle of power. Round and round they went, rising high up above the temple structure to form a gigantic cone of energy. I walked into the holy site, safe in the knowledge that nothing could invade my sphere of perception, especially whilst the alliance of power continued to circle around the sacred structure.

The seven walls of the temple flashed in hues of green azure, as I neared the golden dome. Strange archaic symbols covered the floor, flashing vibrantly with each step that I took. A woman dressed in a veil of brilliant white manifested before me, her hair the colour of the darkest night. She raised her head. Her eyes were the Sun and the Moon. But who was she? I thought. What was she?

Using an elementary vocal technique, I summoned her.

'What is your name?' I said, projecting each syllable forcibly towards her. Silence prevailed. I repeated the inquisition. Still there was no reply. Once again I repeated my question, enquiring whether she held a message for me.

Finally, the spectral form spoke.

"My name is not for you," she announced in an almost hypnotic tone, "it is not necessary at this time for you to know my name," she added. "But look towards the cupboard for your answer. It's behind the cupboard."

The radiant intelligence repeated the curious message as she

The Lady In White

turned to leave the temple.

"What is your name?" I implored.

With this final request, the entity turned around.

"Remember, remember, it's behind the cupboard! It's behind the cupboard!"

The spectral form turned away and left the temple of light. The resplendent images of my curious pilgrimage quickly began to fade. Darkness returned, as once again my consciousness flooded back.

Chapter 6
The Significance of 1947

The conference was at an end. It had been an interesting and enjoyable couple of days. However, centred at the forefront of my mind was the tedious train journey home; home to the heart of the bustling West Midlands. Climbing aboard the busy 4.30pm Euston to Birmingham inter-city train, the ineffable effects of a hectic weekend finally began to take their toll. Moments after I had settled down, the packed locomotive pulled away from the crowded platform, lulling me gently into a deep and relaxing sleep.

Zipping up my jacket and rubbing my smoke filled sleepy eyes, I stepped onto the foggy Kidderminster platform, succumbing to the fact that it was time to begin the short walk home.

It was freezing cold as I left the confines of the station, and to make matters worse, an impervious fog accompanied me as I quickly made my way through the dimly lit local park. Orange sodium streetlights, strategically positioned alongside the narrow pathway that snaked in and around the darkened park, played havoc with my imagination. Spurious anomalous shapes appeared from the cover of the trees; apparitions which governed the night, momentarily revealing themselves, all but hidden within the dense blanket of autumn fog. Reassurance was at hand nevertheless; home was just a matter of minutes away. Calming memories of the conference suddenly flashed across my thoughts, as I quietly walked along the stone paved pathway that led to the front of the house.

Turning the key in the front door, I warmed to the welcoming barks of Sam and Lucy. It was good to be back home, I thought, as I gave Trudie a loving peck on the cheek.

The Significance of 1947

"The girls are still awake," she explained, as I removed my coat and walked into the warmth of the lounge. "They've been trying to stay awake," she said, "so that you could wish them goodnight, when you got back."

Climbing the creaky wooden staircase that led up to the children's bedrooms, I instantly became aware of how excited they had become. Childhood recollections of my own father returning home from a night shift, flashed radiantly across the memories that were imprinted in my own mind. Crossing the hallway, I walked through into Hollie's room. Excitably, she jumped up and ran across her room to greet me. She looked into my eyes. She was so excited she could hardly speak. Catching her breath, she heralded an extraordinary remark.

"Daddy! Daddy! Daddy!" she cried out. "There's a giant behind the cupboard! *It's behind the cupboard!* Daddy! Daddy! Daddy! There's a giant, *it's behind the cupboard, it's behind the cupboard!*" Hollie paused to regain her breath. My head began to throb. Vivid memories of the conference flashed radiantly through my thoughts. Those extraordinary results, spurred on by the museum meditation, suddenly began to reappear within the cognisant area of my mind, induced by my three-year-old's peculiar remark. Eventually, I wished her goodnight, trying hard to reassure her that there were no giants anymore.

Walking across the hallway into Daniella's room, I suddenly began to feel faint. My vision was becoming blurred as a loud buzzing sound clawed violently at my tired body. I grappled for the stair-rail. I desperately needed to sit down. *It's behind the cupboard! It's behind the cupboard!* A vivid image of the Greek galleries slowly began to form within my mind's eye.

"What the hell's going on," I muttered, as I sank effortlessly to my knees.

Trudie called out from the bottom of the stairs. "Mike, are you okay?"

Mentally, I repeated the question. I had to know what was going on.

A worrying thought instantly began to crystallise. What was it that was supposedly behind the cupboard? What on earth did it mean? But more importantly, how could Hollie, my three-year-old daughter, possibly have known what had happened to me during

The Sun & The Moon, The Hill & The Well

that remarkable visualisation within the British Museum earlier that day? I needed answers. It was obvious that something was definitely out of place, but what?

After finally pulling myself together, and after wishing Daniella goodnight, I decided that it was time to relay the series of events, including Hollie's odd welcoming remark, to Trudie.

In retrospect, I thoroughly realise how absurd it must seem to submit the following notion, but to deny it would be to simply contravene my involvement with the story. Would it be so wrong, so unscientific, to propose that if Hollie had not unveiled that bizarre reference to her *'cupboard'* back in November '93, then the collection of subsequent events would surely never have occurred. I guess in many respects, it would be easy to merely dismiss the situation as yet another demonstration of coincidence, but equally, it could also be described as what is commonly termed as an act of synchronicity - a Jungian psychological term used to express an apparent act of coincidence, which seemingly occurs to prove a specific point, or subsequent series of events.

Sitting next to Trudie amidst the warmth and quietness of the darkened lounge, my tired mind began to wander. I could perceive it recalling and scrupulously analysing the curious information pertaining to 1947, including the stranger declaration regarding *'the cupboard'* - both annotations gaining access to the conscious aspect of my troubled thoughts, due to Hollie's welcoming act of synchronicity.

I looked across at Trudie and commented on how tired she was looking. It was quite late, and we both needed to be up fairly early the following morning; we succumbed to the fact that it was clearly time for bed.

I tried to relax. Sleep seemed impossible. Anomalous, alien images of all shapes and sizes, constantly tried to invade the deep reticent areas of my conscious mind. My thoughts were swimming, 1947! 1947! 1947! 1947! Turning and cascading, rising and falling, over and over looped the numerical sequence. Opening my tired eyes, I cast my attention towards the radio alarm. It registered 2.30am. What was wrong with me? I just couldn't get to sleep. Closing my tired heavy eyes, I made one final attempt to fall asleep.

The Significance of 1947

1947! 1947! 1947! 1947! 1947! It had to mean something to me, but what?

It was dark in the forest. Running frantically through the dense undergrowth, I desperately clawed a pathway forward. The foliage encroached and cut deeply into my face, as I audaciously attempted to make my way to the safety of the river and the added custody of the grassy clearing. But why was I panting? And what's more, why was I travelling so close to the ground?

My whole being felt invigorated, I could sense crowds of people behind me, screaming people, shouting people, each armed with torches that flickered in and out of the copious area of trees. Stopping momentarily to turn around, I realised that the hunters were in fact chasing me! But why were they after me? What was it that I had supposedly done? I simply couldn't remember.

Feeling myself tiring, I knew that I would have to stop. It was useless to run, but if I stopped, I knew that they would surely be on top of me, and that, as far as I could see, would mean certain death.

An icy cold chill cut through my body as I suddenly realised the objectives which lay behind the chase. I had my answer. My hands and arms were covered in blood! Warm blood! Collections of archaic symbols decorated my arms and chest. 1947! 1947! 1947! The numerical sequence shattered the tense, wry atmosphere, which surrounded me. My whole being was ready to explode. 1947! 1947! 1947! 1947!

I awoke. Perspiration and a sense of trepidation covered my shaking body. Jumping up out of bed, I switched on the bedroom light. A feeling of relief filled the room. The awesome fear, which had engulfed my unnerving nightmare, gradually subsided. All I could think of was the numerical sequence, 1947, 1947, followed by a recollection of the importance of the number four.

Realising that I was finally calming down, my thoughts slowly began to clear. Could it be that somehow, the numerical sequence 1947, equated numerologically with the mathematical value of 4? I tried the calculation. 1+9+4+7=21, 2+1=3. So, 1947 did not add up numerically to the base value of 4. Well, if that was not the answer, then what else could it mean, and why the sudden

The Sun & The Moon, The Hill & The Well

significance of the number four? Surrendering my tired head back to the comforting call of the pillow, I gradually began to relax. Incoherent images flitted gracefully in and around my thoughts. Looking towards Trudie, I wondered if I should wake her and tell her of the nightmare. She looked so relaxed, so totally at peace, and I understood that I could not. It would be so unfair of me to disturb her. Anyhow, it would soon be morning, I thought, and time to get up.

The past few days, had seen me spending a considerable amount of time merely re-reading, and revising, our growing collection of Baydon data. Each day I tried to locate potential key information; conjunctive links which in some way or another, might prove to be conclusive, or possibly symbolic. A growing inner feeling, an overwhelming intuition, saw me taking the conscious decision to try and locate the implications that 1947 obviously held. I decided that I needed a prominent point from which to start my investigations, but where would I begin? Where was I to start looking? The significance of 1947 was, by all accounts, the most obvious choice at hand. I realised that it must have meant something to me at some stage or other, I concluded. But as to when, where, and in what context, well that was yet another problem.

The troublesome nightmare which I had experienced during the early hours of Monday morning, had really begun to plague me. In fact, it was bothering me to such an extent, that I realised that my entire concentration was beginning to suffer quite dramatically. I found myself flitting from one thing to another, finding it impossible to focus my thoughts towards any one single event for more than just a short period of time. What's more, it was most unusual for me to experience this kind of stereotypical nightmare scenario, and much rarer for me to recall a nightmare with so much detail, so much passion.

Sitting down I began to ponder.

Trying hard to focus my thoughts, buried amongst the usual cross section of sales invoices, purchase invoices and Baydon notes, I swallowed the remaining piece of my sandwich. What was the significance of the numerical sequence, I pondered, and why did the number four feature so prominently? Consuming a mouthful of fresh orange juice, I hastily packed away my

The Significance of 1947

collection of notes, and left the shop.

A tentative thought had arisen. A hypothesis that clearly linked the figure four with certain elements of the nightmare that I had recently experienced. Perhaps the dream had signified an intrinsic link in some peculiar way, a conjunction with the 1947 communications that I had received during my visit to the British Museum. This hypothesis, I believed, required an immediate answer. No-doubt a visit to the local library would be my best course of action, I concluded.

Approaching the local library, deep in thought, my hypothesis slowly began to gestate. Could it be that the answer to my enigma lay covert beneath symbolic philosophy; a study of truth attached to the concept of the number four? I found that in most forms of esoteric teaching, a philosophical link with numbers was thought to exist.

To some extent, it was perceived that numbers were endowed with great and sublime virtues. For example, the number three was considered to be a holy number, a number of perfection, a feminine principle. This opinion is substantiated by the fact that there are three theological virtues in religion. Time can be divided into three; past, present and future, and that there are three aspects of astrological signs - Cardinal, Fixed, and Mutable.

It would appear then, that the symbolism attributed to the number three, offers us a certain stability; a feminine quality exhibited by the formulated geometrical triangle. However, when considering the symbolism of the number four, we find that the Pythagoreans called this number Tetractys, a Greek word meaning four. Tetractys took precedence over all numbers, as it was believed to be the foundation and root to all other numbers.

The number four symbolically represents the first solid figure; the spatial scheme or order of manifestation - wholeness, totality, completion, solidarity, order and justice. Four is inherent within the four cardinal points; the winds, the cross, the sides of a square, the four sons of Horus, the canopic jars and the four elements. In essence, the number four equates perfectly with the important characteristics of solidification and materialisation. The fundamental point being, that it expresses the rule of law.

An important presence within the boundaries of the recent revival in Western Magic, is the constant use and interaction of the

The Sun & The Moon, The Hill & The Well

Hebrew Qabalah. An immense system of cognate classifications which we will return to and consider within due course. However, returning to the symbolism of the number four momentarily, let us venture slightly into the Qabalistic system, in order to perceive how this number operates. The Qabalistic method declares that the number four assimilates to the Hebrew letter Daleth, a letter which when translated symbolically, signifies a door. We discover that amongst its classifications, the letter Daleth represents the purer aspect of the planet Venus; a symbolic planet heralding the concept of universal love, which in itself, forms the most prominent of these ideals. By considering this concluding premise, I conceived that we were dealing with a two-fold classification of both love and law.

Suddenly, I recognised the implications presented within my violent dream. A look of shock enveloped my face; the contents of the dream had come to a symbolic fruition. The number four exhibited symbolically, a direct reference towards law and order and the notion of love. Within the dream, the noticeable parameters indicative of this, were that firstly, I had evidently found myself inundated amidst an enormous aggregation of magical symbols. It also appeared that for some reason, I was playing the role of a 'Wild Beast'. Instantly, I recalled that this information displayed an obvious correlation with the recorded life of notorious Occultist, Aleister Crowley. Crowley, the self confessed Beast, had coined the expression, Love is the Law during the collective writings of his highly acclaimed *Book Of The Law*. My heart began to pound intensively. Adrenaline raced violently through my body. I had to calm down; I needed time to think.

Sitting back, I pondered this latest correlation, accepting the possibility that assuming my hypothesis was correct, then it would appear that a direct analogy between Aleister Crowley and the contents of my bizarre nightmare, somehow existed. But why should this be so? And for what possible purpose? Furthermore, it appeared to make absolutely no sense of the original problem; the year is 1947.

A bitter cold drizzle drenched me as I began the twenty-minute journey back home. It had been a stressful day at work, I

The Significance of 1947

concluded, as the dull ache of an approaching headache radiated violently across my throbbing forehead. With my thoughts immersed in the results of my earlier visit to the local library, a possibility began to gestate. Could it be that the dream was somehow acting as a kind of consequential prompt? Indicating that there was presumably, an unidentified underlying theme lurking beneath the surface of the dream. But if this was so, was it relating in some way or another, to the enigma of 1947?

Sinking effortlessly into the pleasant and relaxing comforts of the armchair positioned adjacent to the glowing fireplace, Trudie handed me a piping hot cup of coffee, I was certainly glad to be back home. After a brief term of relaxation, and a chance to nurse my still aching head, I decided that it was time to continue with my research. Intuitively, I removed a couple of books from the bookshelf. Within minutes, I stumbled upon a couple of initial references that shared some correlation with the year 1947. From my observations, it appeared that 1947 was the fateful year in which the celebrated Dead Sea Scrolls had allegedly been discovered. Hastily inspecting the brief account which I held in my hand, I took note of any references heralding potential links to the Crowley material, but more importantly, the Baydon dossier.

Examining these tentative references, led me to the conclusion that as an avenue of investigation, the Dead Sea Scroll material displayed no obvious clues, well at least nothing of any significance.

Trudie sat down beside me. "How's the headache, Mike?" she enquired, perusing through my notes. "Have you had any luck yet with the 1947 material?" she politely queried.

"No, well not exactly," I courteously replied. She smiled. "Anyhow, I feel that I'm getting closer," I added. "I think it's really just a matter of time."

With the girls both fast asleep, I opened a bottle of chilled 'Soave' and poured us both a drink. Once again my thoughts drifted towards the Crowley research. Trudie interrupted, kindly suggesting that perhaps I had overlooked something quite obvious. Smiling to concede her sympathetic thoughts, I continued to think. Why had there been a sudden Crowley involvement, I pondered? Was it that Crowley shared some correlation with 1947? It was certainly an idea worth pursuing.

The Sun & The Moon, The Hill & The Well

The cluttered pine bookshelf contained many books relating to Crowley's early work, in particular his intuitive outlook towards both the Qabalah and the Tarot. Over the years, I had purchased a wide cross-section of his work. Enough, in fact, to keep me thinking for a good time to come! However, as far as I could recall, I was positive that I had not come across anything that linked him directly with 1947. So what could it be?

Opening up my unread edition of *The Confessions of Aleister Crowley,* an Autohagiography edited by John Symonds and Kenneth Grant, I had the distinct impression that this was where the information that I required, would eventually be discovered. Lightly folding back the stiffened outer cover, I frantically began scouring through the list of contents; searching, hoping; desperately trying to solve both the root cause and significance of 1947. My heart began to race, adrenaline poured violently into my body. 1947! 1947! 1947! It went over and over, again and again. Yet somehow, I just knew that the answer lay there, coveting, hiding, and prostrate amongst the thousand or so pages that lay before me.

Thirty minutes of intense study passed before the obligatory piece of information was finally revealed. It transpired that 1947 was the fateful year in which past Golden Dawn Master Magician, Aleister Crowley, had died. An icy cold shudder infused my shaking body as I realised that this, along with its imaginable implications, was the information which I had painfully sought. Once again logic prevailed suggesting the rather obvious path of mere coincidence. Nevertheless, I was soon to realise that other more crucial elements were about to prove that consonance alone, was not the only factor.

Chapter 7
The Holy Qabalah

Having located the secret meaning behind the enigma of 1947, I realised, much to my disappointment, that this led me no nearer to solving the riddle of Baydon. In fact, initial impressions regarding the whole concept of 1947, seemed somewhat extraneous to those associated with Baydon.

So what was the significance of 1947? Why did it appear so important to me? Call it a hunch, intuition or a sixth sense; but without question, I sincerely believed that a discernible conjunction between 1947 and Baydon Hill existed. But I suppose with hindsight, it was a combination of inquisitiveness and an underlying gut feeling, which encouraged me to elevate the assortment of information - in particular that of 1947, onto an entirely purer, clearer, ethereal line of symbolic thought.

The decision was taken to involve the use of certain aspects of the Holy Qabalah, a magical system of cognate classifications, which clearly interprets, categorises, and synthesises, the subtle energies and influences present within the human body, and those prevailing within the universe as a whole. The Qabalah can be used as a means of explaining the very nature of the living universe, including our inter-relationship with the divine creator. I realised that by reference to the system, I would be able to clearly elucidate supposed analogous symbols, and thereby, test out both the validity and effectiveness of certain areas within my own line of research.

Digressing somewhat, I believed that it was important that a clear, concise, yet nevertheless basic outline of the concepts inherent within the Qabalistic System, should herein be portrayed. This decision was taken, as we shall soon see, in order to exhibit the pure genius congenital within every branch of its mystical philosophy. I perceived that with the inclusion of these classifications, much of my own material would be seen in its true representative perspective.

The Qabalah, when translated, is derived from the Hebrew root QBL - to receive. It is most certainly not a book as some people seem fit to have us believe, but in fact, a vast body of Hebrew mystical knowledge. The Qabalists upheld that mankind could be perceived as a miniature universe, or microcosm, and that overall he was complete with all the forces and factors that constitute the manifested universe or macrocosm.

In one of its many forms, the Qabalah conveniently outlines the structure of the universe, displaying to us principally, the technique by which it was created and then ultimately manifested. Furthermore, on a higher level, the Qabalah exhibits just how those multiform, heterogeneous forces, manifest themselves within our own personal psyche. To the average Westerner, the Qabalah offers possibly the best means of both personal and spiritual development, by awakening and stimulating greater right brain activity, and in so doing, augmenting our intuitive and creative potential.[1]

The Qabalistic doctrine, has, as its primary concept, a belief perpetuating the notion that the point from which this universe and all life herein has evolved, is Ain Soph Aur - the infinite or limitless light. This boundless glory, this eternal splendour, is often perceived metaphysically, as an infinite ocean of brilliance, with all things held as within a matrix, and from which all life evolves and must consequently return.[2]

From within this state of brilliance, or in the words of the Victorian Scientists, the Luminifrous Ether, evolved what is Qabalistically termed as The Tree of Life -The Etz Chim. The Qabalists explained this metaphysical term, as a glyph composed of ten spheres of evolution, or Holy Sephiroth, evolving within space.

The basic outline of the tree, asserts that the ten spheres of evolution are linked with twenty-two interconnecting lines or paths, giving in all a total of thirty two paths of wisdom. To each of the ten spheres or Sephiroth, is assigned the concept of objective empathy, displaying a level of consciousness that resides deeply within each and every one of us. To the 22 interconnecting

The Holy Qabalah

paths of the Qabalistic tree, we ascribe phases of subjective consciousness, or the method by which the soul can unfold its self-realisation of the cosmos. To each sphere and subsequent path, is assigned one or more of the multiform classifications of both gods and goddesses, which in turn, form our indiscriminate selection of collective world-wide belief. Analogous to these attributions, is an integral and comprehensive selection of Spiritual experiences, Angelic beings, Astrological correspondences, Planetary names - complete with their appropriate symbols, Perfumes, Animals - be it real or mythological, various colour scales, the Hebrew alphabet and the Tarot, to name but a few.

In practice we can use this layout, or more correctly, formula of the tree, to act as a type of matrix grid, enabling us to perceive the characteristic similarities of items sharing the same sphere or analogous pathway. To each sphere and successive path, there heralds the potential of expanding our awareness of the universe, and thereby, simultaneously awakening our consciousness to the wide variety of subtle energies that co-exist within the branches of this fruit laden tree. In order to accomplish this task, the individual would usually resort to the extensive study of meditation, visualisation, and a whole host of other psycho-spiritual exercises. Yet to some people, however, this peculiar pursuit would be deemed as nothing more than an extension of the premise of primitive magic. To others, including myself, the Qabalistic process represents life itself.

By first learning how to fully awaken, and as a result, utilise these latent forces, once again we will be able to contact, and consequently inflame greater spheres hidden deep within our own inner nature, thereby allowing the subtle Qabalistic forces to flow unconditionally.

To help convey this concept, let us briefly consider the layout of the ten Sephiroth, complete with its primary attributions. The first and highest Sephirah, heralds the curious title Kether, a symbolic term signifying a crown, and relating to the first manifestation from out of the unknown. In one sense, it would be correct for us to perceive Kether as personifying the deepest sense of individuality, and the absolute root of all substance. Within the human sphere, this principal constitutes the divine centre of human consciousness.

From within this centre, displayed diagrammatically as the pinnacle of the tree, issues the universal concept of duality - the philosophy of polarity. Here, we discover the notion of male and female, negative and positive, each forming aspects to the ideology of the countless opposites that constitute life.

The male or positive principle issuing forth from the crown, is credited the term Chokmah - wisdom, and as a symbol, embodies the impression of the male creative force. Binah - understanding, the third emanation, personifies the negative or female principle and alludes to the sphere of Saturn. This triad, these first three Sephiroth, is special to us in the sense that they represent the Supernals, the super consciousness, or the light of the spiritual self, and subsequently, the root of the lower emanations.

Reflected from within the uppermost trio, is the triad of the human consciousness. Once again these emanations display the positive and negative attributions of both Chokmah and Binah, except that this time, we are faced with a third element, a reconciling principle.

The Qabalistic term attached to the fourth Sephirah, is Chesed - mercy, and into which we discover the sphere of Jupiter and the quest for expansion and solidification. The astrological characteristic Mars is attributed to the fifth emanation, Geburah, representing the destructive force which accompanies the necessary transition of potentiality into actuality. Tiphareth, the sixth Sephirah, forms the centre of the tree, and has attributed to it the Qabalistic concept of beauty. Tiphareth represents the conclusive point of the second triad, and signifies the harmonising and reconciling factor, alluding to the sphere of the Sun. The sixth Sephirah, personifies a direct reflection of Kether, in so much as Kether refers to in one sense, the super consciousness, and rightly so, Tiphareth characterises the ordinary Human Consciousness - the ego.

The third and reflected triad correlates perfectly with the elemental sphere. To the seventh sphere, Netzach - victory, is attributed the planet Venus - the sphere of Aphrodite. While the eighth emanation Hod - splendour, has ascribed to it the sphere of Mercury. The ninth and final component of the third triad, has attributed to it Yesod - the foundation. This Sephirah represents

The Holy Qabalah

the domain of both the Moon and the Astral Plane, and it is at this point that the subtle electromagnetic forces manipulate the final divine plan, the concept upon which the physical world is ultimately constructed.

Malkuth, the tenth and final emanation, is suspended from the tree connected via the 29th, 31st and 32nd paths, and refers to the kingdom. In the physical world, Malkuth represents both man and the temple of the Holy Ghost.

To help convey this metaphysical concept, let us consider the Qabalistic symbolism attributed to the universal shape of the Square. The Square is attributed to the number four, indicating both law and order, and its place upon the tree is positioned at the fourth Sephirah, Chesed. Four equates with the Hebrew letter Daleth, a letter that symbolises the concept of a door. The planet Venus is attributed to the letter Daleth, while Jupiter is likewise credited to the fourth Sephirah, Chesed. The Egyptian deity ascribed to this sphere, is Amoun, while the Greek attribution is Poseidon.

On a final note, it is important to realise that the previous list of classifications, are not placed upon the tree in an arbitrary fashion, but each article shares an affinity with that of its fellow inhabitants. I must stress however, that the Qabalistic approach offers the only 'true' method of comprehending the vast and varied quantity of hidden symbolism, inherent within our collective world mythologies.

Chapter 8
The Serpent and 1947

Having found the correlation between Crowley and 1947, I promptly established that Aleister Crowley's rising birth sign, was 'Leo'. Gathering together my assortment of Qabalistic tables, I quietly sat down and began to thoroughly investigate the path of Leo. The astrological sign of Leo falls upon the 19th path of the tree of life, linking together the Qabalistic spheres of Chesed and Geburah - mercy with might, via a horizontal path. Paths joining together both a male and female Sephirah, as in this case, are termed reciprocal paths.

I turned the page; my eyes meticulously scanned the various columns existent within my well-read Qabalistic text. Adrenaline rushed rapidly through my body. I turned another page. Positioned approximately half way down and set amidst the comprehensive listings of Egyptian deities and their attributions upon the tree, lay the Egyptian Goddess Sekhmet; the same divinity who had introduced me to the 1947 scenario. It transpired that she was likewise attributed to the 19th path of the tree, the path of Leo.

This information personified a major break-through in my research, indicating that some, if not all of the material bestowing direct reference to 1947, evidently did seem in some way to be connected. I began to construct a mental hypothesis; a presumption created primarily from a cross section of the data that we possessed. From my observations, it appeared that during my initial visit to the British Museum, and whilst wandering through the Egyptian galleries totally oblivious of anything regarding the year 1947. I realised that somehow, I had triggered off a current of data alluding to the year 1947. It transpired that this data, Qabalisticaly linked Crowley, the sign of Leo and the Egyptian Goddess Sekhmet.

The Serpent and 1947

Gazing down at the faded details printed upon the page, I had to admit that all of these connections did seem a little absurd; pure coincidence. But equally, I was quick to realise that these tentative links clearly did make some kind of sense, enough at least for me to realise that coincidence was not necessarily the correct prognosis in this instance. I began to consider the implications that lay before me, checking each parameter as to its position upon the tree. By virtue of the fact that no parameters had in fact changed, suggested that my only logical course of action, would be to go with the flow to see where it would lead.

Perusing the pile of books and scribbled notes that were carelessly strewn across the lounge carpet, I posed a valid question. Could it be possible, that perhaps the Qabalistic listings were in fact pointing to something else; guiding me towards a much purer, constructive line of symbolic thought? It was certainly an interesting possibility, I concluded, and a concept that would have to be considered in due course.

I began to think aloud. Could it be that the information I required, did not lie in these individual identities, but perhaps in some form of composite symbol? Alas! Surely this meant that perhaps some other more important aspect of the 19th path held the key to my predicament? Looking patiently through the well worn pages of my ageing copy of Aleister Crowley's Qabalistic masterpiece, '777', I realised that the fundamental attribution given to this particular path, was the Hebrew letter Tith (ט).

A peculiar feeling slowly emanated from the base of my stomach; I felt an instant affinity with the letter. I found myself intuitively drawing its exotic shape; placing question marks against each hastily drawn letter. Something inside, some kind of perspicacious feeling suggested that this was indeed the area where I needed to look.

As we traverse the 19th path of the Qabalistic tree, its principal attribution is the Hebrew letter Tith. A letter which when translated, means Serpent, and when considered symbolically, displays an allusion pertaining to a coiled serpent protecting her eggs, hence the ancient tradition of the serpent guarding treasure.[1]

Further discernment indicated, that by the systematic use of one of the many techniques employed within Qabalistic dogma, we could, for instance, take a single Hebrew letter and then spell

The Sun & The Moon, The Hill & The Well

it out in full, thereby constituting an integral word. This composite word can be further investigated, by firstly considering the individual definitions of each of its component letters, with the effect being, that we can achieve a much greater insight and a much more thorough understanding of our fundamental letter.

For example, and as a simple demonstration of this elementary technique, let us consider momentarily, the first letter of the Hebrew alphabet. This letter is 'A' (א) pronounced Aleph, and should not to be confused with the 'A' of the English language, since it is a consonant and is characterised by a smooth breathing, similar in many respects to the silent 'H' in the word Honour. This primary letter when spelt out in full, forms the Hebrew word Aleph, composed of the letters 'A L P' (אלפ) reading right to left.

To each of these letters, is attributed firstly a symbolic meaning, followed by a possible elemental or zodiacal definition, a planetary alignment, a card of the Tarot, a particular colour, and a whole host of other interwoven attributions.

By returning our attentions towards the Hebrew letter Tith - the initial source of this enquiry, I decided to apply the gematria theory described above. By considering the spelling and symbolic analysis of each component letter of the word Tith, then the following revelatory formula is obtained.

HEBREW LETTERS FOR THE WORD TITH (טית)
T= (ט) = TITH, I= (י) = YOD, TH= (ת) =TAV

Symbolic meanings for the letter Tith: T (Tith) = Serpent, I (Yod) = Secret, TH (Tav) = Cross or Earth. By considering this information, and then organising it in the form of a sentence, we will intuitively uncover the following proclamation:

THE SERPENT HOLDS (OR HIDES) A SECRET
TO THE LAND

This curious manifesto certainly had a peculiar overtone to it, but what did it mean? Furthermore, where, if at all, was it to lead? The answers to these questions were certainly not forthcoming. However, in retrospect, the statement only appeared to increase

The Serpent and 1947

the ever-growing assortment of unanswered questions which Trudie and myself had to overcome. Slowly, and as the days passed by, it appeared to us as though everything was beginning to fall neatly into place, indicating that in time, all would be revealed.

With both the Questing conference and the unresolved tangent relating to the 1947 scenario, comfortably behind us, it was time once again for us to direct our thoughts towards the Baydon saga. Trudie had suggested, that maybe we should file away the notes pertaining to 1947, in favour of concentrating all our efforts towards the Baydon scenario. I knew that she was right. Reluctantly I began placing the notes into the centre drawer of our Welsh dresser. A peculiar sensation stopped me in my tracks. I felt overcome by a lucid perception, a frantic impression urging me to reconsider the hasty decision which we had taken in respect of the 1947 notes. This, we sincerely believed, represented some form of omen.

Realising the odd nature of the events pertaining to 1947, I persuaded Trudie to reconsider the possibility of an apparent connection, a conjunction linking together 1947 and our Baydon thesis. After two hours of intense discussion, we were still under the premise that this supposition amounted to nothing more than pure speculation. Was it just possible that perhaps we were trying to create something out of nothing?

Hardly a moment passed us by during the weeks that followed, when Trudie and myself felt that we were not being mentally drawn to those bleak slopes of Baydon Hill. But as the weeks passed by, we began to sense a growing feeling, a sensation which suggested that Baydon Hill was a site of absolute importance to us, a place that we realised could herald further spiritual growth.

Saturday, 13th November, 1993. The soporific sound of the late autumn rain falling heavily on the lounge window, set the scene for what would hopefully be, yet another stimulating, evening meditation. We had decided to continue our efforts along the lines of a further Baydon meditation, hoping that in so doing, we just might possibly elucidate some of the perplexing questions with which we had been posed.

The Sun & The Moon, The Hill & The Well

With the distinctly summery aroma of jasmine hanging lightly in the air, I curiously watched as the candles, seated upon the pine fire-surround, flashed and flickered. Flames casting eerie shadows danced to and fro, invigorated amidst the walls of our darkened smoke filled lounge. Silently, Trudie walked towards the hi-fi, fumbling in the half-light. She switched on the C.D. player and sat down. The soothing sounds of the Humpbacked Whale, slowly filled the incandescent room. It was time to begin. Closing our eyes we proceeded with the meditation.

I could sense what appeared to be a small handcrafted wooden boat, floating gently through the rolling mists. The vessel drifted slowly towards me, coming to rest at the edge of the sandy shoreline upon which I stood. In a trance like state, I climbed aboard and the wooden boat gently sailed into the great veil of mist, which hung around the tranquil lake. A new image began to form; I was walking along a grassy pathway that led up to the summit of a hill. I was at Baydon. I could clearly see the Georgian folly standing a short distance away, highlighting the pinnacle of the ancient hill.

Walking carefully along the ancient pathway, a figure approached from the domain of a Celtic cross erected at the edge of the old track. The entity moved towards me, dressed in a wonderful veil of silver white. Around her neck she wore a golden chain, a protective amulet.

Gazing upon the translucent image, a sense of innocence pervaded; a peculiar feeling of recognition. The entity spoke.

"Tis I, the one who protects you," said the guide, speaking in a slow hypnotic rhythm. "Tis I, the one who safeguards you. Follow with your heart."

The guide repeated her statement and walked off across the darkened hill. Hesitantly I followed. As the two of us neared the dense thicket of trees adjacent to the crumbling folly, her clothes appeared to change from a shimmering silvery white, transforming into a dense midnight black. The spectral form raised her right arm. She pointed over to the western side of the hill, the site of a sacred pit, a 'Place of the Dragon'.

Returning my attention to the monolith, I became distinctly aware of a strange feeling, an impression suggesting the presence

The Serpent and 1947

of a stone altar, a henge sited where the Georgian folly now stood. A place memory had retained the latent image of the stone alter; a localised personification, within which would have been stored many solar connections. The guide informed me that we were here awaiting a big solar event. She spoke of two names. These she said, were appellations that would eventually become very important to us. The ethereal form spoke, quietly relaying each name over and over. "Yugar, Yuga," she whispered. "Aghma, Akhma," she said.

We approached the small altar and encountered a further image; a male dressed entirely in black and carrying a silver headed staff. This religious implement I felt, indicated his authoritative office.

Opening my eyes, and slowly sensitising them to the darkened surroundings of the room, Trudie greeted me with her usual smiling face. She had been sitting, hastily jotting down a list of accoutrements, items which she had encountered during the various stages of her own visualisation. Likewise, this material based itself fundamentally around the concept of a riddle, a bizarre puzzle that suggested symbolic representations of the Sun. Moreover, the concluding sentence which read, 'there's a twinkling of light before me, visible to me, moving closer, yet freely across this frozen hill,' certainly appeared most perplexing.

I pondered Trudie's remark. What had she meant by her peculiar reference to a frozen hill? Nevertheless, extensive questioning revealed that Trudie had simply felt compelled to put pen to paper. She indicated, that it was as if a guiding voice situated deep within her subconscious, had merely placed the riddle in her waking cognisant mind. From that point onwards, Trudie had simply recorded her feelings regarding Baydon Hill.

I found it hard to settle that night as I lay in bed. I couldn't sleep. Looking out across the darkened bedroom, I forced my eyes to focus on the digital clock. It was three-thirty and I was still wide-awake. Quickly dressing, I quietly crept downstairs. The lounge felt bitterly cold as I sat down and pondered the collection of images which filled my troubled thoughts. I needed explanations. My mind was filled with images of Baydon Hill; representations which desperately sought answers.

The Sun & The Moon, The Hill & The Well

I deliberated the collection of notes and recordings that had been made since our involvement with the hill. I laid each item out methodically across the expanse of lounge carpet. Dimming the lounge lights, I hoped that somehow in the peaceful silence which accompanied me, I might forge that all-important link; that correlation which would add validity to the countless hours that we had spent contemplating the ancient hill-fort.

As I gazed idly through the jumbled assortment of notes, the allusion that I had made pertaining to the Place of the Dragon, seemed strikingly familiar to me. I began frantically scouring through the notes, trying to find a connecting link. Intuitively, my attention immediately turned towards our selection of records which concerned the 1947 scenario, and the British Museum. Instantly, I knew that this was where the connection was to be made.

Reflecting upon the questing conference, I remembered how I had felt compelled to take the peculiar tangent with regards to 1947. I recalled how I had discovered by the use of Qabalistic tables, that Tith - the primary attribution of the 19th path on the tree of life, was linked in an enticing way with the symbolism of the Serpent. Opening up two books dealing primarily with the analysis, and significance of collective symbolism, I quickly discovered that the Serpent was intrinsically linked with the symbolism of the Dragon. Instantly, I felt that I was looking in the right direction. I read on. My thoughts turned towards the comment that I had made during our last meditation, the exposition regarding the Place of the Dragon. Something about that particular comment excited me. But what was it, and what was its relevance? Eventually, I managed to piece together, a comprehensive analysis of the significance of what many believe, the Serpent and the Dragon would have symbolically meant to our predecessors.

Christian iconography, implies that the Serpent, or Dragon, represented a direct personification of evil, Satan, the adversary of God. This we clearly perceive, when we consider that when St George, St Leonard, and many other mythical Dragon slayers, each fought and slew their alleged Dragons, they were perceived by the Christian authorities of their time, as personifying the symbolic victories of Christ against the powers of darkness. But

The Serpent and 1947

looking beyond the ever-watchful eye of the church, we instantly perceive the hidden significance which the Serpent, or the Dragon, reveals.[2]

The pre-Christian pagan people, believed that there were certain locations scattered across the landscape, where Serpent Power, the Dragon - the enigmatic power of nature, could in fact be tapped, or more correctly evoked. These strange and mystical places sacred to the ancient religions, were classified as great centres of spiritual earth energy, i.e. The Place of the Dragon. Recent evidence suggests, that Serpent or Dragon Energy, may have been symbolised upon the landscape by the construction of Serpentine avenues; stone passageways such as those believed to have once existed in Avebury, Wiltshire. The common notion regarding such avenues, is that apparently large groups of people were believed to have danced along these sacred channels, generating bands of subtle energy, alien energy, which was then harnessed and used in a variety of potent fertility rites.

With this information to hand, I continued to grapple with the 1947/Baydon correlation. It appeared that the information pertaining to 1947, had been acting as some form of cryptic message; a memorandum perhaps, which attempted to elucidate the importance of Baydon Hill?

Chapter 9
New Beginnings

Monday, 15th November, 1993. Unquestionably it was time for action. During the course of the previous few days, I had found myself constantly re-reading and re-checking all of the notes that Trudie and I had made to date. Trying desperately to stimulate my memory, I began the painstaking task of checking through the collection of micro-cassette tapes which we had amassed, hoping that I might somehow, stumble across some previously unnoticed lead.

With the hand held micro-recorder whirring away in the background, I picked up one of our earliest sheets of scribbled notes and slowly began to read. I suddenly realised that during our first meditation, I had made a direct statement, or rather postulated, that part of Baydon Hill had, during its elusive past, been used as some form of beacon site. This information, I was glad to say, could be substantiated. No doubt a further act of coincidence? I concluded. But even so, it is far too easy to constantly make continual references to the possibilities of coincidence, thereby losing sight of fact. Let us bear in mind that while coincidence may be invoked once, or possibly twice, the fact remains that when several divergent elements coincide and harmonise, time and time again, then surely, coincidence becomes conformity and thus revokes the idea of chance. This was the mode of thought or rather the state of open-mindedness, of which I was to become constantly reminded throughout the duration of the arduous six months that were to follow.

Simon, my close friend and regular customer from Worcester, telephoned the shop, informing me that he and his girl friend Tracey, had become members of a local Earth Mysteries group. It was interesting to hear that the group were studying aspects of the

New Beginnings

paranormal, subjects which included; Creative Visualisation, Meditation, Haunted House Phenomenon, U.F.O's, Magic & Mysticism, Runes, Historical Enigmas, and the Crop Circle debate. Simon felt quite sure that I would probably benefit from attending one of its monthly lectures. In fact, the next proposed meeting was destined to take place within the next few days.

"Ladies and Gentlemen, thank you for attending tonight's lecture concerning the Rosicrucians," the leader of paranormal research group announced, as the evening lecture drew to an unfortunate close.

"I hope that you have all enjoyed tonight's discussion," he added. "But before we depart, can I remind you all that our next meeting will occur in four weeks time; when I obviously hope to see you all again. Oh, and before I forget, do help yourselves to either a cup of tea or coffee from the machine out in the foyer."

A round of applause accompanied Dave Taylor, the group organiser, as he left the small wooden stage and headed towards the rear of the lecture room. The wood-panelled, gothic style conference room, instantly filled with the friendly hum of idle conversation. Nevertheless, the nagging desire for a hot cup of coffee got the better of me; so, leaving the busy conference room, I passed quietly through into the foyer for a little libation.

From the sheer volume of people who had attended the lecture that evening, I was certainly surprised to see that I was far from alone in my keen interests of life's many mysteries.

Simon tapped me on the shoulder.

"Mike, I'd like to introduce you to Dave."

Turning round to acknowledge them, I shook hands with Dave, and instantly sensed an emphatic link between us.

"I hope you've enjoyed tonight's lecture," he said, pausing for a moment to catch his breath. "It's been great to see a few new faces sat amongst the group," he concluded, turning to bid farewell to one of the group members as she left the Victorian building.

"Yeah, it certainly was an interesting lecture," I courteously replied.

"Simon tells me, that you and your wife have experimented heavily with psychometry," he curiously inquired.

The Sun & The Moon, The Hill & The Well

Acknowledging him, I turned towards Simon.

"I'm sorry Mike," he added. "I hope you didn't mind."

Naturally I didn't. We both laughed.

"Tell me Mike, that's if you don't mind of course, but what areas of the paranormal interest you?"

Precariously, I began a brief synopsis of some of my own and Trudie's experiences. Finishing my coffee, I completed the account by presenting him with a rather vague description of the Baydon Hill scenario. Fascinated by the list of experiences which I had related to him, Dave seemed particularly interested in those relating to Baydon. Making the most of what appeared to be an obvious opportunity to solicit the views and thoughts of a sympathetic, independent person, I popped the question to him.

"So what do you think then Dave?"

"Well," he whispered. "I am certainly interested in some of your thoughts relating to Baydon Hill," he excitedly replied. "I've spent countless hours walking around the old hill-fort, and I suppose you could say, that I actually feel part of it, if you know what I mean." I empathised completely with his comments.

Dave stood still. A look of intrigue briefly covering his tired face. It was obvious to me that thoughts of Baydon were flooding his mind.

"I really would like a chat with you and your wife, if that's at all possible," said Dave. "Over the past few years, I've met up with lots of intuitive people, and you know, every one of them has felt apparently drawn to Baydon Hill."

A peculiar sensation engulfed me as I considered the present situation. It seemed as though, dare I say, that my attendance at the lecture that evening, could in some respects, be construed as an act of fate. Seizing the opportunity to mention Trudie's idea of proposed meditations on top of the hill, I put her interesting proposition to Dave.

"How would you feel about conducting a sequence of meditations on top of Baydon Hill?" I enquired. "Bearing in mind that like myself, you obviously share some kind of affinity with the place."

Dave responded enthusiastically.

"That's a great idea," he added, pausing to wave goodnight to one of the group members. "We could even form some sort of

New Beginnings

group if you like, to help with the meditations."

Great! A working group; that was just what we needed.

Nevertheless, at this early stage in what was hopefully to be a working relationship with Dave and selected members of his group, I decided that it would be very wise to keep most of our experiences tightly under wraps, as I certainly did not wish to influence the thoughts of any key member of a proposed research team.

Walking back into the main conference room, Dave introduced me to a fellow-minded associate, Chris Wright. Chris was a level headed, logical thinking member of Dave Taylor's group, and had being involved with it from its inception. Chris, like Dave, approved of the idea of group meditations, especially I might add, where it was to involve the use of ancient sites.

By the end of that first evening, a small but nevertheless open minded experimental group had been created; a team which consisted principally of Chris, Dave, Simon, Tracey, Trudie and myself. But it was evident however, that in order for us all to become fully acquainted, the necessity of a social get-together prior to any serious fieldwork, was prerequisite. A meeting would also pose as the ideal opportunity, when each prospective team member could gain a detailed understanding of the alleged site in question.

It is my belief, that interacting with people in such a sensitive, open way, always prompts the necessity for social meetings prior to the onset of any serious work. In fact, it is the only way that the obligatory links with each key member; on an integrational, psychic, or emotional level, can rightly be made. Speaking for myself, I was more than aware of the fact that firstly, I needed to be able to trust each person, and secondly, feel confident and relaxed in his or her company. Without this intrinsic link, the prospect of 'opening oneself up psychologically', and in so doing, working successfully within the group, could not be possible. I also realised that without a doubt, Trudie would share in this belief.

Sunday evening was chosen as the most convenient time for the first of our proposed social get-togethers, deciding that our initial meeting should ideally occur within our home environment. This arrangement, I felt, would also help Trudie feel just a little

The Sun & The Moon, The Hill & The Well

more comfortable.

Dave arrived at the house at 8pm as previously arranged. Escorting him through into the lounge, I introduced him to Trudie prior to the rest of the group's arrival. It transpired that poor Trudie had been so concerned about the group get-together that evening, that the stress and worry of meeting unfamiliar faces, had almost made her ill. However, with the arrival of the team, and after a brief period of initial introductions - not forgetting the odd glass or two of chilled white wine to calm her nerves! Trudie eventually began to relax.

Inevitably, the controversial subject of the paranormal, naturally headed the conversation. Dave took up the lead, suggesting that perhaps each member of the group should make use of our first meeting, using it as the ideal opportunity, when we could each briefly discuss our own thoughts and opinions as to the objective reality of the paranormal.

As the evening drew to an inevitable close, our attention turned towards selecting an agreeable date for our proposed night-time vigil upon Baydon Hill. Saturday, 20th November, was the fateful date that the group eventually selected, and it was arranged that initially, we would meet up inside the Rookwood Arms Public House; a hostelry situated on the outskirts of Woodleigh, positioned conveniently close to Baydon Hill.

I lay silently awake in bed. Trudie slept soundly at my side. An unexpected tingling sensation swamped my restless body, urging me, prompting me, suggesting that perhaps I should conduct a further visualisation. I eventually conceded to my innermost feelings, and decided that a further Baydon meditation would be in order.

Assuming a conformable position, sitting upright in bed, I initiated the gradual process of relaxation. The ever-present sounds of passing cars moving past our bedroom window, drifted progressively off into the distant background. I felt alone. Darkness prevailed.

All was still on top of the prehistoric hill. Gradually, I became aware of a female form, an entity drifting close to the location

New Beginnings

where previously, I had experienced the amorphous 'orange ball of light'. Silently beckoning her, she approached. Her appearance seemed somehow familiar to me; did I already know her?

As the spectral image approached, I felt that she was in fact the same mysterious form, with whom I had made contact during the strange incident at the Ruskin Hotel.

The translucent being gently positioned herself before me. She smiled. She was attempting to acknowledge me. Focusing my mind, I projected my innermost thoughts towards the entity. Who was she? I had to know her name.

The diaphanous object spoke.

"You ask of my name?" She gracefully inquired, repeating the question in slow succession. Mentally I replied.

"To some, my name is Marianne," she whispered. This was my chance. I needed to know more, much more. I began by requesting an explanation as to the apparent purpose behind our involvement with the hill-fort, and the reasons for her constant communications ever since our initial visit to the hill. Sadly, there was no reply. I tried repeatedly, but to no avail. Contact was broken. Yet I felt that this would not be the last time that Marianne would contact me. Only time would tell.

Focusing my sleepy eyes upon the familiar surroundings of the bedroom, my consciousness slowly returned. Trudie was fast asleep and I was sitting upright in bed. Picking up the dictaphone, I set it to record and commenced with a synopsis of the visualisation.

Chapter 10
The Hilltop Meditations

Saturday, 20th November, 1993. We left the house at eight o'clock as scheduled, having arranged to meet Dave and the others at around 8.30pm, out on the crowded car park of the Rookwood Arms.

A bitterly cold November wind accompanied us, as we quickly walked down the pathway towards Chris Wright's parked car. Turning towards Trudie, I jokingly remarked that I hoped the heater inside Chris's car was working. She smiled, remembering how hard I had tried to convince her that this adventure would be worthwhile. To Trudie, the prospect of walking across the top of a prehistoric hill-fort in sub zero conditions, and in total darkness, did not constitute a good Saturday night out. Nevertheless, like myself, she was equally intrigued by the curious possibilities that this hazardous adventure might herald, and had been wondering if this was the key to the solution of countless dreams and strange peculiarities, which we had both been experiencing.

It was only after much persuasion that Trudie had finally succumbed to my constant nagging, and had agreed to the proposed meditation. My only concern however, was that she would not be able to set aside her usual fear of the dark, and consequently fail to produce any intuitive results.

A dense mist encircled the base of Baydon Hill as we turned off the busy A492, and headed towards the Rookwood Arms. Conversing with Chris, I couldn't help noticing just how eerie the hill-fort looked that night, as it slowly faded away into the distance.

Chris turned towards Trudie.

"I guess it's a bit late for us to change our minds," he

The Hilltop Meditations

chuckled, as he indicated and overtook the car in front.

Spontaneously, Trudie gave him a scathing look and muttered something about missing her weekly episode of 'Casualty'. Approaching the entrance to the busy car park, Chris noticed that the rest of the group had obviously arrived slightly earlier than planned. There they all were, standing in the freezing cold, waiting for us to arrive.

The packed lounge of the Rookwood Arms welcomed us as we all entered. Chris quickly made his way to the bar and ordered the first round of drinks. With beers in hand, the group followed Dave as he made his way across the smoke-laden lounge, searching for the nearest vacant table. Sitting down, Simon took a quick gulp of his lager and proceeded with a snappy selection of his rather amusing jokes; aimed primarily, no doubt, at diverting our minds from the daunting task ahead.

Gradually, almost reluctantly, the conversation finally focused itself around a discussion of the forthcoming meditations. Casting my eyes across the crowded lounge, it suddenly dawned on me that here we were, poised and ready to face the unknown. I leaned forward to resume the debate. A sudden presence clutched at my shoulder, as Trudie politely informed me that it was time once more for another drink.

Leaving the car well hidden at the base of Baydon Hill, we donned our waterproofs, locked the car, and began the steep incline to the icy cold summit of the darkened prehistoric hill. A layer of crisp fresh frost, glistened all around us as we began our clandestine adventure, the onset of winter truly upon us.

As the group walked scrupulously along the slippery pathway that snaked its way through the quiet woodland, a host of vivid imagery suffused my thoughts; detailed representations of how I believed the hill may have appeared during its distant past Nervously, I climbed the small wooden fence which overlooked the secondary hill upon which the crumbling monolith stood. Trudie turned and gently whispered into my ear.

"Mike, do we really have to go through with this?" she said, speaking in an anxious manner. "You know, I simply can't believe that I am actually going through with this," she added. "What with walking around in total darkness, and in the dead of night. What the hell was I thinking when I agreed to do this?" Endeavouring to

The Sun & The Moon, The Hill & The Well

reassure her, I had to admit that in the dark, Baydon Hill even gave me the creeps!

Eventually, the group finally reached the perimeter fencing that surrounded the Palace of Minos. In turn we quietly climbed over and proceeded to the heart of the Doric style building.

Casting my thoughts towards the proposed meditation, I reached into my hold-all, and produced a petite box containing a porcelain charcoal burner, a bag of planetary incense, and a box of Swan matches. During the course of the proposed meditations, the group intended to invoke both the psychological, and inherent qualities of a sickly sweet smelling incense, a fragrance commonly known as 'Saturn'. It is an age-old belief, that the burning of incense actually rids the immediate atmosphere of unwanted negative energies, subtle currents that could easily interfere with those existent in and around the working domain. The enigmatic use of incense, is also considered in many respects, to cause a certain mental stillness; a tranquillity which could suitably enhance the concentration of the mind.

In most forms of mystical/magical practice, there is a belief suggesting that 'Saturday' or 'Saturn-day', is intrinsically linked to the symbolism inherent amongst the cycle of myths pertaining to the planet Saturn. As our forthcoming meditations were set to occur during the fading hours of Saturday, 20th November, the choice and use of the Saturn incense seemed somewhat appropriate.

Igniting the small charcoal block, out in the open, amidst a host of wintry conditions, did however, pose us more of a problem than we had originally anticipated. After repeated attempts with an increasingly damp box of matches, we did nevertheless, finally manage to persuade the saltpetre block to splutter and spark violently into life.

An icy cold wind invaded the temple as the group tried to relax. Thick spirals of aromatic incense radiated in and around its confines. Desperate minutes slipped by until each member of the team had eventually achieved a fairly relaxed state of mind. Streams of spiralling fragrance, twisted around us as we sat huddled together in a circle, fighting to keep warm and endeavouring to focus our thoughts. Switching the dictaphone to pause, I prepared myself for the forthcoming adventure.

The Hilltop Meditations

Dave had kindly agreed to initiate the first of the three visualisations, by first formulating the traditional psychological circle of protection. Like myself, Dave believed that the use of ritual protection was prerequisite to work containing essentially, magical or mystical overtones. Basically, the protection rite that we had selected, simply required each of the group to visualise a thick, whitish blue circle of light that encased the whole team. Once formulated, we knew that we would be safe, protected amidst the confines of the hallowed circle; shielded within its sanctuary of protective light.

Upon completion of the first experiment, the astral circle was securely closed down, and then each member of the team was requested to relay any imagery, thoughts, feelings or any other information, which was deemed relevant to the constituents of the visualisation. Picking up the pocket recorder, Chris switched it on and slowly began narrating his imagery.

"Well it was bloody difficult relaxing," he said in his typical Worcestershire accent. "Considering how cold it was, and how all I could hear in the background was the constant drone of traffic, I'm surprised that any of us could relax at all!"

Pausing briefly, he appeared to be deep in thought. The silence broke.

"Well, putting aside all the initial hassles," said Chris. "I suppose I could say that it was relatively easy to relax, once we'd started." He paused to look down at the terracotta incense burner, as the white-hot saltpetre block, hissed and spat.

"But after we had visually climbed the hill," he added, "I suddenly found myself surrounded by orbs; balls of light that constantly changed into elliptical shaped objects, which radiated yellow and red rays of light."

An icy blast of freezing fog engulfed us all as Chris continued to relay his imagery. Shuddering, he resumed.

"The temple appeared to be encircled in one of these domes," he added. "Indicating to me that perhaps something was wrong."

Stopping momentarily to regain his thoughts, Chris scanned the walls of the temple before resuming his commentary.

"I feel that the problem here, is possibly linked in some way or another, with that of an environmental nature." Patiently, I looked towards the group as we each listened to his remarks and

The Sun & The Moon, The Hill & The Well

waited for him to finish.

"Suddenly, my thoughts filled with a selection of crosses," he said. "Celtic crosses, crosses in every conceivable shape, size and form. Everywhere I looked, there they appeared; crosses, lots of crosses."

Simon cleared his throat. He picked up the dictaphone and pondered a while before finally beginning to speak.

"Moving visually towards the central sector of the palace," he said, "I somehow realised that it was important for me to be stood by the monolith."

It was growing colder as we sat there, patiently waiting for Simon to continue.

"Repeatedly the guide spoke of Dionysus," Simon explained. "Dionysus, the bringer of balance and harmony."[1]

The tape in the micro-recorder ground to a sudden halt. Fumbling in the half-light, desperately trying to locate Simon a blank tape, my numbing fingers finally fell upon the miniature cassette, buried at the base of my hold-all. I handed Simon the tape, as an unnerving silence appeared to smother the darkened hill.

"Six by nine the hoards marched on," Simon concluded.[2]

His final message baffled me. Pondering his comments, I decided to question Simon as to the significance of his strange comment. However, it was obvious from the look on his face that he simply did not know. What's more, he added that during the reception of the message, he had sensed that the folly seemed to represent a more important location than that held by the defaced Palace of Minos.

It was now my turn to retrace the collection of events which I had picked up, or more precisely, deemed important during my own magical journey. Now this would be interesting, I concluded, as the rest of the group knew very little about the results that we had already acquired.

A flurry of snowflakes danced ingeniously around the temple walls. I picked up the recorder and switched it to record. Returning my thoughts to the visualisation, I finally began.

Following Dave's visual imagery, I found myself situated within the central region of the Temple. It was there that I met Marianne,

The Hilltop Meditations

my guide. She beckoned me to follow her towards the Georgian folly, but for some reason, it was no longer a shrine, it had been transformed into a stone altar; a sacrificial altar!"

With the tape machine still whirring away, recording my every word, I continued speaking, informing the group of an invading tribe of viscous, malevolent looking warriors, dressed in black and white animal skins, and complete with rams skulls affixed to their heads. A sense of growing unease accompanied the tribal imagery. I was convinced that they were here, either to remove something, or someone, from within the vicinity of the ancient hill.

Suddenly, the winds intensified. It was growing colder, much colder. Talking to Trudie and Dave, I inquired whether either of them had discovered anything during the first experiment, hoping that with the inclusion of their information, we might be able to enhance the collective picture of Baydon. To my disappointment however, neither of them had received anything.

Nevertheless, the results that were achieved during the first meditation, certainly needed some kind of explanation. Was I simply fooling myself? Were these results the product of pure imaginative fantasy? Or was it that there really was something lurking amidst the growing collection of information? Whatever the answer, this was neither the time nor the place in which to draw conclusions.

The next experiment had been organised to occur in close proximity to the Georgian folly. The group had decided, that the best place for this visualisation to occur, would be well within the perimeter fence that traversed the outer area of the crumbling folly. Furthermore, we all realised that this decision could herald a certain amount of danger. The powerful cross winds ever present upon the hill, were particularly strong around that remote area of the site.

As the group approached the secondary hill upon which the monolith stood, a cruel icy shower greeted us. Facing the team, I carefully noted their expressions. Morale was low, and the jokes which had passed amongst us were now at an end. This was no place for jokes, it was deathly cold, and all thoughts of catching last orders back at the Rookwood Arms, were fading fast.

As we prepared ourselves in readiness for the dangerous task ahead, even the unthinkable prospect of abandoning the

The Sun & The Moon, The Hill & The Well

visualisation entered our thoughts. The November winds were up on the increase, but even so, we still opted for the rather dangerous decision to continue. But considering the collection of sandstone blocks that lay scattered around the base of the crumbling monolith, this decision, we soon realised, heralded ominous possibilities.

Huddled together and sitting directly beneath the folly, Dave and Simon repeatedly tried to light the small charcoal block. In the half-light, I began to imagine that some anomalous ethereal force, was deliberately trying to put a stop to our clandestine activities. Ten minutes passed by before the saltpetre block finally ignited, bringing with it, an immense sense of relief that could be felt by us all. Trails of perfumed incense cavorted aimlessly around the team, but still we huddled together, stilling our minds and waiting for the meditation to commence.

Akhma! Aghma! But still I failed to comprehend the strange name that resounded over and over inside my mind. Akhma, what did it mean? An intuitive inner voice suggested that the name was male, and closely associated to some kind of religious significance. Maybe the connection represented a priest? Or possibly some form of symbolic worship that had previously occurred upon the hill? But still the name recurred again and again as my consciousness slowly began to abate.

Feeling my attention directed towards a different sensation, a rather unpleasant and powerful feeling, I probed the awning blackness that lay ahead. Something appeared to be encircling the protective sphere that we had created. I sensed myself situated amidst a strong feeling of unease. I felt alone and in desperate need of an answer. Something was out there, moving amongst the dense mask of darkness, travelling slowly around the protective circle. I could feel it. I could hear it breathing, undulating, trying to break through into our sphere of sensation. A cold shiver rushed across my body as I opened my eyes. Sensitising them, I cautiously began exploring the physical darkness, which encroached. But whatever it was, it was there waiting.

Clearing my thoughts, and then redirecting them towards the protective circle of light, I began to visualise it glowing with a vibrant selection of electric blue and dazzling white hues, each reinforcing my sensation of mental protection.

Something was happening. The power of the circle was working. The dark entity appeared to be subsiding. Now there were different feelings here by the ancient folly, positive sensations that were solar in origin. This was a place that I believed had once been a centre for solar worship - reverence in honour of the Sun. But what of the mass of negative energy which had gathered around the outer circle, and had been trying to break through? Whatever it was, it appeared that the power of the circle had temporarily dispersed its negative qualities.

Visualising the summit of the hill, I found myself confronted by the image of a henge, a prehistoric structure positioned due east and occupying the position of the crumbling shrine. Concentrating intensively, I began to sense an intuitive feeling that seemed to confirm my belief, in that the henge had once been some form of sacrificial altar.

Chris picked up the dictaphone, an air of serenity accompanied him as he switched the portable machine to record. A flowing sequence of white vapour trails gently left his mouth. He began to highlight a brief account of how, during the meditation, he had been confronted once again, with material which related to crosses; in particular 'Celtic crosses'.

He cast his thoughts across the hill, and stated that during the meditation, his symbolic crosses were hovering horizontally above the landscape. This, he concluded, was indicative of some form of geomantic landscape.

Having recorded the results of the second astral investigation, one item appeared particularly significant. It seemed that during the initial stages of the experiment, each member of the group had independently felt distinctly uneasy. Simon added, that it was as though something, or possibly someone, was actually moving around the outer perimeter of the circle. Trudie took up the gauntlet, continuing where Simon had left off, and commenting on how that she had felt the presence of some form of opposing entity, an anomalous negativity approaching us from the vicinity of the nearby woodland. What ever it was, Trudie was adamant that she had felt it move slowly around the outer area of the circle, searching, coveting, hoping to find a way in.

The Sun & The Moon, The Hill & The Well

With an enquiring look upon his face, Simon turned towards Dave. "Come on then, matey," he calmly enquired, "what do you know about this particular hill?"

Dave pondered Simon's question.

"Well," said Dave, "I've always held a keen interest in the site," he hesitantly exclaimed. "I suppose you could even say that I feel there's something quite magical about it," he said, pausing as he looked out upon the hill. "What's more, I tend to agree with Mike - you know, the placement of a stone shrine prior to the positioning of the monolith."

Dave appeared deep in thought as he inhaled the icy cold air. He continued.

"I find it fascinating to know that Mike's not alone in his belief concerning a small henge," said Dave, as he began to explain how the idea of the henge had recently grown in popularity. A feeling of serenity enveloped the hill, as Simon stood in silence and considered Dave's final statement.

Kneeling down, Dave picked up the micro-recorder. Speaking slowly and rhythmically, he began by first outlining a theme in which three Druid figures approached him from the vicinity of the woods. These images, he informed us, were of two males and a female. An impervious wind blew across the hilltop, as Dave deviated from the description of his imagery, in order to inform us of an event which had occurred on October 31st - the Celtic festival of Samhain, Halloween night. Apparently, it was alleged that a group of local pagans, or so he informed us, had been up on the hill conducting some form of sacred rite; a group ritual in which their sole objective had been to evoke what they believed to be the 'Site Guardian of Baydon'.

The team turned towards Dave, intrigued by his remarks. He continued. From his comments, it appeared that the anonymous group was going to such lengths, in order to form a kind of astral protest; a demonstration aimed directly at opposing the proposed area development plan. Silence prevailed as Dave briefed the team on the selection of details that he had regarding the proposed project.

Suddenly, I realised that the development plan which he spoke of, could in one sense, form the root cause to the vivid imagery to which Trudie and myself had been initially subjected. Bearing this

The Hilltop Meditations

in mind, was it so wrong therefore, to assume that the hill was simply releasing what could be best described as a series of distress signals? Beacons that could easily be encountered by an individual or group, unaware that the hill was summoning a saviour, a sort of knight in shining armour to interpret these signals, thereby disclosing the many secrets associated with the hill.[3]

An agitated, nauseous feeling enveloped my body. Dave handed me the data recorder. Refocusing my thoughts, I directed my attention towards the darkened hill. I knew that it was time to acquaint the group on the collective material that Trudie and I had acquired, ever since our initial involvement with the hill.

The final stage of experimental meditations, was set to occur in close proximity to what the locals had rightly termed as the old yew tree, a tree, which by all accounts, was purported to be somewhere in excess of 1500 years old.

In silence the questing group began the slow walk towards the darkened woods. An eerie sensation accompanied them as they travelled along the indistinct footpath that snaked itself through the dense woodland. Up ahead lay their final destination, the cluster of antiquated yews.

The darkness suddenly drew closer. Chris switched on his torch, as the blustery winds appeared to grow in pitch. Simon, trying his best to keep Trudie relaxed, fired an amusing assault of his witty comments back and forth amongst the team. Nevertheless, we were all aware of just how frightened she must have felt, as we continued onwards into the darkened abyss. Yet somehow, Trudie managed a smile, but it was obvious from the look on her face, that she would rather have been sat at home, as opposed to walking along an ancient pathway in total darkness, searching for possible clues to a forgotten prehistoric custom!

The team positioned itself directly before the cluster of ancient yews. The powerful beam from Chris's torch outlined their ghostly forms. Scenes from Steven Spielberg's classic film, Poltergeist, flooded my thoughts - particularly the scene in which the old tree smashes through the young boy's bedroom window. I shuddered as an icy cold shiver ran violently down my spine. It was time to begin.

The Sun & The Moon, The Hill & The Well

Settling the team, I commenced with the protection ceremony. The vibrant words of the simple ritual, reflected back and forth across the mass of darkened trees. Looking out beyond the blackness, heightened senses became aware of ten thousand eyes, each watching us as the trees bowed back and forth, screeching amidst the rising gale force strength of the barbarous wintry winds.

The exercise was eventually completed and the circle securely closed down. It was freezing cold out in the woods, and no doubt every one wanted to get back home.

Simon knelt down and picked up the data recorder, switching it to record.

"There appeared to be a small ball of blue light, which darted in and out of the trees and veered off towards the monolith," he excitedly announced. "As it reached the folly," said Simon, "I watched it travelling vertically and I felt compelled to follow it."

Simon thought intensely about the collection of disjointed images that had invaded his elated thoughts. He continued.

"A peculiar flying sensation completely engulfed me," Simon added, "and I found myself situated directly above the folly, watching as a further two balls of bluish light suddenly linked up with the first one."

Dave interjected.

"That's funny," he said, "I've had a similar experience - small balls of blue and white energy moving really quickly amongst the trees."

With a look of concern radiating around her face, Trudie added that likewise, she had also felt the presence of the strange balls of light dancing in and around the trees. What did this imagery mean? I queried. These were certainly not the results that we had expected. Obviously I needed to discover if there could be any significance in the chaotic balls of blue light, but at least that could be done from the warmth and comforts of home.

In retrospect, and with regards to that cold November night, I believe that through a particular combination of visualisation and place psychometry, the group was able to penetrate the countless memories imprinted within the hill. These place memories were

The Hilltop Meditations

perceived, for want of a better word, as accumulations of information, which over the course of time, had become impregnated within the localised energy matrix. Subsequently, these memories were acknowledged in visual, audible or sensory form, and usually occurred due to the positive or negative effects of past human interaction with the site.

With regards to the apparent negative feelings, which we had each independently encountered as we sat huddled together alongside the folly. I believe that these were forces which had been magnetically drawn towards the team, perhaps even trying to feed off the positive energy which the group had raised during the initial stages of the visualisation.

I felt positive that something was obviously wrong within the site on a subtle, psychic level, and I sincerely believed that the contents of the yew tree experiment, confirmed this opinion without a doubt.

Another curious item that was touched upon, was the strange image of the altar positioned in the location occupied by the folly. This, the group considered, personified an excellent example of *Subconscious Signalling;* a term used to denote the positioning of an object subconsciously, in such a way as to highlight an object of similar symbolic meaning, thereby, monopolising the same locality geographically, except occurring within a different time continuum.

On a final note, one other item of particular interest came about as a result of the monolith experiment, that being the inclusion of what appeared to be a secondary site, a sacred site that was in some way closely linked to Baydon Hill. This concept came about as it had become apparent that the area surrounding the monolith, had been used as a site for solar worship.

Chapter 11
The Plot Thickens

Sunday, 21st November, 1993. I was awoken with a turbulent start. Turning over, I glanced towards the radio alarm. The unholy hour of seven-thirty registered upon its face.

After quickly dressing, I crept downstairs and switched on the kettle. Thoughts of Baydon flickered aimlessly through my troubled mind, as the onset of an approaching winter cold nagged incessantly at my over dry throat. The sudden click of the electric kettle as it switched itself off, shattered the tranquil illusion, as the refreshing smell of ground coffee wafted effortlessly throughout the kitchen. All thoughts of Baydon faded.

Having spent most of the morning recovering from the tiring effects of the previous night's clandestine adventure, mid-day abruptly arrived. Sitting quietly at the dining room table, the painstaking task of checking through the collection of results obtained during the Baydon meditations, finally began.

After analysing the results of the first two meditations, my thoughts were immediately drawn towards the information pertaining to the strange 'balls of light', apparitions that we had all apparently experienced. Deciding to make a closer, more detailed examination of this information, I finally put pen to paper and began my research.

To begin with, I decided that it was well worth considering the reports claimed by countless other investigators, who, during similar situations, had experienced results not dissimilar to our own yew tree experiment. Further insight promptly revealed that the presence of electrical 'balls of light', seen to be dancing in an apparent chaotic frenzy - partially around the remains of an ancient site, strongly suggested the presence of some form of astral imbalance, a type of psychic frenzy.[1] Common belief within

The Plot Thickens

the questing fraternity, suggests that this situation can often befall a site, particularly where conflicting religious beliefs have transpired. It is generally believed that the subtle balances held within the localised energy matrix,[2] can, during such situations, be thrown into a state of total chaos.

This information certainly did seem to agree with, and confirm certain aspects of our earlier beliefs; developments that prompted me to consider a deeper and more detailed observation of the religious history assigned to the hill.

According to Dave, it was common knowledge that certain groups had, and were still using the hill for the re-enactment of shrouded rites, ceremonies which seemingly occurred at various set intervals within the calendar year. This information bothered me considerably. I began to wonder if any of these mysterious groups, had ever bothered verifying as to whether their beliefs were both suitable, and harmonious to the requisite working polarity present within the hill. Considering the distinct probability that a percentage of those groups were perhaps not working in the best interests of the hill, then naturally, this led me to conclude that this 'conjured' up energy, could in fact be detrimental to the localised energy matrix present around Baydon. Of course it must be remembered, that these conjectures were based entirely upon a subtle psychic level alone.

A brief telephone call to Dave and the others followed, and it was decided that we should conduct a sequence of follow up meditations still based around Baydon, but this time, the objective was to hopefully locate and identify the elusive 'Site Guardian' of Baydon Hill.

Amongst the beliefs put forward, surrounding the Earth Mysteries and Psychic Questing fraternity, there exists an interesting doctrine, a belief which upholds the view that the network of prehistoric sites covering Britain's ritual landscape, embody the concept of Guardian Spirits - Genius Loci. These 'intelligences', are usually associated in some form or another, with a localised ancestral spirit, an intelligence which has become attached to an area in general. It is common practice for these 'entities' to be perceived as being entrusted to countless pre-reformation Christian edifices, stone circles, long barrows, holy hills, sacred springs, and ancient trees.[3]

The Sun & The Moon, The Hill & The Well

The Guardian Spirit/Genius Loci can, in one sense, be considered as a geomythical or totemic entity, and include a cross-section of the elemental beings and the fairy folk so commonly found amongst the mythological tradition. Clearly, it must be understood that when we refer to the notion of an alleged 'Site Guardian', we are in fact, fashioning a direct allusion to a series of thought forms or elemental forms, created and set up either intentionally by a priest/magician, or accidentally by the protracted devotion of local religious and/or mystical belief. When 'set' into position, these guardians can be considered in one form or another, as an overall protecting influence towards the prehistoric site in question.[4]

Trudie picked up the bundles of incense, inhaling the subtle fragrances offered by each open packet. She had decided that she would select an incense to burn during our evening visualisation. Having gently inhaled each subtle aroma, Trudie finally opted for the scent entitled Mercury. Her choice that evening turned out to be an interesting one. The planet Mercury is associated esoterically, with the workings of the mind, wisdom, and all forms of Higher Magic.

Perfumed smoke delicately began to rise. Once again the room became infused amidst the familiar and overwhelming smell of burning incense. Finding myself rapidly falling into a state of tranquillity, I switched the dictaphone to record and commenced with the meditation. The calming, droning words of the visualisation, drifted softly, peacefully, out across the smoke laden expanse, which engulfed and electrified the darkened lounge; propelling the team once more into a deep and settled state of repose.

A pin-spot of dazzling white light, travelling through the great expanse of space, slowly descended upon the group. Remaining perfectly still, it appeared to hover above each of their heads. But the travellers were not alarmed by the presence of the radiant anomaly; instead, they merely concentrated intensely upon this single manifestation of consecrating light. Watching from within their mind's eye, the sphere of light vibrated intensely, becoming fringed with an outer hue of electric blue.

The Plot Thickens

The single manifestation of light gradually began to rotate. Six beams of radiant light descended upon the team, coming to rest at the base of their spines. A short, sharp, jolt was felt by all as the inflamed beams of light began to travel the length of each spinal cord. As the point of light arrived at the base of each skull, the stem of burning brilliance slowly entered the temporal region, causing a strange tingling sensation; a feeling of pending pressure; a sensation felt by all.

Without warning, the beam of light gently began to deviate right, leaving the temporal lobe of each group member to connect with the left-hand lobe of the person sitting to his or her right. A glowing white circle of light travelled in and around the group, as a tremendous sensation surged throughout the team. The circle of light was in place, its protective power felt by them all.

Reluctantly, Trudie knew that she had to speak out, she recognised the importance of what she felt. Eventually she spoke, her mind filled with a low-pitched resonant humming sound, a tone that reminded her of the peculiar sensations she always experienced, prior to the onset of a bad dream.

"My thoughts are filled with strange noises," she nervously whispered. "I can hear a word forming, in fact, it's more a case of feeling it form."

Closing her eyes once more, Trudie tried to come to terms with the imagery that was invading her inner eye.

"The word – it's getting louder," she announced. "Ingthon! Ingthon! Ingthon! What does it mean?"

Dave lifted up his head; he wanted to know more.

"I am beginning to feel the word changing, becoming," said Trudie. "Ingon, yes that's it, Ingon."

The peculiar words repeated over and over, louder and louder, causing her consciousness to shift. A feeling of nausea overwhelmed her. Trudie knew that she had to let go of these invading thoughts, yet strangely, she seemed to sense the importance hidden within the contents of the words.

"I sense a new image forming," she reluctantly exclaimed. "The words have each faded, but there's something else here, I can see it; summer. Yes that's it, it feels like summer here by the old Norman church."

A puzzled look radiated across her face.

The Sun & The Moon, The Hill & The Well

"Something is calling out to me," she added. "It wants me to walk across to the wooden archway at the front end of the church, the area overlooking the church yard. I know that I must follow the voice."

Trudie revealed that the guiding voice had positioned her in such a way, that she was able to look through the wooden lychgate and view the oldest section of the church. A tree-lined pathway led her attention towards the entrance porch of the Christian edifice. What's more, this place she realised, was a place which appeared to hold such happy feelings; a pathos reminding her of a long forgotten child-hood memory; an impression of a secret garden.

"Another voice is calling me back," Trudie nervously announced. "Calling me towards the confines of the lounge, but I can sense something else," she added, "a loud voice, a word."

The sonorous inflection amplified the word wheelbarrow! Wheelbarrow! Over and over. But how was this related to the guardian of Baydon? I pondered. Switching the dictaphone to pause, Trudie passed the portable recorder on to Tracey, who was intrigued by Trudie's peculiar reference to a Norman church. Tracey cleared her throat and began.

"Visually I climbed up towards the summit of the hill," she remarked. "In front of me stood some kind of guide, but I couldn't ascertain whether it was male or female."

Tracey informed us, that as she approached the shrouded figure, it turned around to reveal the composite image of the body of a man, complete with the head of a falcon.

"The guide tried to communicate with me," she said. "Its words rang through my head - RESTORE THE ATEN! YOU MUST RESTORE THE ATEN!"

Relaying his poignant message, Tracey noticed that the falcon headed guide had begun pointing towards the ground. There, positioned close to the Georgian folly, and pushed deeply into the moist earth, was a large broadsword. Three diagonal rays of brilliant sunlight each radiated magnificently from within its leather bound hilt. Tracey informed us that she sincerely believed that at one time, there were two precious jewels bound within its hilt!

"Was it that these gems were symbolic allusions to the Sun

The Plot Thickens

and the Moon?" she curiously enquired.

As Tracey turned around, she became distinctly aware of two large horns; bullhorns. She tried desperately to maintain and hold onto this fading image, hoping to obtain further insight. However, the imagery at this stage appeared difficult to interpret, and she slowly lost contact with her astral guide. The vision was lost. Dave looked towards Tracey, questioning her words. We needed to know what her knowledge of the item that she termed as the Aten was. Did she realise what she was implying? The possibility that ancient Egyptians had once travelled up to the top of Baydon Hill, whatever next! But nevertheless, Tracey had certainly unearthed some very interesting imagery, information that would definitely require further exploration.

Simon picked up the hand held data recorder. He focused his thoughts, and carried on from where Tracey had ended.

"During the meditation," he said. "I became aware of a white farm-house, situated near a place known as Turner's Hill." Simon paused to ponder his thoughts.

"I also believe that it is somewhere close to water," he added, as he switched the recorder to pause.

Chris interjected.

"Don't get too excited," he said. "I am afraid that all I can offer is more information relating to Celtic symbolism."

Chris claimed that during the meditation, he had evidently found himself standing alone by some form of ancient bridge, a crumbling building that was covered in Celtic latticework. He strongly believed that perhaps something relating to Celtic lore, was the correct course for the group to follow.

I was deep in thought as I turned to face Dave. A growing succession of questions had filled my consciousness. For instance, why had no one picked up direct information pertaining to the identity of the supposed 'Site Guardian' of Baydon? The only glimmer of hope seemed to lie in the rather curious imagery experienced by Tracey.

A look of concern radiated across Dave's troubled face, something was obviously bothering him. Rubbing his aching temples, he collected together his assortment of scribbled notes and succumbed to the fact that it was now his turn to narrate the contents of his astral experience.

The Sun & The Moon, The Hill & The Well

"After reaching the crest of the hill," said Dave. "I focused my thoughts and mentally summoned the Site Guardian of Baydon. Silence prevailed, so I repeated the question."

Dave Paused, giving himself enough time to quickly check through the order of his notes.

"I suddenly felt as though my whole being had been intoxicated within a riddle," said Dave. "An enigma which involved flying across from Baydon Hill and onto the nearby village of Clent." I picked up a fresh sheet of paper and jotted down a selection of Dave's intriguing remarks.

"Once there," he said, "I found that I was standing amongst the grounds of an old church. This imagery prompted me to believe that the church was in some way important."

Dave's allusions towards a church, suddenly reminded me of the fact that Trudie had also made citations to some kind of church during her visualisation. Could it be that the church of which they both spoke, really did hold some kind of clue for us? This I felt, was apparent in the look of intrigue that flitted across Dave's face. What was he thinking?

In total silence, he handed me the dictaphone. Switching it to record, I picked up my jumbled collection of scribbled notes, and quietly began.

Darkness surrounded me as I made the final ascent of the hill. Standing before me was my familiar guide. She greeted me and I projected the question to her. Who was the Site Guardian of Baydon? Silence. The guide failed to speak. Once again I asked her the question, but she still refused to answer. After one final attempt, the female form eventually spoke out.

"The information you request cannot be given," she exclaimed. "You are not yet ready to know. You are not prepared."

Projecting the question again heralded the same reply. Disheartened, I cast my attentions to the hill. Standing proud upon the hill, positioned quite close to the Georgian folly, stood a large animal; an immense bull with very large horns. It seemed as though the animal acted as some form of mascot, or religious icon. The guide went on to inform me that this was the time of the 'Great Rains'. Once again I became aware of an invading tribe, raiding and ransacking the ancient hill...

The Plot Thickens

With the coffee and biscuits out of the way, the group began discussing the results of the meditations, the big question being, that no direct answer had been obtained regarding the true identity of the guardian of the hill? As far as I was concerned, this lack of positive result attested to the notion that something was possibly wrong within the infrastructure of the group. Maybe it was just a simple case of expecting too much, too soon. Equally, it could also have been that as a working group, we were being put through some sort of psychological test; an investigation designed to test the group's integrity and commitment towards the project.

But then what gave us the right to presume that the site should readily reveal three thousand years or so of its covert history, just because as a group we wanted it to. This line of thought led me to the conclusion that belief in the quest had to be the single most important factor. It was an avenue of belief of which I had certainly become aware of during the course of the previous ten years, and an ideal to which the group would have to become sensitised; particularly if success was to occur.

The hypnotic sound of heavy rain falling fiercely against the shop window, brought an instant end to an otherwise busy Monday morning. It was lunchtime. I unwrapped my trusty cheese and onion sandwich, and began perusing the set of Baydon notes that lay strewn across my untidy desk.

As the endless stream of words flooded through my thoughts, the shrill sound of the telephone broke my concentration. I picked up the receiver. It was Dave. It appeared that he had obtained some information which he felt would be of real interest to me. He proceeded to outline the curious tale, of how upon arriving back home after our last get-together, he suddenly felt compelled to check through some of the mail which he had received during the course of the previous few months. For what it was that he was searching, he did not know, but he was soon to realise however, that it would be well worth the effort.

Within minutes, Dave had stumbled upon a neatly folded letter, a correspondence written by Alan Cole. Dave informed me that Alan lived in Milton Keynes, and had written to Dave airing his concerns regarding the possible fate which awaited Baydon Hill, well that was assuming that the proposed development

The Sun & The Moon, The Hill & The Well

project would go ahead. Dave explained how Alan had been directing a stream of positive thoughts towards Baydon Hill, desperately hoping that in some strange way, he might positively influence the probable outcome of the sacred site.

Having listened to what Dave had to say, It was certainly interesting to note that during his meditations, Alan had allegedly encountered a series of images that displayed the undeniable presence of a large bull, standing on the pinnacle of the hill – *'On top of the hill stood a proud and noble bull'*.

Dave awaited my reply. He knew that this information formed an important development, an independent confirmation implying that someone else had received information similar to ourselves.

After a tiresome day at work, I arrived back home to the usual greetings from Trudie and the girls. Sitting down, I slowly began to unwind. Those familiar tension pains radiated painfully across my forehead. But it was so good to be back home.

Eventually, I decided to relate the curious contents of Dave's telephone conversation onto Trudie, concluding the discussion with my decision to hold yet another meeting; a rendezvous set to take place sometime during the forthcoming weekend. It had been arranged for this meeting to occur within the grounds of a local church, the church to which both Dave and Trudie had evidently alluded. After speaking with Dave, it appeared that he had been able to successfully identify the church suggested by Trudie's imagery, as St Kenelm's Church, a Norman chapel situated in the picturesque village of Romsley, Clent, and accessed via an interconnecting country road titled St Kenelm's Pass. Keeping this identification to ourselves, we decided not to mention this to Trudie - fate would play a hand in that!

Leaning back, I slowly sank into deep thought. Something about the link that Dave had proposed regarding St Kenelm's Church, somehow began to feel important. Was Dave correct in his assumptions? Did the church hold some sort of key for us? Was our forthcoming visit destined to guide us on to the next leg of our quest?

Chapter 12

In The Sanctuary of The Well

A sense of urgency accompanied me, as I stood silently, motionless, positioned amongst the dense undergrowth that choked the surrounding sanctuary of the small holy well. The leaves on the trees swayed back and forth, amidst the gentle breeze that blew quiescent amongst the sheltered remains of the old pagan well. The welcoming sight of a winter robin, watching cautiously from the invulnerability of a nearby tree, broke my concentration. Was its presence here to act as a portent - a symbol of what was to come?

Looking deep into the still waters of the well, I realised that I was not here to sample the pleasantries on offer. No; I was here to accomplish a task; a specific purpose of the utmost importance. Placed around my feet and forming a triangle, lay the three broadswords. Scrupulously, I picked up each weapon and intuitively proceeded to plunge the end of each sword deep into the murky green waters of the well.

An inexplicable tingling sensation traversed my entire consciousness. Somehow, I realised that my task here was to charge up each of the swords in readiness for some kind of mystical operation; a procedure that I was to learn about in due course.

Gradually, the three swords began to assume a glow, an effervescence bathed in a brilliant hue of golden yellow. It was then that I realised that the swords were fully charged.

Stillness engulfed us as we stood on the crest of the sacred hill; the arrival of spring paving the way. Three members of the team, including myself, formed the familiar shape of a triangle around the base of the folly. With our minds focused, we each held aloft a sword. Plunging the tips of each blade deep into the ground, we watched in awe, as golden rays of energy rushed forth

The Sun & The Moon, The Hill & The Well

from the pinnacle of each weapon; radiating deep into the land. Healing the land. The process of replenishment had begun.

Before me stood the familiar entity whom I had encountered so many times before. But why was she here? I thought. She beckoned me to open my hands. A loud cracking sound shattered the tense silence. A cascading cloud of golden glitter filled the atmosphere. I opened my eyes. Hovering just above my outstretched hands was a golden dagger, its decorative hilt shaped to the symbolic form of a Serpent. The guide informed me that we would obtain this sacred artefact, thereby marking the end of the quest.[1]

I awoke drenched in perspiration. It was all too much. I had to wake Trudie. I needed to talk with her. I needed to discuss the vivid dream that I had experienced. Relaxing somewhat, I realised that our pending visit to St Kenelm's Church was beginning to play on my mind.

Saturday, 27th November, 1993. The incessant ringing of the telephone broke the silence. I lifted the receiver. It was Simon. It appeared that he had managed to locate Turner's Hill on an Ordinance Survey map - the location that had previously featured in his last visualisation, and was trying to organise a prompt visit.

Aerial masts pierced the clouded skyline as the car slowly approached the summit of the hill. Turner's Hill was encompassed within the confines of a desolate quarry. A look of horror filled our faces. It was easy to visualise how at one time the hill would have commanded a truly wonderful position; a location offering superb views of all the surrounding countryside, including Baydon Hill and its associated area. Nevertheless, all that had changed, and whatever subtle energies it had once retained, had evidently been destroyed and lost forever.

A short walk around the remaining area of the hill-top signalled a hasty return to the car. Perhaps a similar fate lay in store for Baydon? I concluded.

Within minutes of the team arriving at the house, the traditional bottle of chilled white wine had been opened, prompting Simon to initiate his usual ritual of crisps, garlic mini rolls, and Philias

In The Sanctuary of The Well

Fogg Tortilla Chips. As the evening continued, the varied events of the previous few weeks inevitably formed the main topics of conversation, including the somewhat ill fated visit to Turner's Hill.

As the group finished off the assortment of savouries, which by this stage, had somehow become an integral part of our evening gatherings, eventually, the conversation finally directed itself towards the proposed evening meditation; the primary objective this time, to locate the identity of the alleged Site Guardian of Baydon Hill.

The flickering candles cast otherworldly images on all four walls of the lounge. There was something quite bizarre, almost hypnotic about those abstract images as they danced, aided by the gentle spirals of fragrant incense, which occupied the incandescent room. The white-hot saltpetre block, hissed and spat, as the smouldering incense liberated its sweet odour. Watching patiently, straining my tiring eyes amidst the half-light which imbued the tranquil room, those familiar, haunting helical streams of pungent smoke, slowly began to infuse the lounge, signalling that we were at last, ready to begin.

The familiar image of Baydon Hill formed before me. Spring had arrived, though the trees were still bare and an icy cold chill embellished the crest of the sacred site. To my right, I noticed a figure approaching. It was Marianne, my guide. She drew closer. I called her, hoping that she would answer my questions.

Speaking softly, I projected my inquiry towards her. A brilliant white starburst of light, radiated gently from within her vitreous form, as my lingering words rippled gently across her translucent form.

"Who is the site guardian?" I cried out. Silence enveloped the ancient hill. I projected the interrogation once again. Still nothing. "Who is the Site Guardian of Baydon Hill!" I forcibly called out. Suddenly, a glowing symbol appeared before me, an emblem that resembled the familiar shape of the number five. The symbol, placed directly in front of the guide, glowed in ever changing hues of red and white. Repeating the inquisition, resulted once more in the appearance of the curious symbol.

A dull vibratory sound, slowly emanated from within the

The Sun & The Moon, The Hill & The Well

heart of the sacred hill. Something was evidently happening in response to my question. A malevolent tremor shook the hill. A huge, Greco-Roman god-form, arose from the heart of the hill. The gregarious figure slowly turned towards me. Pulling myself together, I attempted to look directly upon its face. Placed upon its head were three horns, one situated on each side of its head, and a third sited within the central confines of its face.

Eventually, I managed to leave the influence of the god-form, and slowly became aware of some kind of activity occurring on the far side of the hill. I could clearly see five people seated within a circle, sitting positioned amidst a radiant pentagram of fire.

I turned towards the Georgian folly. Once again it had been replaced by the recurrent image of a stone altar; its cold stone surface covered with an abundance of dried, wild flowers. Streams of congealing blood whirled haphazardly down the scabrous edges of the grey stone altar, congregating in an array of sparse pools scattered upon the ground. Positioned recumbent, lying adjacent to the altar, was a priest, his throat lacerated and the wings of death firmly upon him.

My visualisation had ended. But nevertheless, a series of questions remained. For instance, who was the Greco-Roman entity that I had encountered? Could it be that this image represented the real guardian of the hill? Or possibly some form of key to the true guardian? Furthermore, with the subsequent discovery of the archetypal icon, to what effect would this current discovery have upon the direction of our visceral quest?

These, along with an assortment of other ideas, were added to my growing collection of notes; left in place to act as mental prompts, opinions that included the notion that the pagan icon could have represented, not only the present guardian of the site, but also the possibility that it may have acted as some form of key.

Dave switched on the recorder; he cleared his thoughts and focused his mind, preparing himself in readiness to embark upon the difficult task of reliving his astral journey.

"As I reached the top of Baydon," he said. "I encountered a female form dressed entirely in black." Sighing, he paused.

"I felt that initially, she didn't want to help, but even so, I

In The Sanctuary of The Well

persevered with the proposed line of questioning."

A sudden cracking noise shattered the silence, the saltpetre block had split in half. Nervously, Dave continued.

"Formulating the obligatory question," he added. "I projected it towards the anomalous form. There was no answer. So I repeated the request, trying continually to obtain answers." Dave closed his eyes, searching for the right words with which to describe his encounter. He continued.

"Succumbing to the fact that I was getting nowhere fast, I decided to clear my mind and simply re-direct my thoughts. Suddenly," he added, "the role of Mike's broadswords appeared to have a deep significance in the final outcome of the quest."

My ears pricked up.

"It appears that we need to obtain what I will loosely describe as the three keys of equilibrium," said Dave, as he fumbled with his jumbled collection of notes. "It appears that these keys can be located by ritually charging the three swords, and then placing them at specific locations upon the summit of Baydon Hill."

Dave's words resounded over and over. Instantly I recalled the dream sequence that I had encountered, which had featured three members of the team, complete with the three swords laid out forming the shape of a triangle. He continued.

"Beginning the journey back home," said Dave, "induced a peculiar feeling of anger, confusion, and even war which radiated across the entire surface of the sacred hill." Dave turned around to pour a small quantity of incense onto the glowing charcoal block.

"To be quite honest, the whole affair unnerved me." He said, pausing as he looked across the darkened lounge.

"I turned to face the monolith," he added, "and a huge god-form arose from within the hill." I turned my attention towards Dave. "The sensation could only be described as Egyptian in origin," he concluded, knowing exactly what I was thinking.

Simon leaned forward and took hold of the dictaphone.

"Testing, testing," he joked, clearing his throat and continuing with an exposition of his own personal encounter.

"After reaching the trees," said Simon, "you know, those positioned at the top right hand side of the hill. Well, I found myself being drawn to the region of the old yew tree."

Tracey turned to face him.

The Sun & The Moon, The Hill & The Well

"AMROG! AMROG! Does anybody know what it means?" Simon enquired, taking note of our reactions.

"Well anyhow, whatever it was, it was being repeated over and over, growing louder and louder."

Pausing momentarily, Simon began to pour himself a glass of Coke.

"Suddenly," he added, "I became aware of something lurking behind me; hiding amongst the shadows. I turned. I knew that I had to run as fast as I could!"

A look of concern flooded Tracey's face as she pondered Simon's experience. Composing himself, he continued.

"Slowing down, I found myself under the safety and protection of the folly, but then almost immediately, I was situated back amongst the Yew trees. This scenario repeated itself again and again." Swallowing a mouthful of Coke, Simon reached over to the packet of blank tapes and placed a fresh cassette into the dictaphone.

"What must I do?" he remarked.

"You do not possess the obligatory keys!" the voice reluctantly replied. Simon opened his eyes. His intriguing encounter had ended.

Switching off the portable recorder, the magical circle was securely closed down, while each member of the team silently contemplated the collection of results that we had accrued. Quietly, Dave began re-listening to the recordings taken during the meditation. He picked up the mass of scribbled words and sketchy drawings that we had each composed, and finally began with his hasty review.

"Who was the curious three horned deity?" he muttered, as Simon opened up his final bag of savoury goodies and reluctantly poured them into the waiting dish, placing them upon the cluttered pine coffee table.

A look of concern radiated across Dave's troubled face.

"What on earth is its link with our quest?" he queried, hoping for an answer as he picked up a handful of crisps.

I looked across at Dave; it was odd that the pair of us should simultaneously experience images pertaining to some form of archetypal deity. Picking up the collection of scribbled notes, I decided that there had to be a link.

Chapter 13

St Kenelm's Church

It had been raining during the night, I concluded, as I opened the bedroom curtains and viewed the world below. We were all very excited at the prospect of our forthcoming visit to St Kenelm's Church, later that day. However, my only concern was whether the heavy rain forecasted for that afternoon would cordially refrain. It appeared to me, that so many of our answers apparently lay hidden within the church, particularly having been informed of the fascinating legend which accompanied the church.

It was two o'clock by the time Dave finally pulled up outside the house, and with the winter sun still shinning, we made our way down to the car; initiating the start of our afternoon adventure.

Dave indicated taking the right hand turn that was to lead us into Clent. As we approached the quaint Worcestershire village, I somehow sensed that St Kenelm's Church would soon be in view.

Suddenly, Trudie's expression froze; a glazed, almost frightened grimace covered her wry face. She looked terrified. Dave turned to face her; he had noticed Trudie in his rear view mirror and had decided to stop the car.

"What's wrong Trudie?" he enquired.

She failed to speak.

"What's wrong? Are you okay?" I anxiously enquired

Silence. I repeated the question.

Eventually her frozen expression changed. Her usual colour came flooding back. At last she was able to speak.

"It's, it's the church," she nervously exclaimed. "I can't believe what I'm seeing – it's amazing. It's just how I saw it."

Saw what? I pondered.

The Sun & The Moon, The Hill & The Well

Dave looked totally puzzled as he glanced towards me. "What's wrong with Trudie?" he remarked. "Is it the church?" he curiously remarked.

A fleeting thought invaded my consciousness. Something suddenly clicked into place as I realised what was happening to her. During the visualisation, just one week earlier, in which the team had requested information regarding the site guardian of Baydon Hill, Trudie had found herself describing and sketching a series of images that appeared to be based around a specific church. However, as she relayed this imagery onto the group during the meditation, it appeared to us as being simply misplaced. Nevertheless, to Trudie, its appearance was of paramount importance. Dave smiled, realising that he had been correct in his assumptions. It appeared that St Kenelm's Church, was in fact the church that had featured in Trudie's earlier visualisation. The shocked expression, which had shrouded her face, served only to confirm his speculation. It appeared that Trudie had located an inanimate image of her church, except that this was no fantasy situation, this was a very real place, and a location that she had never visited before.

Cautiously stepping out of the car, Trudie turned around. Once again she examined the solid image that resided before her eyes, scanning every crevice, fully absorbing the reality of the eerie image which stood before her. She knew, however, that the reality of the church would be a difficult one to accept. The latent image which she had carried around during the course of the past week, matched in every way with that of the building which currently stood before her. It was real - there could be no way of denying it, but how could she accept this, she thought. How could this really be so?

A screech of brakes broke the silence as another car came to a sudden halt on the small church lay-by. The rest of the group had finally arrived. Dave walked gingerly towards them as Chris stepped out of his car. Dave explained to them all of Trudie's extraordinary experience regarding the church. A look of intrigue covered Chris's bewildered face; he needed to know more.

Simon got out of the car and strapped his video camera firmly around his shoulder. I removed the 35mm camera from its protective case and switched it on. Lifting up the video camera,

St Kenelm's Church

Simon attempted to film. Nothing. He tried once again. Nothing. He changed the battery and tried once more. Still nothing.

"What's going on?" he cursed, as he pointed the camera and tried once again.

Focusing the lens of the Minolta 35mm camera, I gently squeezed the shutter release. Silence. I tried again. Still the same. Simon confirmed that both the main battery and his back up battery, had somehow drained. Likewise, this was also the case with the Minolta. We checked for any obvious answers as to the apparent power failures, yet failed to arrive at an adequate result. Upon reflection, it appeared that the only logical explanation as to the apparent failure of the two cameras, lay in the rather obvious fact that as it was fairly cold in the grounds of the church, we had to accept that camera batteries in extreme cold weather, can and do, quite often lose their charge. Nevertheless, this freak occurrence still struck us as being most bizarre.

With no actual working method for recording still or moving pictures, we succumbed to the fact that the visit to the church would simply end up as a pleasant, but chilly afternoon of sightseeing. If nothing else, we had at least been able to confirm that Trudie's visual image of an old church, viewed from the location of its lych-gate, was in fact St Kenelm's Church, the very church besides which we were all congregating. What's more, Trudie was of the premise that for some reason or another, it seemed obvious to her that the group had been guided there. But after questioning her as to the apparent purpose behind the visit, she had to admit that could offer us no suitable explanation.

St Kenelm's Church is situated within the quiet, sleepy village of Romsley, Clent, lying deep within the heart of the West Midlands. The church, considered by many, to be the 'mother' church of eight similar temples each dedicated to the mythical memory of St Kenelm, is placed geographically upon the site of the alleged assassination.

The pathway to the church is by way of its decorative wooden lych-gate; an impressive structure built during 1919, and designed by the architect, Sir Harold Brakspear. Entrance into the Romsley chapel, is via the Tudor porch way, which in turn, houses the Norman doorway and protects the sandstone tympanum. The

The Sun & The Moon, The Hill & The Well

magnificent, crumbling grey tower, dates back to 1475, and stands forward of the Norman west wall, exhibiting one light bell opening complete with blank canopied windows and a panelled parapet.

One of the most predominant features of the church, must be in its intriguing collection of gargoyles, which are found positioned at the corners of the church roof and at its west angles. The fascinating remains of a carved sandstone figure, believed by many to be a depiction of St Kenelm, can also be seen placed upon the southern wall of the church.

The sacred spring, allegedly marking the spot where the young Kenelm was murdered, is believed to have originated at the eastern end of the church. However, the spring currently emerges from a bank sited to the north-east of the church.

As the legend of St Kenelm grew in popularity, a sizeable village, Kenelmstow, eventually arose. The village consisted of a selection of some thirty houses, including a hostelry entitled the 'Red Cow'. Once a year on St Kenelms day, 17th July, it is written that an annual festival occurred that added greatly to the prosperity of the village. But with the enforcement of the reformation and its devastating effect upon the pilgrims, the prosperity of the village rapidly declined. Local history suggests that the final factor in Kenelmstow's slow decay, was the eventual completion of an important turnpike road that led from Bromsgrove to Dudley.

The short walk leading us down to within close proximity of the small holy well, was a hazardous journey. A thick layer of ice partially covered the overgrown pathway, making our journey towards the well all the more perilous. As the group neared the sacred well, my attention drifted towards the familiar selection of devotional offerings attached to the nearby trees; overhanging and shielding the sanctuary of the sacred spring.

Trudie knelt down and looked lovingly into the still waters of the sacred well. Slowly, her attention drifted, as a collection of incoherent images flashed and flickered throughout her thoughts. Chris stooped down; he had noticed something protruding out of the moist grass, positioned close to the hallowed spring. A closer, more detailed examination, revealed a selection of thin white

St Kenelm's Church

candles firmly pushed into the soft earth. It was obvious by this discovery that certain ancient rites still occurred within the boundaries of the holy well.

High above, hidden amongst the copious tree which covered the sanctuary of the sacred well, a young robin watched our every move. Daniella and Hollie found the whole experience particularly interesting, especially the devotional offerings left hanging from the branches of the leafless trees. I tried to put forward a simple explanation, but the girls nevertheless, preferred the notion that the trees simply enjoyed dressing up!

3.55pm and already daylight was fading fast. The group slowly began the short journey back towards the two-parked cars. I turned around and took one final look at the well. There was definitely something quite enchanting about this place, I concluded; it was so peaceful, so serene.

Upon reaching the car, a peculiar sensation began to overwhelm me. Somehow, I just knew that the well was to form a crucial constituent in our ever-unfolding quest, but as to what, when, and how, I simply failed to realise.

The clock registered 1am. I felt as though I had been awake for hours. Trudie had dozed off some time earlier, leaving me to ponder the mixed collection of ideas and visual images that plagued my troubled mind. For some reason, the visit to the church that afternoon, had seemingly triggered off what I knew to be an important aggregation of notions and images. It was imperative that the legend that accompanied the inquisitive tale of St Kenelm, just had to be investigated. I felt positive that concealed within the boundaries of the legend, we would find the guiding light that would point us towards the real purpose of our quest for truth.

A passing car interrupted my concentration. It was no good, I had to get up. Sitting on the lounge carpet, together with a cup of tea and a biscuit, I gathered together the mass of notes that Dave had handed to me. I found myself perusing a handful of notes, each pertaining to manuscripts purporting to offer a detailed synopsis of the Kenelm legend. Reading carefully through the commodious pages of the text, I decided to concentrate all my efforts towards one particular document, a fascinating paper

The Sun & The Moon, The Hill & The Well

entitled the *Douce Manuscript*. The transcript represented an exposition, which was believed by many to have derived from Wlfwin, a monk and disciple of Oswald, Archbishop of York (972-992). This particular work, portrayed the legend of St Kenelm in such a way, that I hoped would warrant valuable insight into the symbolic allusions that I believed were displayed within the boundaries of this curious tale.

Popular belief amongst the questing fraternity, suggests that semblances of truth are often preserved within the confines of local legend, folklore, and superstition; however degenerate this material may well have become. For instance, in the analysis of certain place names, Worcestershire beauty spot, the 'Devils Spade Fall', has the common Devil' pre-fix. Perhaps this is a term, which may have been attributed owing to its particularly unusual physical features. However, It could also imply an indication of the possibility of some form of recurring anomalous phenomenon. It is quite common for place names attributed with a Devil' prefix, to be applied to unequivocal locations connected with the veneration, or worship, of non-Christian spirits or nymphs. These sites would doubtless have included holy wells, standing stones, and sacred mounds. In the eyes of the early Christian church, any such site that acted as a locality for non-Christian 'pagan' worship, was regarded as 'of the devil'. In our example, therefore, it is easy for us to perceive an image forming; a countenance allowing the bright light of truth to illuminate many of the myths attributed to our 'Devil' place name.

This method of analysis represented just one of the many techniques that I administered to the legend of St Kenelm. However, before we can proceed with my hypothetical breakdown of the tale, I feel it best to incorporate a synopsis of the legend of St Kenelm, based upon that given within the *Douce Manuscript*.

Top Left The Goddess Sabrina - Deity of the River Severn. Statue of Goddess positioned overlooking the Severn as it passes through Bridgnorth

Top Right The final design of the Solar Talisman. *(drawing: Dave Taylor)*

Lower Top Right The completed design of the Lunar Talisman. *(drawing: Dave Taylor)* Both amulets were hand crafted & decorated with its appropriated design, prior to consecration and placement at the sites.

Bottom Right The view from the wooden Lychgate at St Kenelm's Church, Clent, as seen psychically by Trudie during a group meditation. *(photo: author)*

Top   Author's picture showing the suspected site of the 'true' St Kenelm's Holywell.

Middle   Photograph of the upper pool, as seen from the lower pond.
(photo: author)

Bottom   Image of the lower pool, as seen from the upper pond.
(photo: author)

Top The view of the enigmatic hill-fort, Baydon Hill - the source of the quest for: *The Sun & The Moon, The Hill & The Well*. (photo: author)

Right Photograph displaying the pagan well decorated with votive offerings, situated at St Kenelm's Church, Clent.
The picture shows the pathway leading away from the well, where two members of the team encountered the vicious assault of the Black Guardian.

Top — Photograph of the Rollright Stones, Oxfordshire. The group were led to the ancient stone circle after the author had received detailed imagery from 'Marianne', pertaining to a circle of ancient stones.
(photo: Dave Taylor)

Right — Photograph of the River Stour.
(photo: author)

Chapter 14

The Legend of St Kenelm

The legend of St Kenelm began during the ill-fated year of 819, when Kenulph, St Kenelm's father, died, leaving his young son Kenelm - who was endowed with every grace of body and mind, as his heir, along with his two sisters, Quendryda and Burenhilda.

The allegory explains how Quendryda, Kenelm's sister, inflamed with an enraged jealousy and an overwhelming desire to reign herself, plotted against her young brother. By all accounts, Quendryda apparently bribed Kenelm's guardian, Askobert, beseeching him to kill Kenelm on the understanding that great rewards, including the prospect of sharing the throne with her, would result. However, Kenelm is said to have experienced a prophetic dream, a portent that he felt compelled to discus with Wlwene, his nurse.

Allegedly, Kenelm's dream featured a vast tree, which is said to have reached high up into the heavens; having seemingly appeared to him positioned by his bedside. Kenelm explained to Wlwene, that having climbed the tree, he realised that he could see all things, and proclaimed that the tree was a most beautiful tree, having wide spreading branches, and covered in all kinds of buds and flowers, each glowing with innumerable lights. But the image was not to be long lasting, and as he marvelled at this glorious vision, Kenelm saw that some of his people had begun to cut down the tree which had stood beside him. Consequently, it fell to the ground with a great crash, and the young Kenelm is purported to have received the white wings of a dove as he flew up into heaven.

Wlwene, Kenelm's nurse, who was said to be wise in the ways of dreams, offered Kenelm an analysis of his strange dream. She insinuated that the image of the falling tree represented the

The Sun & The Moon, The Hill & The Well

annihilation of his life, as a direct consequence of the sinister plot which had been pre-planned by his sister and his guardian. But the young Kenelm paid no heed to Wlwene's prophecy, and when Askobert sought the chance to carry out his intended crime, he took Kenelm out into a woods on the cruel pretence of a hunting trip.

As the fateful Kenelm approached the weald of trees, he unexpectedly became very tired, and upon which, got down from his horse and promptly fell into a deep sleep. Secretly, Askobert dug a shallow grave, a sepulchre in order to hide the earthly remains of the young king. Nevertheless, the child being just seven years old at that time, awoke with prophetic mind, pronouncing that even though a grave had been dug for him, he would not rest there but in a far distant place which only God could provide. As a sign of his pending plight, the young Kenelm planted his staff, and to this day a vast ash tree is depicted which bears out the memory of the holy Kenelm.

After Askobert had committed his murderous crime, the legend attests that he placed the lifeless body of the young king into the shallow grave which he had dug; concealed within a valley between two hills in a wood called Clent. There, under a single thorn bush, Kenelm's head was savagely removed. It is said that a white dove, a holy bird with wings of gold, is reputed to have left the remains of the murdered Kenelm and flown up into the sky as prophesied within the dream.

Interestingly, the manuscript states that Askobert sincerely believed that he could hide the evidence of his cruel barbarous crime; concealing it amidst the great wooded wilderness. Yet the legend resumes, stating that an anomalous column of brilliant white light was often seen marking the remains of the boy king's carious body. Shortly after the treacherous crime had occurred, the legend informs us that a large white cow was seen to leave its pastures high upon the hills, and slowly make its way down to the hidden grave of the holy Kenelm, where allegedly it remained. It is written, that whenever the herd grazed near the site of Askobert's hideous crime, they often produced a double supply of milk. In due time, the holy site became known as Cow-vale.

Quendryda, Kenelm's evil sister, having acquired the kingdom at the costly price of her brother's blood, ordered the penalty of

The Legend of St Kenelm

death to any person, or persons enquiring as to the whereabouts of her kingly brother. Nevertheless, the divine light which was so violently extinguished in England, burned like a raging inferno in Rome, and while Pope Leo Junior was celebrating mass before a great crowd of people, a white dove bearing a scroll written in English appeared from above. The holy man beheld the unknown words with fear, and asked what they might mean. As luck would have it, the allegory attests that a crowd of Englishmen was at hand, and the constituents of the letter were interpreted as follows:

In Clentho vaccae valli Kenelmus regius natus,
Jacet sub spino, capite truncatus

Apparently, as the legend states, Pope Leo sent out an emissary to Wilfred, the Archbishop of Canterbury, and the many bishops of England. He informed them that Kenelm, the young king, the future martyr of God, should be transferred immediately from his unworthy grave, and taken forthwith to the church at Winchcombe.

As the decaying body of St Kenelm was exhumed, it is purported that a spring burst forth from within the unnatural sepulchre of the young child, flowing away in a stream and bringing health and merriment to the many whom drank from it. But as the earthly remains of Kenelm were being transferred to Winchcombe Abbey, carried along by the inhabitants of Gloucester, it appears that an armed group of people tried to prevent the removal of their holy treasure. It is said that an agreement was eventually forged between both parties, stating that whoever awoke first at the dawn of the following day, would have all legal rights over the saintly remains. The Douce transcript then informs us, that the people of Gloucester won the saintly prize, and had travelled a great distance before the inhabitants of Worcester arose.

Driven by anger, they followed. But when the fugitive's saw them close at hand, calling on the name of St Kenelm, they rushed panting along a pathway, concealed beneath a barrier of protective foliage. Approaching Winchcombe Abbey, and overpowered by a desperate thirst, they sank breathless onto the anointed turf where it is recorded that a sacred spring burst forth from beneath a

The Sun & The Moon, The Hill & The Well

neighbouring stone, and from which the assembly drank. What's more, it is interesting to note that the miraculous spring of water, still flows down into the river to this day.

The account continues, explaining how a look of terror descended upon Quendryda as she stood in the upper part of the western end of St Peter's Church, watching the multitude of people running down the hill. Apparently, Quendryda seized a Psalter and began to recite the 108th Psalm in reverse. But the legend states that her evilness turned against her, and as she reached the conclusion of the verse, 'let this be the reward of my adversaries', allegedly, her eyes promptly fell from their sockets onto the page which she was reading. Shortly afterwards, Quendryda died.[1]

Departing from my Kenelm synopsis, in order to initiate the process of analysis; let us not forget the words put forth within our previous delineation, in that semblances of truth are often preserved within the boundaries of local legend, folklore and superstitions, however degenerate they may well have become. But before we can effectively evaluate the characteristics of the legend, firstly, we must deliberate as to what proportion of the tale can be construed as historical fact, and what proportion can be perceived as legend.

Once again I found myself calling upon Dave. In passing, he had kindly mentioned that should I require any further information, particularly factual material relating to the fascinating legend of St Kenelm, then I was simply to call him. The conversation which we eventually shared, left me adequately armed with superfluous fragments of information; items that we both believed would add weight to my own discerning line of thought.

It is well documented that in the 9th century, Saxon Kingship was not hereditary in the sense of passing from father to son. For instance, we read that upon the death of Offa, his son Egfrith was crowned king for the short duration of twenty weeks, after which it was presumed he was killed in battle. He was succeeded in kingship by a distant relative, Kenulph, who had three children, two daughters, Quendryda and Burenhilda, and an only son, Kenelm. Common belief warrants that Kenelm was born during the year 786, and was 'hallowed' by Kenulph in order to ensure

The Legend of St Kenelm

his succession to the throne after his death.[2]

With regards to the apparent age of Kenelm at the purported time of his death, the legend states emphatically that he was murdered at the tender age of seven. However, research reveals a somewhat different story, in that during the year 798, Pope Leo III supposedly sent a letter to Kenelm, thus suggesting that he was twelve years old at that time. Furthermore, during the year 799, Kenelm is seen to witness a deed concerning a gift of land to Christ Church, Canterbury. In fact, there is substantial evidence to suggest that Kenelm was still alive right up until the year 811, when we see the Kenelm seal being used for possibly the last time. This information directs us to the indisputable fact, that if Kenelm was born during 786, then presumably, he was twenty-five at the time of his death; a far cry from the seven year old child inscribed within the boundaries of the popular myth.

Investigations reveal that Kenelmstow, the village that was evidently built upon the site of the purported martyrdom, came into existence, approximately one hundred years after the Kenelm murder seemingly took place. History confirms that the aforementioned hostelry, The Red Cow Inn, did in fact exist, built to apparently commemorate the 'old lady's cow', which had left its herd in order to stand patiently over the spot marking the young king's untimely death.

During 1815, it appears that two coffins were discovered at Winchcombe Abbey, the contents of which were believed to be those pertaining to the mortal remains of Kenulph and Kenelm. Winchcombe Parish Church currently plays host to the regal pair, being situated to either side of the west door.

Having explored the historic aspects of the legend, it was time to contemplate the use and interaction of conspicuous symbolism, attributions that I believed, lay at the heart of the age-old allegory. After reading carefully through the account, and then considering the facts, certain items heralded a particular significance. For instance, my historical research clearly revealed that Kenelm was *not* seven when he supposedly died. Therefore, having shed doubt upon the boys age as encased within the myth, warranted the belief that perhaps the young Kenelm never in fact visited Clent; but then why insinuate that he did? Was it simply that the Kenelm name, along with its accompanying tale, represented nothing more

The Sun & The Moon, The Hill & The Well

than just a Christianised perspective to a much earlier, localised pagan belief? Of course these questions cannot readily be answered, but by the appliance of intuition and the systematic application of symbolic analysis, I attempted to elucidate, and put forth an alternative perspective to this age-old anecdote.

To begin my research, I contemplated an elementary analysis of the Kenelm name, realising that St Kenelm was, and still is, personified as a divine Solar King. Using basic etymology, I decided to sever the Kenelm name into two halves; examining each segment independently.

Having consulted various sources, including Nigel Pennick's excellent book, *Practical Magic in The Northern Tradition*, certain facts were readily disclosed. It would appear that Anglo-Saxon Kings often chose Runic names, believing that they could embody the magical power personified within their chosen Rune. This belief perpetuates the notion that symbolically, these apparent magical qualities, could, in one sense, be utilised within the superstructure of their own name.

The first segment of the Kenelm name, KEN (Cen), represents symbolically, the torch of illumination, the pine, but more importantly its 'cones' - deal apples. These 'cones' were deemed to encompass within their structure, the sacred geometry of the 'Fibonacei Series'. Furthermore, I quickly discovered that 'cones' were often used to tip the wands used by Celtic priests, and that the magical wand sacred to the fertility god Freyr, had a deal apple affixed to it, signifying the generative power, the will, the male creative force, including aspects of the tarot trump, the Fool.

The remaining portion of the name, ELM, implies, when referring to the Nordic tradition, a direct personification of the first woman. But let us not loose sight of historic reality, in that the Elm tree was used extensively during the manufacture of coffins. So bearing this in mind, I perceived an allusion towards the female gender, in particular, an emphasis pertaining to the death aspect of the Earth Mother.

Furthermore, by considering a collective union of the definitions of both 'Ken' and 'Elm', I found myself directed towards the following annotation:

'THE GENERATIVE POWER (OR THE LIFE FORCE),

The Legend of St Kenelm

MOVING INTO THE SPHERE OF THE FEMALE (EARTH MOTHER), AND THUS INITIATING HER DEATH ASPECT'

Perhaps the Kenelm allegory was an allusion towards ritual sacrifice? Was it just possible that an ancient custom of this nature occurred in Clent? Accepting momentarily that this radical exponent was a possibility, clearly introduced the curious dogma of ritual re-fertilisation of the land; an area which I would investigate, later within the quest.

Next it was time to contemplate the apparent age of St Kenelm, realising that if we accepted that a certain amount of truth did exist amongst the historical facts, then clearly, we must embrace the belief that Kenelm was not seven at the time of his legendary death. Intuitively, I began to consider the esoteric importance of the number seven, in so much as the observable effects that this avenue of thought might bestow upon the parameters of the legend.

To our Saxon ancestors, the number seven personified an important number, a numeration that appeared to manifest a significant effect within divine kingship. More importantly, was that seven was seen to be a symbol of rejuvenation and rebirth; manifesting within itself the essence of female lunar devotion.

So would it be illogical to propose that in some respects, the Kenelm legend was attesting to the remnants of a forgotten Lunar Cult, a pre-Christian religious sect, which had been sited around the picturesque confines of the sacred well? The possibilities of which can be clearly seen, in that the number seven, like nine, are figures that resonate with a powerful bearing towards female lunar devotion. Mystical texts allude to the significance of the scale of seven, indicating that in ancient times, seven sacred planets existed. These, listed in magical order, are Saturn, Jupiter, Mars, Sol (Sun), Venus, Mercury, and Luna (Moon). The importance as far as I was concerned, was that the seventh planet on this list is the Moon.

By directing my attention towards the Qabalistic tree of life, I quickly discovered that amongst its ten Holy Sephiroth, Venus is stationed at the seventh Sephira, Netzach, while the Moon, Luna, is positioned at the ninth Sephira, Yesod. Here I perceived an observable interplay between the numbers seven and nine, particularly I must add, when we recall that the magical number attributed to the Moon is seven.

Using Egyptian symbolism, I quickly established that the Isis of Nature, or the more commonly known Hathor, is attributed to the seventh Sephira, Netzach, and the sphere of Venus. Furthermore, when considering the tree from a Greek perspective, I instantly realised that Aphrodite, the great goddess of love, equated admirably with the symbolism of the Egyptian Hathor.

Turning my thoughts briefly towards the Roman system, heralded Venus - the great goddess of love. While research into the Druidic system displayed Keridwen - the great mother goddess of nature. Interestingly however, was that each system of belief offered us a lucid transformation of the consolidated icon of the goddess of nature. Even the traditional image of the Virgin Mary we find derived from an aggregated semblance of this goddess figure. We can perceive this symbolic link, as we consider the familiar image of the goddess Isis and the suckling baby Horus, together with the analogy of the traditional image portrayed by the Madonna and the infant boy Christ. It would appear therefore, that both goddesses are clearly upholding an interrelationship with the Moon and the constellation of Ursa Major, the seven stars of the northern sky.

To the Pythagoreans, the number seven was perceived as the number of Virginity. Consequently strengthening my symbolic link, in that the feminine principle can be equated with both the Moon and the number seven. Furthermore, it is also worth mentioning that the ancient Egyptian festival of Isis/Sirus/Ursa Major, falls upon 22/23rd July. Let us not forget however, that the traditional feast day of St Kenelm was said to be the 17th July. A possible interplay perhaps?

A further parallel must also be considered, in that by adding together each component number, lying within the range of the number seven. Strangely, we arrive at 28 (1+2+3+4+5+6+7=28) and are faced with the analogy of the twenty-eight day revolution of the Moon, and of the female menstrual cycle.

The Kenelm legend also displays allusions indicative of lunar symbolism, when we consider the embodiment of the cow that stood patiently besides the buried body of the Saint. The inclusion of cow symbolism within the charters of folklore and world

The Legend of St Kenelm

mythology, has often been considered as a citation towards the ancient lunar symbol. For instance, the familiar representations of Isis and Hathor, often depicted displaying their 'crescent moon' head-dresses, forms an obvious correlation of the lunar conjunction; itself an additional corroboration of the reciprocity of the female.

By considering the tree that appeared before Kenelm during his ill-fated dream, here, once again, we see a sequence that resonates to a lunar theme. Traditional symbolism suggests, that a tree depicted in either a flower, or fruit bearing stage, identifies a direct personification of the female gender.

But what of the holy well, and the possibilities of a pre-Christian Luna Cult existing in close proximity to St Kenelm's Well? To pursue this avenue, I directed my attention towards the fascinating subject of the holy well. After Reading excerpts from Janet and Colin Bord's excellent publications, *Earth Rites* and *Sacred Waters*, I was able to produce a consolidated image purporting to the significance and interaction of the holy well.

It would appear that our ancestors used to visit the well, requesting cures to various aliments. But more importantly, women would often visit the well in search of magical remedies for their childlessness. The worship of the Mother Goddess, who was incidentally, believed to be situated at the holy well, revolved around a common notion proposing that the well was a concealed entrance into the body of the Earth Mother. This aspect of both the life giving and/or procreative characteristics of water, gradually united, instilling the conviction that the holy well was the origin of fertility. Objective study, reveals that devotional artefacts such as 'Bent Pins'- the natural symbol of childbirth,[3] have been discovered concealed amongst the remains of various wells, left no doubt, as hallowed offerings in honour of the fertility goddesses.

So called 'lunar sites', were attributed to all hallowed water locations. These included springs, holy wells and waterfalls, with a belief that these consecrated sources alluded to the perspicacious energies, which have always been considered female in polarity.

St Kenelm's Well posed us with a conceivable problem, in that it appeared to revolve around a male saint, hence creating subtle energies that resonated in a positive, masculine way.

The Sun & The Moon, The Hill & The Well

Nevertheless, Janet and Colin Bord's excellent book, *Sacred Waters,* in my opinion, appeared to suggest an appropriate answer to this awkward predicament. It would appear that it was quite probable, that male saints were often confused in respect of the correct deity of the well. So although the Christian priests perhaps had within their parishes, holy wells dedicated to supposed male saints, there is a distinct probability that the people who would have visited them, possibly felt more comfortable offering their supplications towards a pre-Christian feminine deity.[4]

Within holy well lore, those surviving legends which signify paganism mixed together with various aspects of the Christian doctrines, demonstrate that, without doubt, the pagan practices were not instantly abolished. Those legends or allegories, which indicate the appearance of a holy well at sites where the severed head or body of a saint had laid and/or fallen to the ground, are the most indicative of this declaration.[5]

As a final contention to the presence of what I believe represented a lost lunar goddess, concealed within the picturesque surroundings of St Kenelm's Church, Clent, then let us pay due respect to that aspect of the legend pertaining to the alleged dove which left the remains of the murdered boy's body. The symbol of the dove clearly personifies an attribution of the higher spiritual nature of Venus, itself offering us further confirmation of the female emblem.

So what exactly is it that the legend purports to display? Is it merely local folklore embodying the rather unpleasant tale of a young king travelling to Clent, a pilgrimage that resulted in his assassination? Or is there something more factual encased within the tale? Perhaps an allusion to the presence of a pre-Christian cult, lunar in origin, followed by possible citations to ritual sacrifice? From my earlier analysis of the Kenelm name, this would appear to be a possibility - remembering how Kenelm was considered by many, to equate with the role of Solar King. With this in mind, let us take for instance, the fascinating legends of the Egyptian Osiris, and those relating to Christ, both of whom were perceived as fertility kings, and ultimately put to death in a way most be-fitting their role as fertility king.

So in conclusion, let us propose that during the history of the well, a polarity mix up did occur. We can perceive this as we

The Legend of St Kenelm

deliberate the allusions characteristic of the feminine symbol, particularly those embodied within the charters of the legend. But let us also recall at this point, of how the 'well' is universally accepted as a feminine symbol - lunar in origin. So, are we then to assume that with the arrival and subsequent murder of the young Kenelm, or, masculine energies in the form of a Solar King descending upon the sacred grounds of a Lunar site, indicative in one sense, of ritual sacrifice and re-fertilisation of the land. Then perhaps we are correct to propose that a change did occur, an incident which transformed the subtle energy balance ascribed to the area, and then re-emerging later, eternalised within the geomythical account of St Kenelm?

But then where did this leave me? What with Trudie identifying the church and consequently linking this portrayal with her earlier visualisation, I decided that perhaps the legend of St Kenelm, embodied some form of symbolic link; a conjunction with that of our current involvement with Baydon Hill.

Chapter 15

The Crone

Thursday, 2nd December, 1993. It had been another tiring day at work, I concluded, as I sighed, collapsing back into the subtle comforts of the armchair. Repeated late nights during the course of the previous few weeks, were finally beginning to take their toll.

Trudie walked through into the lounge, momentarily breaking my train of thought as she handed me a cup of coffee. She sat down. The familiar smell of jasmine hung effortlessly in the air, as we both began reminiscing on some of the more inspiring areas of our investigation. It had emerged that we had opened up many fresh avenues of research, each of which demanded special attention. But nevertheless, the question as to where it was all leading, still remained.

Opening up my day-to-day diary, which contained each and every aspect of the quest to date, Trudie proceeded to browse through it, aided by the gentle flickering light of the candles. The full moon suddenly burst into life, peering from behind a covert blanket of dense cloud, its rays of lustrous light shimmering gently in through the open lounge window. Tentacles of silver light enveloped Trudie, creating a halo effect that engulfed the unmitigated span of her flowing blonde hair. The candles flickered and gently faded. I focused my innermost thoughts towards her. I was at peace.

A strange resonant sound vibrated incessantly throughout my entire being. Firmly gripped in my hands was the smallest of the three swords. The magical weapon appeared to radiate some form of electromagnetic pulse, an oscillation that travelled up my arms and down into my abdomen. I was surrounded by absolute

The Crone

blackness. Where was I? I began to fear for my sanity.
Frantically, I endeavoured to find a point of focus, resting my tired weary eyes onto anything that moved amidst the boundaries of the great abyss. Inevitably, I succumbed to the fact that I was alone.
Suddenly, I sensed something approaching. I attempted to focus my eyes onto whatever it was that lay out there, intimately bound up amidst the choking abyss of darkness. The quasi-translucent image of an Old Crone, her wry face ablaze against an aura of silvery blue, slowly materialised before me. She turned towards me, growling like the howling winds that accompanied her, her twisted greying hair writhing like serpents. The foul image cackled and laughed. The serenity of the abyss was shattered. Who was this malevolent entity which stood before me? What was she?
Lifting the sword high above my head, I prepared for my defence. The crone cackled and hissed as the sword hung motionless, positioned directly above her head. I watched in dismay as she suddenly grew in size, and proceeded to run her blackened tongue along the entire length of the sword. The crone was much stronger than I was, the sword appearing powerless against the malice that she wielded. Her cackling grew louder, much louder, like the rage of distant thunder. I raised the weapon, preparing...

I awoke. It was 5.30am. Daylight ruled once more over darkness. I just hoped that the terrifying ordeal was merely a dream, not a portent of what was to follow.

Saturday, 4th December, 1993. Shutting down my home studio, I turned to acknowledge Dave, agreeing that we were at last finally pleased with the results of the relaxation tape. Initially, we had decided to put together a simple tape, so that each member of the team would at least have the opportunity to practice visualisation exercises within in the comfort of their own homes. However, we soon realised that the tape would also work in countless other ways.

The recording consisted primarily of a varied selection of abstract musical noises, supplemented with additional live sounds,

The Sun & The Moon, The Hill & The Well

including whales, water, birds, and complete with a carefully added, pre-planned voice over.

From the listener's point of view, the tape was designed fundamentally to act as a type of image director, enjoining the listener with a chosen location or selected plane. In this instance, we had decided that for the initial circumscription of the tape, we would use St Kenelm's Holy Well as our chosen point of focus. We assumed that the rest of the group would also agree with this choice.

Dave looked briefly at his watch. We only had half an hour left before the rest of the group were due to arrive. But then to make matters worse, only four of the required six tapes had been duplicated! Trudie walked quietly through into the dinning room, laden with a tray of coffee and biscuits. She believed, rightly or wrongly, that she deserved a sneak preview of the tape prior to the other's arrival, particularly, she added, as she had kept us both equipped with a constant supply of refreshments!

"So this is why you've been burning the midnight oil," she exclaimed, nodding in approval. Acknowledging her, I continued preparing the final two copies of the tape.

The familiar tap on the front door signalled the arrival of the group. Placing the last of the required tapes into the recorder, Dave introduced the concept of the relaxation tape to the rest of the team, briefing them on its usage.

With the six tapes complete, we were ready to begin. After discussing the possible location for the first our of experiments, it was good to hear that everyone agreed that St Kenelm's Holy Well as the initial source for the investigation, offered us an excellent choice. Chris dimmed the lounge lights as a copy of the relaxation tape was placed into each of the six Walkman's. Pressing play, each tape whirred into life, as one after another of the team, suddenly found themselves locked into the subtle idiosyncrasies which the tapes emitted. The smell of planetary incense filled the incandescent room, as a slow succession of spectral phantoms, cast off from the burning candles, danced idly across the leading wall of the chimney-breast.

Chris settled himself, succumbing to the fact that the results in his Sports Argus, would have to wait until later! Slowly, he began to distinguish a selection of strange disjointed images,

The Crone

representations that emanated from the depths of his subconscious mind. Gradually, he allowed his thoughts to lock-on to the relaxing, hypnotic pulse created by the collection of ambient sounds present upon the tape.

In a trance-like state, Chris drifted into the subtle sounds presented upon the tape, guided by the suggestive mesmerising voice which gently caressed his thoughts.

The swirling mists cleared, and the pen that he was holding moved silently across the A4 lined page. Words formed within his consciousness, thoughts suggested by the combination of sound and voice recorded on the tape. Chris began to scribble down his thoughts. 'Sacred water source, trace the flow - beneath the bridge is your goal'.

His hand stopped moving. The pen stood still. A fresh collection of words slowly invaded his tranquil thoughts. Again, the pen began to move. 'Blessed are the waters, use them as protection use the waters, then you will be safe'.

Unfortunately, his concentration was beginning to wane. Chris was finding it increasingly more difficult to maintain contact with the intelligence which had seemingly controlled his thoughts. He tried to preserve the link that had been forged, but to no avail. Interaction with his spiritual guide had ended.

A sudden flurry of anomalous sounds gently invaded my thoughts, as the soothing words contained upon the tape, guided me carefully into an ever-increasing state of repose.

Slowly, the misty began to clear. I could perceive the familiar image of my guide slowly approaching. Calling out to her, I informed her that I had hoped that she would accompany me on a brief visit to St Kenelm's Holy Well. A wry look of concern covered her face.

"You know 'tis safer on the sacred hill," she nervously announced, 'tis much safer up on Baydon." I informed the guide that as part of the quest, I had to go to St Kenelm's, and that I felt that she should be there with me. Reluctantly, the guide finally agreed to my request. Immediately, we found ourselves situated outside the wooden lych-gate guarding the entrance to St Kenelm's Church. Facing the guide, I became aware of a conspicuous change occurring within her translucent form. The female entity appeared to be losing her vitality. Suddenly, the grounds of the churchyard lost their timeless beauty, being replaced by a poisonous green slime, which covered the surrounding trees and flowed down into the ground, swallowing up all that it encompassed. Hastily I performed a simple protection ritual, calling upon the protective power of the Qabalistic Cross - a magical rubric that invoked the guardianship of the divine cross of light.[1]

We headed off towards the holy well; a cross of divine light planted firmly amidst the astral body which I had mentally created. We had to reach our destination at all costs, I concluded. It was there that I felt we would ultimately attain our goal.

It was dark as we approached the perimeter of the well. The friendliness that the team had experienced during our physical visit to the site, was certainly not here with me now. A powerful magnetic sensation slowly began to envelop me, a sensation that left me feeling drained. I sensed that something existed within the confines of the ancient well. Once again I felt compelled to call upon the protection of the Qabalistic Cross.

A flash of light illuminated the area surrounding the pagan well. An elongated sphere of orange yellow light, radiated upwards from within the depths of the sacred spring; hovering gently above the ground. Cautiously, I began to look upon the elliptical mass that hung above the well. A low droning voice called out from within its epicentre.

"We have been waiting for you," the anomalous voice announced. "Waiting here for you."

Slowly the words changed.

"It is I, the one who protects you, 'tis I, the one who protects you."

Looking deep into the heart of the oval-shaped entity, I intuitively realised that I needed to pass through it, I had to travel out beyond the confines of the well. Walking slowly through the body of light, placed me instantly upon the summit of Baydon Hill. The well, it appeared, acted as some form of astral gateway.

I began to recall the unusual occurrences that I had experienced during my short stay at the Ruskin Hotel, back in November. It seemed as though the feminine entity which I had

The Crone

encountered then, and during all subsequent meditations, was in fact, the same as the ethereal form now present within the well. What's more, the female apparition that I had encountered during my visit to the Ruskin Hotel, had left me with the distinct impression that it had a strong association with water!

I opened my eyes; my visualisation had ended. But what was meant by the strange comment suggesting that someone, or something, had been waiting for me down by the well? And why did the guide feel so reluctant to visit the well?

With everyone completing a written account of his or her visual and audible anomalies, the circle was securely closed down. Once again, I found myself faced with a further collection of material to plough through. Sitting down, I decided to scan through the collection of notes before everyone left. One item instantly seized my attention. It was something to which Tracey had made an allusion. 'Remove the Crown! Remove the Crown!' she had written. I quizzed her about her comment, and her response was that during her visualisation, she had clearly seen a kingly crown being removed from inside the well. Unquestionably, Tracey's information tied up nicely with an area of thought currently under consideration.

It was time for lunch. It had been very busy in the shop that morning, and I just hoped that it would quieten down sufficiently to enable me to at least sit down and successfully eat my lunch. Sitting there, half expecting someone to walk through into the main showroom, I allowed my thoughts some free association. The bizarre dream concerning the 'Old Crone' had really begun to bother me. For some strange reason, it had suddenly re-appeared and burst back into my conscious thoughts. But why?

Within the group, the final preparations for an in-depth Winter Solstice meditation had just been completed, this in itself, added to my concern. The objectives behind the visualisation were fairly straightforward; the idea being that the group would symbolically charge up the three swords at St Kenelm's Holy Well for possible use later in the investigation. Leaving the well behind, the plan was that we would then proceed to Baydon Hill, and once there, invoke a known Solar deity, to which a series of questions pertaining to knowledge of the true site guardian of the hill would

The Sun & The Moon, The Hill & The Well

then be posed. Furthermore, if my assumptions were correct, then the nightmare that I had experienced which had featured the 'Old Crone', could in fact, symbolise a possible portent, a premonition attesting to the charging of the swords on the 21st December. A sickly sensation grappled at the base of my stomach. I sincerely hoped that I had merely misinterpreted this information.

The data was beginning to pile up, but I still lacked the all-important information relating to the identity of deities which had been worshipped during the homeric past of Baydon Hill. We also needed to unravel a fair amount of the psychic material, which was still in desperate need of conformation. Needless to say, I decided to re-read all of the notes which we had accrued, followed by a re-listen to the countless hours of micro-cassette recordings; hoping to highlight something new, an item that may have been overlooked.

The following few days found me experimenting with further visualisations, with the most interesting of these being an allusion towards the supposed 'Golden Serpent Dagger', the elusive artefact upon which I had touched earlier. Apparently, or so Marianne my guide informed me, this ceremonial dagger was in many respects, linked with a place named Mean Hill, and that this hill was to be of some importance during the final aspects of the quest.

Chapter 16

The Winter Solstice

Tuesday, 21st December, 1993. Harsh frost covered the ground that morning as I left the house with the two dogs, ready to embark upon our usual early morning walk. I needed time to think, time to reflect upon the collection of events which were destined to occur later that day. Sam barked, breaking my concentration, excited no-doubt at the prospect of his daily walk through the misty woods.

As we reached the purlieus perimeter field, which meandered gently into the wooded grove, an awesome sight greeted us; a superb image of the winter sun as it burst boldly through the darkened tree line, its deep and warming rays desperately trying to penetrate the early morning frost.

Lucy and Sam ran off energetically, allowing me just enough time to conduct a brief, but nevertheless, successful relaxation exercise. I raised my arms and stood perfectly still, drawing in a successive series of deep and calming breaths. I gradually relaxed and invoked the resplendent power of the early morning sun, realising that from this point forwards, the winter sun would begin its gradual ascent into the December sky, thereby marking the approach of our imminent ritual meditation. A sensation of well being developed within my psyche, I knew that I was ready, prepared for whatever the outcome of the meditation would be.

In most traditions, the Sun is heeded as the universal Father, with his consort, the Moon, as the Mother. Symbolically the Sun personifies many ideas. I soon discovered that traditional solar symbols have included the revolving wheel, the disk, the swastika, a radiant face, an eagle, a hawk, a phoenix and a lion.

In an attempt to explain the apparent objectives lying at the heart of the solar cycles, antediluvian civilisations strove to

The Sun & The Moon, The Hill & The Well

develop an incredible collection of convoluted religious myths and ritualistic ceremonies. At best, these solar rites can be defined as psychological intrusions, endowing the mortal with immortal faculties.[1]

The Egyptian Sun-God, Ra, considered by his followers as a direct personification of the Sun, and representing life, creation, and spirituality, forms a perfect example of early solar reveration. Amongst Christian tradition, Christ is said to share an association with the Sun, this we see in the allusion to the sacrificed lamb - the Sun of salvation. Interestingly, both the Aztecs and the Incas equally considered themselves as 'Children of the Sun'. Seen Qabalistically, the Sun is perceived as the abode of the Archangel Michael. Amongst the Muslim faith, Allah the all seeing, the all knowing, can also be perceived as an exponent of the Sun. Pagans however, ancient and modern, consider their horned god as an interesting variant on the traditional, consolidated image of the Solar deity.

Tradition warrants that at the Winter Solstice, the time when the Sun begins its long journey towards warmer and thankfully longer days, the Great Mother, the Queen of Paradise, gives birth to the Son of Light, the mythical Sun-God. Likewise, it is seen as the period when Virgo ascends in the East, and the time when the full Moon is perceived at its nadir. To the Romans, the Winter Solstice represented an established celebration date, a feast day that subsequently changed with the introduction and implementation of the Christian concept of Christmas. Today, however, the Winter Solstice is commonly recognised under its Celtic pseudonym, Yule.[2]

As a group, we hoped that we would be able to invoke the primal power of the Winter solstice, tapping directly into its archetypal current, and hopefully, if all went according to plan, use it firstly to consecrate the three swords, and then secondly, to locate the illusory site guardian of Baydon.

Chris indicated, veering cautiously off the busy dual-carriage way, and onto the quiet, tree-lined, caliginous country lane. A glistening layer of crystalline ice delicately coated the austere hedgerow, as the phosphorescence of the car headlights illuminated the periphery of leafless, stygian trees. Ghostly

The Winter Solstice

images cavorted aimlessly amongst the ice-tipped carious branches, invigorated amidst the sudden flood of brilliance that probed the awning blackness.

Easing off the accelerator pedal, Chris slowly drove the car left, illuminating the familiar line of umbrageous conifers, which eclipsed the crumbling tower of the small Norman chapel. He indicated and carefully manoeuvred his vehicle up onto the gravel-paved pull-in. Dave was already there, patiently awaiting the arrival of the team, parked on the makeshift lay-by, positioned adjacent to the rustic church.

An eerie sense of unease enveloped the group, dampening our spirits as we prepared ourselves for the commencement of our shrouded quest. Walking quietly through the churchyard, down towards the hallowed grounds of the sacred well, Chris, trying his best to monitor our hazardous journey, switched on his torch. Ahead of the team hung a dense rolling mist, a heaving fog that consumed the pathway, smothering the lowly domain of the devotional holy well.

Carefully, Simon placed his hold-all down upon the ground. The group had decided, partially as a matter of safety, to secretly transport the three broadswords under the protective sanctuary of Simon's green fishing hold-all. Silently, he removed each of the weapons from their protective cover, laying them carefully on the ground. My heart began to pound. I suddenly recalled the peculiar dream that I had encountered, which had featured the Old Crone, and the possibility that somehow, it had represented a portent of things to come.

Chris picked up the largest of the three swords and walked slowly towards the well.

"Are we ready then?" he curiously enquired, as both Simon and myself, each picked up a sword and walked silently towards the still waters of the sacred well. As we gathered amongst the pitch-black surroundings of the hallowed site, an air of tranquillity, gently released us from the feeling of trepidation that had ensnared our sensorial minds. It was time to begin.

Forming a triangle around the perimeter of the sacred spring, in turn the three swords were held high above the hallowed waters; honouring the site in readiness for the consecration of each weapon. The team stood in silence. A wintry breeze moaned

The Sun & The Moon, The Hill & The Well

belligerently amongst the darkened branches of the leafless trees. Silently, we contemplated the subtle energies of the well, as Dave began the visualisation.

Exonerating our minds, the group gradually began to relax. It was so quiet, I thought, so easy to simply drift into the state of repose that surrounded the ancient well. Clearing our minds, as we ceremoniously raised the three swords high above the still waters of the peaceful, hallowed well, we simultaneously centred our thoughts on invoking the guardian of the well. Almost immediately, an orange being slowly began to form, an image built up and contained within each of our minds. A powerful tingling sensation rushed rapidly through my body, as the spirit of the ancient well, grew in strength.

With the sword holders confirming the presence of the astral entity, they beseeched the essence of the well, requesting that the consecration ceremony should begin.

Chris focused his thoughts, directing them towards the single concentration of light which had invaded his mind's eye. Silently, he called to the guardian of the well. An image formed before him, a radiant figure dressed in a shimmering veil of brilliant light. The entity reached forward, embracing the raised sword which he held tightly before him. Chris reeled backwards as an anomalous tingling sensation rushed violently through his body. The sword became engulfed amidst a glittering aura of golden light, protective light; consecrating light...

Believing that we had successfully accomplished the consecration and subsequent 'charging up' of the three weapons, we left the domain of the sanctified well and headed towards the car; preparing ourselves for the forthcoming experiments on Baydon Hill.

The dazzling glare of passing headlights illuminated the darkened interior of Dave Taylor's stationary car. Inside, the team sat in silence, focusing their minds, preparing themselves for the next leg of their quest - Baydon.

Dave looked at his watch - 11.15pm. He knew that the group had to be up on top of the hill well before midnight, particularly if their hopes of tapping into the archetypal, Yule time current, were to be a success.

The Winter Solstice

A gruelling wind lashed out at the team as they began the gradual climb up towards the pinnacle of the ancient hill. Layer upon layer of compacted ice, hindered their progress, making the climb towards the Georgian folly a hazardous experience. Fingers of icy cold wind, penetrated their frozen, pallid faces. Nevertheless, they had to accomplish their goal.

Crossing the makeshift wooden stile that looked out towards the crumbling monolith, once again the group were reminded of the dangers that faced them.

Eventually, a suitable place that was both sufficiently sheltered from the wind, and close enough to the folly for the meditation to work, was successfully located. Four terracotta dishes were each filled with incense, ignited and then carefully positioned upon the ground, forming a circle. Dave called the group together, ready to begin the process of initiating the protective circle; completing the operation with the embodiment of an adoration to their chosen Solar deity.

Spirals of climbing incense scrolled upwards, as each member of the group rigorously invoked the 'falcon headed' Sun deity. Slowly, the horizon changed from a dense blackness into a warm pink hue, a colour indicative of early dawn and the presence of their chosen deity. A brilliant flash of light illuminated the horizon line. The colossal image of the Sun god suddenly appeared before them, the ground shaking like thunder as he strode towards them. The deity turned, his eyes like the Sun and the Moon. Flickering and faltering the image of the god stood still. Something was wrong, the primal, raw energy that they had all initially felt, now appeared much weaker. But still the group revered the divine image.

Hopelessly, they each tried in vain to maintain the faltering image of their chosen Sun god. But the Solar King still failed to approach the hill, and gradually, the deity began to wane. They had failed.

Disheartened, the group sat quietly amongst the busy surroundings of the quaint country pub. Loud music blared away in the background, as Dave arrived back at the table with a tray loaded with drinks. I lifted up my glass and swallowed a mouthful of cold Guinness, fully aware of the fact that no one had spoken

The Sun & The Moon, The Hill & The Well

during the short journey back from Baydon. So what had gone wrong, I pondered, as my thoughts recalled the collection of disturbing images pertaining to the 'Old Crone'. Could it be that my dream was in fact a portent, a premonition relating to our present failure at Baydon Hill? I looked across the table towards Dave. A solemn silence hung above the table.

"Okay then, what went wrong?" Chris announced, breaking my train of thought.

"To be honest, I'm not really sure," I replied, as I lifted up my half empty glass. "But I know we should have achieved something more positive."

Simon interjected.

"Maybe we're mistaken believing that the hill is a solar site after all," he added.

Dave looked up. As far as we were concerned, Baydon Hill had to be a solar site. But if that was the case, then what had we done wrong? I pondered Simon's question, realising that perhaps my initial thoughts regarding the hill were correct. Right from our initial involvement with the hill, I strongly believed that perhaps something was out of balance, and as a result, had affected the energy matrix inherent within the site as a whole. By applying this concept to our current situation, and by assuming that the energy balance of the hill had been modified in some way, then perhaps this was the reason as to why our chosen solar deity, when invoked, was denied access to the hill? With this in mind, I felt that I was correct to infer that the nightmarish dream of the 'Old Crone', confirmed this belief.

The customary Yule time break, had seen the group each going their own separate ways, celebrating Christmas in the company of their respective families. What's more, ever since that fateful December night, the group had failed to mention, in any great context, the non-events of the Winter Solstice meditation. However, a fresh sense of enthusiasm had begun, and I felt that the time was right for positive action.

The shrill pitch of the telephone rang out. Trudie picked up the receiver. The familiar and friendly voice of Dave Taylor, radiated gently throughout the receiver. She greeted him.

"Hi Trudie," said Dave, "I hope that you've all had a super Christmas?" he politely enquired. Acknowledging him, she

The Winter Solstice

handed me the receiver. Both Dave and myself realised that what we really needed, was a further meeting, a chance for us to check out the reasons as to why the solstice meditation had turned out to be such an apparent failure.

"How about tomorrow night?" I enquired, "that'll give us the ideal opportunity for a few beers and a chat," I concluded. Instantly he agreed, the riddle of Baydon flowing once more through our veins.

The porch door opened. It was 7.30pm. Trudie immediately stood up and welcomed Dave inside. After a few cans of cold Guinness and an overly large dish of tortilla chips, the fun packed events of Christmas were re-lived once again. Walking through into the kitchen, I opened up the last bottle of Trudie's Chianti, no doubt she would soon be drinking the beer, I concluded!

The three of us shared a truly wonderful evening that night, but it was time once again to direct our thoughts towards Baydon Hill. Trudie turned towards me, the weary look that enveloped her wry face implied that she was suffering the ill effects of a long and tiring day. I smiled, indicating that perhaps she should leave us and go off to bed.

Dave poured out two glasses of red wine, and the two of us plunged headlong into a detailed debate, centred primarily, on the growing enigma of Baydon Hill and St Kenelm's Church.

In the light of the Winter Solstice meditation, it was agreed that we should conduct a post Christmas mediation, basing our thoughts around St Kenelm's Church, or more precisely, the holy well. Once again, the familiar smell of burning incense radiated gently throughout the darkened lounge, as the pocket micro-recorder whirred away in the background, recording our every word. Dave initiated the visual ritual.

Following the tiny pathway which snaked its way forwards, heading out towards the deciduous Norman church, cautiously, I began to touch its outer northern wall. This, I realised, was an attempt to psychometrise the chapel, and hopefully gain useful insight into the legend that surrounded the shrine. A bolt of blue light shot out from the wall and passed right through my body. I sensed a female voice crying out, shouting out, enforcing a

The Sun & The Moon, The Hill & The Well

selection of disjointed words, and repeating them over and over.

"REMOVE THE CROWN! REMOVE THE CROWN!"

Something stood behind me. I turned around. It was the silvery image of Marianne, my guide.

"YOU MUST REMOVE THE CROWN!" She insisted. "YOU MUST REMOVE THE CROWN."

Walking slowly towards the edge of the well, I gazed deeply into the watery abyss. Marianne appeared from behind the well. She beckoned me to follow her. I found myself walking away from the well, travelling out into the open fields that accompanied the hallowed site. The guide suddenly stood still, resting at an old stone bench positioned mid-way across the barren field. Intuitively, I felt that I was about to become privy to something important. Something felt distinctly odd, I concluded. I could almost sense it. I simply knew that the answers that we sought, regarding both the holy well and Baydon Hill, would soon be within our reach.

Chapter 17

The Golden Arrow of Sabrina

Friday, 7th January, 1994. Folding back the crumpled pages of my day to day diary, Trudie curiously skipped through the jumbled collection of loose papers that outlined the most recent developments of the quest to date; each page obviously in need of thorough documentation, and subsequent transfer into our main journal.

"Do you think we should try another meditation?" she suddenly announced, peering briefly through the assortment of scribbled notes that highlighted our plight to locate the alleged site guardian of Baydon. I pondered Trudie's request, intrigued as to the reasons why she believed that a further experiment might herald an aggregation of more conclusive results. But after thoroughly discussing these notions with Trudie, her answer was simple – "it just felt right;" believing that in this instance we would gain information, which we as a group, had seemingly failed to achieve.

The tenebrous room, suffused amidst the radiance of flickering candles and the effervescent odorament of pungent incense, set the scene for our imminent visual exploration. Spirals of incense cavorted freely amongst the lifeless shadows that filled the quiet, incandescent room. Spectral apparitions, invigorated amongst the allaying sounds of Tangerine Dream, imbued the semi-darkened, smoke-filled lounge. Slowly, we both began to relax, our thoughts drifting into a timeless impression of calm.

A pin-spot of whirling light descended upon us, hovering just above the central point of our sacred circle. The sphere of light slowly began to gyrate, growing in size as it slowly spread around us, enveloping us in a protective orb of radiant light.

The cone of light gained momentum, forming a circle of

The Sun & The Moon, The Hill & The Well

protection, a cone of power,[1] bathing us in its benevolent transplendency. Suddenly, a vast doorway formed in front of me, a shimmering portal that I felt compelled to walk through.

The windswept slopes of Baydon stood before me. I evoked Marianne. There were so many things which I needed to know; so many answers that I knew only she could give. Forcibly I called out her name. She appeared.

"What do you want from me?" I curiously enquired.

Equanimity prevailed. I repeated the interrogation.

Silence.

I reiterated my request. She answered.

"Jump high into the sky," announced the guide, as an air of intrigue flashed vibrantly across her translucent form. I looked towards her, and she repeated her peculiar petition.

"Jump high into the sky," she cried.

Following her bizarre request, and in true questing spirit, I literally jumped up into the sky and realised that I could fly.

The familiar images of the hill-fort rapidly faded as I soared high above the open countryside. Baydon was no where to be seen. Around me lay the grumous etiolation of the great abyss. Where was I? What was this place? I invoked my guide - but to no avail. I was alone.

Gradually, a fresh image slowly began to form. The sorrel hues of a vernal dawn flooded my elated consciousness. My thoughts were filled with light. I could perceive an image forming, a detailed representation pertaining to a circle of ancient stones hidden amongst a fiendish periphery of tall, thinning, windswept trees. Adjacent to the circle, positioned amongst a freshly ploughed field, stood a second group of large grey stones.

"Where was this place?" I enquired, calling out to the translucent guide. It was certainly a place that I had never visited, or for that matter, ever seen before.

I descended into the centre of the ancient circle; an overwhelming sensation flooded my tired body. Walking amongst the ring of prehistoric stones, I called out, continually enquiring as to the reasons as to why I had been brought to such a place. A female voice spoke out, shattering the tense atmosphere which had accompanied my visit to the sacred stones.

"YOU MUST LOCATE THE GOLDEN ARROW OF

The Golden Arrow of Sabrina

SABRINA!" the female voice proclaimed. "YOU MUST LOCATE THE GOLDEN ARROW OF SABRINA!"

Marianne stood patiently by my side.

"There is much more to this clue," she calmly announced, as the distinct image of an old church, a small parish church, a Christian edifice surmounted by a spiral tower, and complete with an integral covered porch, filled my mind's eye. Surrounding the outer perimeter of the ageing churchyard, stood a Cotswold style brick and slate-topped wall. Marianne informed me that I had to go to this place.

"You will discover a white gravel pathway leading up to the church," she said, pausing momentarily as I began to reflect upon her request. "You *will* receive a clue in the form of a crossed Indian feather," she added.

Marianne continued.

"These are events which are out of your hands," announced the guide, "affairs that have already been set in motion."

The imagery changed as the visualisation progressed. I found myself standing alone, situated along side St Kenelm's Holy Well. Again Marianne appeared, beckoning me to follow her. We walked away from the confines of the sacred well, out across the open fields that stretched beyond the reaches of the hallowed well, stopping momentarily at the old stone bench which I had perceived during my previous visitation.

"Why here?" I inquired. She carried on walking. But as we approached the top of the incline that formed the boundary to the field which we were in, I became conscious of two pools of water positioned around a plateau. One of the pools, the larger of the two, appeared to be situated upon a much lower ground level than that of the smaller pool. Overhanging the larger lagoon stood an old tree, its ageing, carious roots, exposed as it leaned and stretched out across the barren expanse of water.

I turned to Marianne.

"A young girl drowned here once," she curiously announced. "And to commemorate her juvenile death, pins were thrown into the pool, devotional offerings, hallowed sacrifice's given in honour to this, the REAL HOLY WELL."

I couldn't believe it. At last everything seemed to be making some sort of sense. But did the pools exist? I looked towards

The Sun & The Moon, The Hill & The Well

Marianne; I had to discover who she really was.

I propelled my inquiry towards her. The entity responded.

"This is a riddle which you will solve," she remarked. "But until such time, Marianne will suffice."

I opened my eyes. Trudie sat reposed, she smiled as an air of excitement beamed across her face.

"I just knew that we'd discover something important!" She exclaimed. I remained motionless, mentally assessing the accumulation of images that I had received. I picked up my note pad and sketched a rough outline of the old tree that I had perceived, leaning, stretching, reaching across the larger of the two pools.

I picked up the portable recorder, and relayed the details of my visual experience to tape. But what of the two pools, did they exist? Well let's suppose momentarily, that perhaps they did, and were situated beyond the fields that lay behind St Kenelm's Church. But surely, the possibility of locating the overhanging tree as bestowed within the visualisation, now that would be an impossibility. And what of the evidence to suggest that devotional pins had once been thrown into the pool, indicating that the pool could have been a holy well; St Kenelm's Holy Well? Only a visit to the well would either confirm, or dismiss the real findings of the meditation.

I decided to contact Dave, knowing full well that like myself, he would no doubt be curiously interested in these particular developments. Furthermore, something felt distinctly authentic about the results of this particular visualisation, even though I was fully aware of the fact that the findings of the meditation would mean absolutely nothing, until an actual confirmation had been obtained.

After a lengthy conversation with Dave, it was agreed that a further visit to St Kenelm's Church had to be organised. He, like myself, felt more than a little intrigued, particularly as he recalled that back in early '93, Chris had supplied him with a collection of details pertaining to a meditation which he had participated in, an experiment that had allegedly centred around the location of a collection of artefacts, items which included a 'golden arrow', a 'crown' and a 'pool'. Instantly, we both realised the potential that this information heralded. Was it that the group was onto

The Golden Arrow of Sabrina

something big? But who was Sabrina? And what was her Golden Arrow?

The return trip to St Kenelm's Church was scheduled for Sunday afternoon. Dave had contacted Simon, Tracey and Chris, and had established that thankfully, they could all attend the prospective visit. Unfortunately however, Trudie was unable to join us. She had been recovering from the ill effects of a bad bout of flu, and had decided to leave the prospective treasure hunting up to the rest of the group.

As the car approached the crumbling Norman church, a feeling of elation welled up inside my stomach. Turning towards Dave, I realised that he knew exactly what I was thinking, hoping that the return trip to the church would herald a positive identification at the back of the well.

The lifeless fingers of the bitter sweet winter sun, crudely infiltrated the rows of barren hedgerow, trying its hardest to invigorate the team as we strolled across the bleak, exposed field, that traversed the rear of St Kenelm's Church.

Simon pointed out that from where he was standing, he could see Turner's Hill, this, he realised, was due to the collection of aerial masts that stood high upon its desolate pinnacle. We continued forward, marching heartily across the unkempt muddy field, heading towards the outer perimeter fence. Eventually, we encountered a slight incline, a gentle arc preventing us from viewing the fields that followed. Pools of congealing mud made our journey that much more unbearable, yet we were all well aware of the fact that we could not give up, we had to see what lay ahead.

Tracey was the first to notice what looked like the two visualised pools.

"Mike," she said, "look over there." She pointed into the field that followed. "There are your two pools!" She excitedly announced.

I looked up; a sense of shock reeled across my body. It seemed as though Tracey was correct. Just ahead of us lay two fairly large pools of stagnant, murky water, with the largest of the pair positioned upon a much lower ground level than its smaller compeer. Even the writhe tree that I had spoken of was there,

The Sun & The Moon, The Hill & The Well

leaning, stretching, and reaching across the expanse of insidious solemn water. Euphoria surged throughout my entire consciousness as I gazed upon the two pools, it was a truly wonderful sight.

Regaining my thoughts, I suddenly realised that something about this heavenly image somehow appeared familiar to me, but I couldn't quite place it. Turning to the others, I asked each of them in turn, if the present image of the pools meant anything to them. I quickly realised that it did not. Two pools of water, one of which was situated within a ditch, and with bright rays of light emanating off its surface, what did it mean? I assessed the image once more. Still without a positive result.

Dave spoke, breaking my train of thought.

"You know, it's a real pity that Trudie was ill," he said, gazing upon the pool, "she's certainly missed out on a great find."

A radiant image of the two pools quickly flashed throughout my thoughts. Suddenly I remembered. Way back in October, just prior to the formation of the group, Trudie had described in detail, the fascinating image of the two pools during one of our earliest Baydon meditations. It was during that particular experiment, that she had made an allusion towards 'two pools of water', one of which she believed, was situated within a ditch, complete with golden rays of light emanating off its surface.

I was completely speechless. Oh, how I wished that Trudie had been well enough to share this experience with us, I thought, as I continued examining the two pools. Looking out across the larger pool, it was interesting to note that it did actually have an old tree leaning out across its tranquil surface, with most, if not all of its decaying roots exposed. Furthermore, despite the fact that some of its branches had been removed, the image positioned in front of us was nevertheless, just how I had sketched it.

"Well come on then," said Simon. "Who's going to risk falling in," he sarcastically exclaimed, "searching for those devotional pins?" Simon looked at us all, waiting for a response. Eventually, it was Chris who decided to take on the watery challenge.

"Guess it looks like I'll have to give it a go," he remarked, with a hint of humour ringing through his words. He climbed over the frail wooden fence that protected the pool. Carefully, he

The Golden Arrow of Sabrina

scoured the perimeter of the well, paying specific attention to the collection of exposed roots that stretched out across the watery expanse. Chris looked towards me, realising that if there really was something still lying hidden amongst the pool, then surely, its only hope of retrieval would involve getting soaked. Indignantly, he accepted the challenge, deciding that as the meditation involved a tree that was seen to be leaning out across an expanse of water, then this had to be where his investigation should begin.

Placing his hand deep inside the only visible entrance point that granted access into the ageing roots of the dank, decaying tree, he carefully began pulling out large clumps of rotting vegetation; desperately trying not to displace a possible artefact.

Tension was rising. Again Chris reached into the deathly remains of the old tree, and produced a further clump of debris. Still nothing. He pulled out yet another. Nothing. What was going on? It had to be there.

He spent a further twenty minutes trying to locate the devotional pin, or something that bore a close resemblance to it. But still nothing.

The soft afternoon sunlight was gently beginning to fade; Chris realised that he would have to stop his search. It was getting dark. But why had he not discovered the pin? Chris reluctantly concluded that he could not locate anything concealed along the waters edge, or for that matter, anywhere within the remains of the tree trunk.

A sense of disappointment descended upon us all, as he climbed over the small wooden fence that surrounded the pool. Disheartened, yet nevertheless pleased by the discovery of the two pools, the team began the arduous walk across the muddy fields that ushered us towards the rear of the Norman church. Reaching the cars, we made the arrangements for our next group meeting, fully aware of the fact that in leaving St Kenelm's Church behind, we were also withdrawing from whatever mysteries were concealed within the depths of the larger pool, the real holy well.

Pouring out two glasses of 'Chianti', we all sat down ready to begin our evening meal.

"Daddy, the telephone's ringing," said Daniella, as the perpetual wailing of the telephone caught her attention. I walked through into the lounge and picked up the receiver.

"Hi Mike, it's Dave, I'm sorry to disturb you during meal time" he began, "but I thought you'd like to hear the information which I've just got."

Trudie called out from the kitchen. "Who are you talking to?" she enquired.

"It's Dave," I replied, "apparently he has got some interesting news for us."

He continued.

"You remember that devotional pin? You know, the one you felt certain would be discovered hidden amongst the pool?"

I certainly did.

"Well get this," said Dave. "A close friend of mine who's a local archaeologist of sorts, apparently worked on an investigation that centred around those two pools, some years ago. Apparently, a religious artefact was recovered, a bent pin to be precise, discovered within the larger of the two pools."

He paused, giving me time to ponder the effects of his last statement.

"Mike, believe it or not, the artefact was discovered quite close to the old tree, just as you had indicated!"[2]

Now that was interesting, I thought. It certainly gave us the necessary evidence that I believed, could prove both the existence and location of the correct holy well, along with the evidence of a much earlier Lunar Cult.

Within minutes of replacing the handset, I decided to quickly re-evaluate all of the data currently in our possession. There were still far too many questions that remained unanswered. For instance, who or what was The Golden Arrow of Sabrina? Did it in fact exist?

Furthermore, one point stood out well above the rest, this being the apparent lack of a definitive time period into which our collective series of intuitive results could have possibly occurred. So where was it all leading? I felt sure that we were on the right track, even though we still lacked that special something, that unique insight which would hopefully unite all.

Spending a further couple of hours reading through the growing collection of data, I noticed an abundance of information denoting a direct connection with the Celtic period. It was

The Golden Arrow of Sabrina

apparent, as far as I was concerned, that a further visit to the local library was now a necessity.

Leaving the local library, complete with a vast collection of books each relating to the Celts and their fascinating mythologies, I eventually set about the task of compiling a concise synopsis, paying particular attention to the gods and goddesses revered during that epoch. I decided that I needed to gain a feel for the Celts, it was imperative for me to at least understand something of the deities which had played a major role in their day to day lives, including their various methods of worship. Glancing briefly through each of the books that I had managed to borrow, I was able to finally construct a fairly detailed image of the Celts.

Trudie sat quietly in the armchair, drifting in and out of sleep. The topic relating to known deities somehow stood at the forefront of my conscious mind. I began to feel that one particular god had appeared, or so I thought, to remain fairly prominent throughout my brief investigation.

The Celtic God Lugh, or Luga, appeared uncannily familiar to me, yet for some unknown reason, I couldn't recall as to why this should be so. Lifting my head up briefly, I realised that poor Trudie had fallen asleep. She must have been bored silly, I concluded, just sitting there listening to my incessant mumbling!

As I lay buried amongst the warmth of the duvet, I simply could not rid my tired mind of the curious godly name, Luga. Backwards and forwards the name cascaded, over and over, yet still I failed to realise as to why, or what it meant to me. It must have been a good hour or so before I was relaxed enough to enable me to drift off into some sort of vague sleep. Drifting deeper and deeper, slipping off into that great voyage of the unknown, once again, the Celtic God Luga took predominance over my semi-conscious mind.

I glanced at the radio alarm. It was 3.45am. My weary mind was filled to the brink, swimming with the repetitious cycling of Luga, Luga, Luga, Luga, Luga, *Yuga*, Luga, *Yuga*. I awoke! The conjunction was made. Jumping out of bed, I quickly made my way downstairs, fully aware of the reasons behind the correlation with Luga. Yuga, an exotic word 'picked up' during the meditations that had occurred throughout November 93, formed the inevitable link. Since the dawning of the investigation, I had simply failed to locate what I considered to be the befitting identity of this unusual word. What's more, I had certainly not considered the possibility that perhaps I might have either misspelt, or merely misinterpreted this strange word.

To the Celts, Luga was heeded as a god of light. His name, I soon discovered, was cognate with lux and light, and was worshipped widely throughout Ireland and central Europe. The Celtic festival attributed to Luga, was Lughnasadh, August 1st - the first full moon in Leo. Over the years, this ancient festival date eventually transformed into familiar celebration of Lammas, and then ultimately, the Harvest festival.

It is interesting to note however, that in Welsh, Luga becomes Lleu, and literally means Lion, this being an obvious astrological allusion towards the sign of Leo, remembering that Leo is ruled by the Sun. This conjunction formed an exciting and unusual twist to the saga, as the whole investigation had its fundamental basis surrounding the series of events relating to Sekhmet, 1947, and Aleister Crowley's rising birth sign, each centring upon the astrological sign of LEO. Let us also remember, that my initial contact with the angelic entity occurred in London - perhaps a further allusion towards Luga?

European mythology attests that the worship of Luga occurred, or so it is believed, upon various hills or mounds which appear to have been artificially enhanced. Luga was commonly perceived as the shining one, a mason, a goldsmith and a magician. Within the realms of Christianity, I promptly discovered that the Celtic god Luga transformed into St Michael, thus identifying him with the Qabalistic Archangel of fire, and the angelic hierarchy of the Sun. By projecting my thoughts towards the Qabalistic tables, I found that the Archangel Michael is positioned upon the eighth Sephira of the tree of life, thus identifying him with the planet Mercury.

At last we appeared to be on the right track, and if my current observations were correct, it was conceivable that Luga was in fact connected with Baydon Hill, hence confirming that the hill was Solar, or male in origin.

A further, independent piece of information, which curiously demonstrated the effectiveness of the Leo/Baydon link, was passed on to me via my close friend, Chris Whale, the person who

The Golden Arrow of Sabrina

had originally introduced Trudie, the girls and myself, to the ancient hill-fort upon Baydon Hill.

Chris had informed us, that during a recent meditation which he had conducted, that involved using the ancient hill-fort as a visual point of focus. Surprisingly, he had found that he had become aware of a series of thoughts pertaining to the astrological star sign, Leo, together with an apparent conjunction with Baydon Hill. However, I must stress emphatically, that Chris, at this point, was totally unaware of our obsessive interest in the shrouded history of the prehistoric site.

Ever since our preoccupation with the quest, I had discovered countless allusions, which each in their own particular way, hinted at the presence of a 'Solar' cult having existed upon Baydon Hill. In summarising to the effectiveness of this symbolic association, I decided to re-dress these facts, supplementing our earlier material with additional data, material which I believe effectively explains the symbolic image of the Sun.

The first reference that we had collected, indicative of an apparent 'Solar' theme, was that of the wheel - collected during early October. From around 1500BC, the wheel became a common symbol of the Sun. I suppose in many respects, it is fairly easy for us to understand this conjunction, simply by considering its shape and its embodiment of movement.

Sunday, 21st November, brought with it the intriguing allusion of the Eagle and/or Falcon headed deity. The results of this particular experiment, produced a remarkable correlation concerning the Roman Sky God and the Celtic Sun God. To the Celts, the familiar image of the Eagle was perceived as one of the select attributes of the Sun God. At this point, it is well worth noting that the Bull was also seen as a companion of the Sky God. Perhaps, here we may in fact be witnessing either a possible intensification of the celestial symbol, or perhaps some form of shape shifting between the Bull and the Eagle. The probability of the Sun God ascribing to a form of shape shifting, can in fact be confirmed within the annals of early Welsh mythology. Amongst these legends, we read that Lleu, or Luga, changed into an Eagle after having received a fatal blow from 'Gronw'.

As a final note, I would like to briefly re-dress Bull symbolism. Within classical and oriental religion, the Bull is closely associated with the 'Sky Gods'. It is a common practice to observe many gods of human form, depicted with Bull-horns. In Roman/Celtic Europe, representations of the Bull were often depicted with an additional third horn, this it was believed, could instil a form of 'sacredness' to the common image of the Bull. In Celtic Britain, there is a strong belief suggesting that an intrinsic link between both the Bull, and the Celtic Sun God, did in fact exist. My own research revealed that the Bull was believed to symbolically represent fertility, virility, and strength, with the Druids paying special attention to this animal. As an added twist, let us not forget the letter that Dave had received from Alan Cole, outlining his inclusion of Bull symbolism during meditations centring on Baydon Hill.

As a concluding note, I also recalled how the Palace of Minos, located upon Baydon Hill, displayed obvious allusions towards Bull symbolism in the mythological legends of the Minotaur. It is also worth stating, that the crumbling monolith located upon the hill, is also a direct symbol of the sun.

As far as I was concerned, this information appeared to direct us towards the notion that Baydon Hill would have been a logical site for 'Solar' worship. This opinion strengthened considerably, particularly when I recalled that most springs, rivers, holy wells, etc. pertain to a female principle, whilst standing stones, hills etc. were said to allude to the male principle.

This was all very well, I thought, but why should we have suddenly become so intensely involved with the legendary tale of St Kenelm? What was I to conclude from this involvement? Was it simply that a link between Baydon Hill and St Kenelm's actually existed? Or was it something deeper, more profound?

Chapter 18
Saturn, Old Father Time

Upon confirming the apparent Baydon Solar link, my attention swiftly turned towards the curious symbol that had resembled the number 5. This intriguing emblem had been collected during the group meditations of 27th November, '93, when the team had tried to locate information pertaining to whom, or what the current site guardian of Baydon actually is. The results that were obtained however, were certainly not what we had expected. But upon reflection, and after finally recognising the true identity of the symbol, all notions surrounding the investigation, finally began to fall neatly into place.

Having spent a considerable amount of time verifying every possible attribution that the symbol conveyed, the most obvious of these had unfortunately been temporarily overlooked - I should have known better. The correct identity of the emblem, signified a corrupt form of that commonly used to personify the planet Saturn. It was also, on a lighter note, the common logo used by the popular seventies rock band, Blue Oyster Cult.

After successfully identifying the meaning of the symbol, and with this information planted at the forefront of my mind, certain symbolic notions finally became apparent; in particular, the station or Sephirah, which the planet Saturn held upon the Qabalistic Tree of Life. This symbolic implication represented an important find, a necessary acquisition that was to substantiate an element of truth in most, if not all of the answers that we as a group had interpreted during our countless experimental visualisations.

The planet Saturn is attributed to Binah, the third Sephirah on the Qabalistic Tree of Life, a word which when transliterated, means understanding. To this station, we find designated the passive female or negative quality, 'Aimah', the Great Mother, Great Sea - the Mother of all living. Binah, in many respects, personifies the archetypal womb through which life is inevitably manifested. To this third Sephirah, are ascribed a variety of goddesses that included such names as Mary, Cybele, Rhea, Frigga, Demeter, Here, Hecate, Juno and Selene, including many aspects of the commonly known Isis; each indicating in their own particular way, the idiosyncratic personification of the Great Mother.

Considering the implications suggested by the discovery and subsequent identification of the Saturn emblem, it became obvious to me then, that some kind of change, for want of a better word, had occurred upon Baydon Hill. But let us for a moment, reconsider the question put forward by the group, during the visualisation to identify the site guardian of Baydon Hill, and how that the answer which we eventually received, was given to us in the form of a symbol.

Initial thoughts regarding the concept of the Saturn symbol, suggested the rather obvious possibility that it was some kind of cryptic clue. However, further research revealed that this belief was in fact correct, the Saturn emblem indicated that a goddess sharing the attributions of the Qabalistic Binah, was in fact the current site guardian. But how could we ever effectively prove it?

It is interesting to recollect what's more, that during that same visualisation, I had experienced a vivid series of imagery suggesting the one time presence of a three horned deity; the identity of which still baffled me. Nevertheless, the point that I was trying to state, was that during that particular experiment, I had come to realise that a change of belief *had* occurred during the history of the hill. This caused me to conclude that the three-horned deity, denoted reverence of a *past* tense, and consequently, implied that the hill was now at the hands of some other deity. If we consider the Saturn symbol collected during that same session; hence, it would appear that the elusive deity was perhaps that of a goddess.

Right from the onset of the investigation, it had emerged that some form of psychic imbalance had, and was still occurring on Baydon Hill, insinuating that something, or someone, had disrupted the subtle energy balance attributed to the area. As far as

Saturn, Old Father Time

I was concerned, this information strongly upheld the opinion that the proposed disorder was due to a change of belief, and therefore, the key to our quest.

Our evidence had indicated that Baydon Hill was rightly a Solar or male related site, and that due to some form of transformation, the hill had become a female or Lunar related site. It is well documented that the worship of the female deity during the pre-Christian era, was related in many respects, to the passive inherent energies of the Moon, just as the male dominant principle, was usually associated with Solar worship.

So was Baydon Hill under the influence of a goddess? If so, we needed to find out who. So, by directing our attention towards Baydon Manor, of which Baydon Hill forms part of its estate, I discovered that located within it, are a variety of depictions, each relating to the goddesses Flora and Cybele, both of whom incidentally, come under the attribution and ruler-ship of Binah, home to our peculiar Saturn symbol.

With this material at hand, I proposed that perhaps it was correct for us to assume that what we were in-fact encountering, was a localised variation of the female deity Cybele. Furthermore, it was whilst working upon this aspect of the quest, that I stumbled unknowingly, upon what I believed to be the correct identity of the three-horned deity.

The Celtic Solar God, Luga, appears, in many respects, to share an affinity with the pagan deity Mercury; it being one of the more popular gods revered during the annals of ancient Britain. Interestingly, I discovered that depictions of this particular pagan god have recently been unearthed, displaying three heads, three horns etc, and with one particular representation well worth mentioning here. It has been clearly documented, that representations of the god Mercury, have been evidently discovered, which depict him complete with three phalluses; one placed upon the head, one positioned in place of the nose, and the third situated within the usual genital region, thus indicating potent fertility.

We can clearly expand upon this link, when we recall how Mercury is situated at the eighth station upon the Tree of Life, the location commonly attributed to the Archangel Michael - the angel of the Sun. Hypothetically, we are then led to believe that the visualised three horned deity, represented a localised configuration of the 'Luga/Mercury' connection - the Sun God.

With all this information falling neatly into place, was there any hard evidence to suggest that there was a connecting link between Baydon Hill and St Kenelm's? Was it just possible that both sites were in some way inter-linked? Whatever the answer, it was time to re-investigate the Kenelm aspect of the quest, in particular, Trudie's incredibly accurate description of St Kenelm's Church, along with the allusions that she had made concerning the words, Ing-thon and Ing-on.

Having failed to attribute suitable identities to either of these curious words, a prompt visit to the town library heralded the following information. 'Ing' was regarded as the divine progenitor of the Germanic Ingnaeones, an ancient race who had once inhabited the Baltic coast. The symbolic meaning of Ing, alludes to the notion of a lance or a yew, and suggests a correlation with the patronal deity of England; equating with the fertility god Freyr. According to an Anglo-Saxon Runic poem, the god Ing was connected with the eastern Danes and corresponded to the 'Yngoi' of the Scandinavian tradition. History postulates that the Vandals were responsible for the subsequent arrival of the cult of 'Ing', here upon the shores of ancient Britain.

If we recall my analysis of the Kenelm name momentarily, in it we will discover a selection of references indicative of a subtle current alluding to fertility. So would it be correct therefore, to suggest that this information verified a uniting link with Ing/Freyr, posing an analogy with the fertility god Cernunnos, the 'Horned God' - the Green Man?

To the Celts, the worship of Cernunnos - the Horned god, was wide spread. He was perceived as an ancient deity of nature, and was usually portrayed complete with horns or antlers and long curling hair. The most common symbols attributed to Cernunnos, were the Stag, the Ram, the Bull, and the Horned Viper. On an alternative note, my research also revealed that the Horned God also shared in the universal personification of the Divine Solar God.

But how could 'Ing' - the Horned god, have been closely linked with St Kenelm's Church as Trudie's information had apparently suggested? After thoroughly examining our complete

Saturn, Old Father Time

collection of notes, I was at last able to formulate my hypothesis. It emerged that right from the onset of our involvement with Baydon Hill, there appeared, or as far as we were concerned, to be a strong possibility that some form of energy imbalance had occurred within the locality of the hill-fort. But what were the origins of this alleged imbalance? In our opinion, we believed this to be a consequence in respect of the constant interaction of incongruous worship to a Lunar, or female deity, as opposed to the reverence of what we believed should have been a Solar - male deity.

With this in mind, was it just possible therefore, that what were in fact looking at, was a time in history when the Celts, who had inhabited Baydon, were driven off their sacred solar hill. History nevertheless, does seem to suggest that this event could have occurred; being instigated by the Romans, who as we know, seemingly did inhabit the hill-fort.

So with the Celts losing their sacred site to the hands of the Romans, I propose that they finally found refuge in and around Clent, and it was there that a new centre of religious worship was finally brought about. After descending upon the picturesque surroundings of Clent, in particular Kenelmstow, along with their Solar deities, I believe that the accumulation of feminine energies, indicative of the Lunar Cult which had once resided alongside the well, were then thrown into a state of complete and total chaos. The subtle feminine current was then either absorbed into the rival Solar Cult, which now occupied the well, or alternatively, magnetically drawn towards the Roman Dianic, Lunar based centre, which I propose then resided upon Baydon Hill.

So are we to assume that the myth of St Kenelm actually embodies this ideal, a Christianised double barrelled perspective, that emphasised aspects of two much earlier pagan religions, and with the life and trials of St Kenelm personifying firstly, a Lunar Cult based around the sacred well, and secondly, the arrival of the Solar Deity - the Horned God, Ing, Freyr, Luga and St Kenelm?

Considering our evidence regarding the proposed Kenelm Lunar Cult and the later arrival of the Baydon Solar tribe, I felt happy with my conjecture. However, let us renew ourselves of some of the more important aspects of this premise.

The Kenelm legend spoke of the young king being seven at

The Sun & The Moon, The Hill & The Well

the time of his death. But this, as we now know, is a number closely associated with the Moon and reverence towards the feminine principal in general. Regarding the old hag's cow, immortalised within the myth, and which stood patiently by the deathly remains of the young king, here, once again, we have allusions indicative of a Lunar current.

It is an interesting fact that Venus-Aphrodite, the goddess of love, is acknowledged as being born of the sea foam, and that the Virgin Mary is known by the Catholics as 'Stella Maris' - star of the sea, the link here being, that Venus is attributed to the seventh Sephirah, and seven plays a prominent part within the Kenelm legend. Seven, I must add, is also the total number of hills situated in and around Clent, this alone suggesting an apparent link with the female Lunar belief. The list is endless.

Equally, the Baydon Hill solar connection clearly categorises this theme, in that hills, mounds, and standing stones, are considered to allude to the male or solar principal, and with the presence of the Druids, Luga and Serpent energy, empowering this hypothetical perspective.

As a group, we firmly believed that incongruous devotion had continued at both sites right up until the present day, and that some form of energy re-dress would have to be effected, if the correct harmonious energies required within the site, were to flow inhibited once again.

Everything pointed towards the probability that our task was to involve re-dressing the subtle energy balance at both sites in order to re-establish what we perceived as being the correct polarity required within each location. I recalled how Tracey had clearly informed us that we had to 'remove the crown' from St Kenelm's Holy Well, believing that we were required to remove the Lunar devotion inherent at Baydon, and then re-locate it at its correct locality, this being the pool situated to the rear of St Kenelm's Church.

The Solar dedication would also have to be symbolically moved, and subsequently repositioned within close proximity to the monolith. Obviously, we had no right to simply march into both sites, only to destroy the accumulation of devotion, which had amassed at each location; doing so under the pretence of reinstalling them to their correct polarity. However, I believed that by simply moving this misdirected energy, the subtle energy matrix that had harmoniously governed the surrounding area, would once again function more effectively and efficiently.

But what of the female entity that had continually invaded my thoughts? As to the guide herself, and after many hours of reading, I was finally able to confirm her association with water, and therefore her link with Kenelm.

By analysing the constituents of her name, her conspicuous water association became quite apparent. Marianne was in fact, the temporary name given to me by the guide, and in it, I found my clue. By turning my attention towards the Semitic languages, I found that the word Marah, symbolised the Great Sea, and also formed the root base to the name Mary. Here, once again, we have a curiously interesting attribution of the third Sephirah, Binah; the name Marianne being related in one sense to Mary, and in so doing, sharing some, if not all of its properties.

So it would appear, therefore that Marianne was some form of water spirit, and let us not forget that the entity had stated that this name only represented what she was, *not* who she was.

Chapter 19
The Temple Of The Sun

Thursday, January 27th, 1994. Were we correct with our assumptions? I thought, as I gazed idly up at the star-lit winter sky. But nevertheless, I felt sure that before any corrective work could occur at either of the two sites, a further meeting with Dave would have to occur, in order to clarify the overall objectives of the quest.

The scented candles flickered momentarily, invigorated amidst the growing whirls of burning incense that danced effortlessly around the golden glow of the incandescent flames. The two dogs pricked up their ears, the sound of the porch door opening, catching their attention. Dave had arrived.

It had been quite a time since our last meeting, I concluded, as Dave handed us both a copy of the rough notes which he had been composing; thoughts that outlined his feelings towards the quest so far. Eventually, we settled ourselves down and the debate began, centring itself initially around cross checking each and every piece of data which we had acquired, and taking care to ensure that each fragment had been correctly assigned to its respective corresponding domain.

By the time we had finally agreed upon the theory that, as far as we were concerned, the information that we had accumulated *did* warrant a problem at each of the two locations, Dave suggested that a final meditation should take place, believing this to be prerequisite to any ritual work actually occurring at either of the two sites.

As to the nature of the visualisation, this was easily agreed upon. We needed to confirm the identity of the deity, or guardian of the hill. Trudie handed me the packets of incense, and we set about creating the appropriate atmosphere conducive to a meditation.

The Temple Of The Sun

The candles glimmered enduringly, as the planetary incense crackled and spat; bursting into life as it suddenly fell upon the surface of the white hot block of charcoal. The subtle aromas emanating from the smouldering incense, filled the darkened room, instilling a deep and lasting state of repose, a tranquillity which travelled amongst us all.

Closing my eyes, I found myself drifting deeper and deeper, falling into the tranquillity which had engulfed us. It was time to begin. From within the depths of my heightened consciousness, Dave's hypnotic voice could still be heard, guiding me back onto those familiar slopes of Baydon Hill.

Reaching the summit of the hill, I called out to my guide. It felt so different as I stood amidst the hill-fort. An overwhelming impression of calm, gently radiated across the surrounding landscape. Looking up towards the cloudless, radiant blue sky, once again I called out for the help of my guide.

"Who is the correct deity of the hill?" I shouted.

Silence prevailed. I repeated the interrogation.

"Who is the correct deity of the hill?" I enquired, this time projecting the question out across the entire hill. Patiently awaiting some form of response, I caught sight of a small figure approaching me. As he neared, I became distinctly aware of his defined facial features - a wide beaming smile and pointed ears. As the curious dwarf-like character advanced, he eventually spoke.

"You would like to know who the site ruler was?" He enquired, looking deep into my eyes.

"You would like to know who the site ruler was?" he announced, in an almost agitated manner.

"Yes!" I exclaimed!

"Then follow me," he said, "but you must be quick."

Inquisitively, I began to follow him. The guide burrowed his way through a curtain of leafy foliage, a passageway that revealed a secret entrance, a hidden tunnel which led into the core of the sacred hill. Following the guide, I found myself entering an earthen corridor, a pitch-black chamber that led us deeper into the hill. The two of us began to move quickly through a complex maze of darkened tunnels, guiding us towards the heart of the ancient hill. Suddenly, my peculiar pathfinder stood still. He

The Sun & The Moon, The Hill & The Well

turned around and spoke out.

"This is where my ruler lies," the little person announced.

We entered a vast, dimly lit anti-chamber, a gallery that led into a huge secondary chamber. Positioned mid-way across the far corner of the cavern, stood the figure of a golden monarch, a king seated upon a magnificent golden throne. The divine figure appeared to be in a suspended state of stasis. I looked towards the guide, he continued.

"My king has been forced underground," he said, staring me straight in the face. I kindly asked him for the name of his king, but his answer was that I already possessed this information. Once again I questioned the little person, this time with regards to his name.

"To some, my name is Sun-face," he quietly remarked, "but to others, Oghma."

I thanked him for his friendly help, and realised that it was now time for me to leave the underground domain of the sacred hill. I had achieved my goal.

I opened my eyes. Thankfully, I was still sitting amongst the protective circle. After relaying the selection of events onto Dave, Trudie, and the dictaphone, I eagerly awaited an account of Dave's visual experience.

"Having reached the top of the hill," said Dave, "I made my way out towards the folly, except that it had now changed into a stone altar surrounded by a large circle of ancient grey stones."

Dave paused, contemplating the array of vivid imagery which had invaded his thoughts. Reluctantly, he continued.

"The group were standing outside the perimeter of stones," Dave exclaimed, turning over his page of scribbled notes.

"But for some reason, the guide simply stood before me, dressed in dark red robes."

A swirl of incense invigorated the darkened room; the candles flickered to and fro, casting ghostly images upon the walls of the lounge.

"I projected a question to the guide," said Dave, "requesting permission for us to gain access into the inner sanctum of the magical stone circle."

Dave paused, trying to recollect the images of his encounter.

"The guide finally granted my request," he added, "but as we

The Temple Of The Sun

cautiously entered the sacred circle, a ring of azure flame engulfed the perimeter of the circle."

A sudden clank signalled the end of the tape. Dave loaded a fresh cassette into the hand held recorder, and once again he continued speaking.

"A horned deity entered the imagery," Dave added. "I focussed upon the image, attempted to discover who, or what it was, and believing that this figure was possibly Luga."

He looked up, contemplating the images cast by the candles as they each danced idly, brought to life amongst a delicate shroud of shadows.

"Who is the correct site guardian of the hill?" Dave questioned, returning his attention to his notes.

"The gigantic figure swept me up and held me high above the stone circle, answering my question in the form of a symbolic image."

Dave was quick to realise that this symbol resembled the familiar attribute of the wheel - the emblem of Solar force. We closed down the protective circle; our encounter was at an end.

"Mike, the reference you made to going underground with that little person - you know, the one you named Oghma," said Dave.

Trudie looked up.

"Well that's really interesting," he said, looking out across the smoke-filled room. "Because in Celtic Mythology, it was believed that the old gods, or to use a Celtic term, the Tuatha, were given dwellings inside the Barrows or hillocks. These hidden, magical locations were known to the Celts as the Sidhs."

Dave added that according to mythological tradition, it was considered common belief that the divine race of the Tuatha - the good gods, were driven underground and forced to live amidst an underworld environment, where it was said that they established otherworldly kingdoms, hidden deep beneath the sacred hills. Tradition states that the Dagda - the father of the gods, assigned each member of the Tuatha to one of these sacred mounds or Sidhs.

Dave opened up his hold-all. He felt sure that hidden amongst the cluttered collection of books, which he had brought along with him, he had to have something covering these aspects of the Celtic tradition. Eventually, and after a thorough and detailed search, he finally produced an amazing assortment of information, material which outlined the belief that the burial mounds of the Neolithic and Bronze ages, were perceived as the dwelling places of the gods; believing that these mounds would act as astral doorways, magical passageways granting access into the underground realms.

Dave paused momentarily, stopping as he opened up another fascinating book.

"Oh, this one looks interesting," he said, glancing down at the page. "The Dagda was considered to be the good god, the lord of life and death, and shared many of the attributions of both the Sun and the Earth god."

He turned the page.

"It appeared that the Dagda had four mythical palaces," announced Dave, "each one situated deep within the realms of the hollow hills." He leaned forward, pouring a small quantity of incense onto the brown terracotta dish. Dave continued with his account, stating that the Dagda had several children, one of which was Oghma, or Sun-face, and sharing similar attributes to the Greek hero Hercules. He also added, that Celtic tradition asserts that Oghma invented the Ogham script, and was a poet, an artist, a musician, a Sun god and a god of magic and spells.

Upon hearing what Dave had to say, Trudie and I were both pretty astonished. Our thoughts instantly recalled the results that were obtained during one of our earliest meditations, a visualisation in which we collected impressions that we now realised, related directly to Oghma. During that particular experiment, Trudie had made a direct reference to a Sun-face, whilst I had highlighted a peculiar name which sounded something like Oghma, in that Aghma or Akhma and Sun-face, were obviously direct references to the Celtic Oghma.

Next, we turned our attention towards the contents of Dave's visualisation, in which he had made references to both 'Fire; and 'Wheel'. Our research revealed that symbolically, fire was considered as a gift of the Sun in antiquity, with the pagan fire festivals Beltane, 1st May, and Samhain, 1st November, illustrating these critical points within the solar year, and serving as an acknowledgement of the life giving power of the Sun.

The Temple Of The Sun

We were now totally convinced that our assumptions pertaining to the masculine, Solar polarity of Baydon Hill, were correct. This notion could be substantiated, by considering the results of our meditational experiments, in that the Aten, Eagle, Fire, Leo, Luga, May-Day festival, Oghma, Sun-face, and the Wheel, verified this belief.

Finding myself literally swamped amidst Solar symbolism, and believing that we were correct with regards to our Baydon Hill Solar conjecture. I knew that it was time for us to begin considering the techniques that the group would employ, assuming that we decided to re-dress the imbalance associated with both sites.

A meeting of the group was hastily arranged. We needed to update the rest of the team in respect of all current developments, and conceived that this would also act as the most suitable opportunity, in which to put forward a detailed synopsis regarding the corrective procedure that we planned to administer to both sacred sites.

"I propose, that should we decided to correct the energy problems at Baydon Hill and St Kenelm's, then frankly, I feel we should construct some sort of emblem, something to personify the Celtic concept of the Sun and the Moon."

"Leave that to me," said Dave, as he began to quickly sketch an assortment of designs that he felt represented the masculine, Solar energies, including a similar collection, indicative of its feminine, Lunar compeer.

"With the two objects psychically charged up," I exclaimed. "I believe we should then place each charged artefact in a pre-selected secret location, a covert hiding place set within the grounds of each site."

Simon piped up.

"What happens to the objects then?" he enquired, pouring out another glass of wine.

I answered his question, stating that it was my opinion that the talismans had to be left in situ, for a period of nothing less than fourteen days. The idea was that with the help of the team, the two concealed artefacts would absorb a characteristic quantity of the subtle energies retained within the locality of each site. To

The Sun & The Moon, The Hill & The Well

help substantiate this process, I proposed that the group should conduct a series of daily meditations, ritual visualisations designed to attract the inherent energy present within each site, re-directing it towards each applicable talisman.

I then explained to the group how that the charged Solar symbol would be then placed amongst the grounds of St Kenelm's Church, concealed in a position which allowed it to accumulate the Solar energy present within the site. Following this, the Lunar symbol would be concealed on Baydon Hill, positioned like the Solar amulet, set amidst a locality that would aid in the symbolic recovery of the subtle feminine energies.

With the talismans charged up, and then covertly positioned amongst the grounds of each site, a congenial date for the completion ritual then had to be decided upon. I proposed that this date should be non-other than the Celtic festival date, Beltane, May 1st. Right from our initial involvement with the quest, the concept of a May Day festival had appeared to play an important role within the intuitive information that we had amassed. Dave instantly agreed with my choice, believing that we should inform the group of the benefits and beliefs associated with the Celtic fire festival, Beltane.

The conversation continued, concluding that under the cover of darkness, the two charged talismans were to be ceremoniously separated from their ephemeral locations. This would be accomplished by the use of a specially designed ritual, a rubric to which I had given the title: The Sun & The Moon. At this point during the re-balancing rite, the charged artefacts would then be ceremoniously re-positioned, sited within the grounds of each sacred site, with the understanding that the talismans would naturally liberate their collective charges; empowering the localised environment, and replenishing the depleted energy matrix.

With each aspect of the ritual effectively executed, it was my opinion that the consequence of these actions, would result firstly in the symbolic release of the Sun god, Luga, from his prolonged period of enslavement, deep beneath the sacred hill, and then the whole process would be counterbalanced by the ritual re-establishment of the Lunar goddess, which we felt had once reigned over the site that currently housed the archaeological

The Temple Of The Sun

remnants of the ancient village of Kenelmstow.

Assuming that the re-balancing ritual went according to plan, then to all intents and purposes, I felt that there should be a physical improvement within the area as a whole; indicating that by virtue of our actions, the subtle bands of energy that had once flowed undisturbed, would be free to do so once more. To complement the effectiveness of the ritual on a long-term basis, I proposed that the two talismans should be situated within the confines of a Celtic Earth Shrine - a hallowed site, set up so as to receive devotional offerings pertaining to a particular god, or goddess.

With the 'Earth Shrines' concealed within the grounds of each ancient site, and the planting of a living votive offering to seal our plight, it was my belief that the process of ritual cleansing and replenishment could then successfully occur. The group sincerely believed, that with the ceremony completed, it would warrant a lasting impression upon the localised energy matrix - that collective configuration of perspicacious energy patterns that are ever present within the landscape as a whole.

Wednesday, 2nd February, 1994. It had been a distressing night for Trudie, as she lay awake in bed, desperately trying to drift off into some form of concocted sleep. She had lost count of the numerous occasions when she had felt the need to lift up her head, trying to catch a passing glance at the time displayed upon the radio alarm.

It was 5.30am, and Trudie had succumbed to the fact that it would be impossible for her to fall back to sleep. It was no good, she thought, as she idly tossed from side to side, she would have to get up and make herself a hot drink.

Trudie sat up in bed, allowing herself just a few moments in order to fully awaken prior to going downstairs. Suddenly, to her total amazement, her consciousness became inflamed amidst a vivid selection of images - semblances that related directly to St Kenelm's Church. She rubbed her sleepy eyes, half expecting to wake up, but she quickly realised that she was in fact, fully awake.

A picture slowly formed before her, an image into which she was being magnetically drawn. Trudie could see herself walking

The Sun & The Moon, The Hill & The Well

slowly through the churchyard which accompanied St Kenelm's Chapel, traversing the entire length of the grounds, and making her way down towards the domain of the sacred well.

Beginning the steep descent that led down to the sanctuary of the well, Trudie suddenly began to experience a change occurring. She noticed that her clothing had changed, and that she was taking on the physical characteristics of the young king, Kenelm. Cautiously, she approached the well. In solemn silence she knelt down and covertly began to pray. A fierce, malevolent wind suddenly arose from amongst the confines of the sacred site. Darkness encroached, but still the young Kenelm knelt deep in prayer.

Trudie began to feel nauseous, a heavy, sickly sensation grappled at her chest, she could envisage the approach of a negative entity, an insidious blackness; a foul faced emptiness that consumed all life within the sphere of the sacred space. The intruder probed the blackness, its baneful menacing fingers, reaching out from beyond its abyss of darkness. She quickly turned around, aware that someone, or something, was watching her.

Trying to focus her weary eyes onto the old pilgrim track, which veered gently away from the church, Trudie caught sight of the guardian; a cowl clad black knight with sword raised uppermost. She needed to know more. She needed to be sure that it *was* just a dream, and not a portent of what was to occur. Disturbed by the occurrence, Trudie got out of bed and made her way downstairs. She needed to think this one out. She had to inform the others.

Chapter 20

The Rollright Stones

Friday, 4th February, 94. Heavy rain lashed maliciously against the lounge windows, as I poured out three glasses of chilled dry white wine, and surrendered to the fact that we still had a busy evening ahead of us. Passing Trudie a glass of wine, Dave returned his attention towards the selection of drawings, which by this stage, had filled up four pages of his sketchpad. Throughout the evening, the three of us had independently been trying to concoct a varied selection of symbolic blueprints, rough ideas that could be attributed to the proposed designs for the forthcoming Sun and Moon talismans.

"What about these?" Dave enquired, as he lowered his half-filled glass.

He passed his sketchpad over to Trudie and awaited her response.

"What do you think then?" He curiously enquired, as she carefully glanced at the collection of images that filled the cluttered pages of his A4 drawing book. Suddenly, her eyes settled upon two rather fascinating Celtic stylised drawings.

"I like these two!" she exclaimed, nodding in approval, "I think I can honestly say that these are definitely the ones!"

Trudie leant forward and handed me the collection of drawings. Instantly I found myself tending to agree with her rather spontaneous choice. The distinctive images that Dave had quickly sketched, appeared in many respects, to personify the idea of what we as a group believed, constituted suitable symbolic representations of both the Sun and the Moon. Once again Trudie was correct with her assumptions, it appeared that these were exactly what we were looking for.

With the three of us agreeing in principle, as to the basic

The Sun & The Moon, The Hill & The Well

theme of our chosen designs, it was time for us to focus our attention on the other more pressing aspects of the quest; in particular, the collection of sketches pertaining to the ancient stone circle, and the information referring to the conjectural Golden Arrow of Sabrina.

I handed Dave my collection of intuitive drawings; a bewildered expression radiated across his face.

"Dave, are you okay?" I curiously enquired, picking up my assortment of sketches in the hope of realising what he had obviously seen.

His facial expression slowly changed and he finally began to speak.

"I think I can identify your stone circle," he announced, as he looked me straight in the face. "The bizarre thing however, is that only yesterday, I found myself planning a trip for us all to this particular site!"

Dave looked perplexed, as he mentioned that in the rear of his car, were a collection of books and photographs which he felt, illustrated the site perfectly. With a curious look still radiating across his face, he questioned me again, checking to see if I had in fact, ever visited the site depicted within my drawing. I replied, stating that as far as I was concerned, it was a site that I had never visited before, and I must add, had no previous knowledge of, but did the site actually exist?

"Well, if I'm not wrong," he calmly declared, "I believe that you have actually produced a fairly detailed rendition of the Rollright Stones," said Dave, "an ancient monumental site situated within Oxfordshire."

I felt intrigued; I needed to know more.

Returning from his visit to the car, fully armed with an incredible assortment of historic paraphernalia, Dave picked up my humble collection of drawings and set about the task of comparing each sketch against the selection of photographs that he had, which featured the Rollright Stones.

"Look here," said Dave, pointing to the assortment of images scribbled upon the page.

"The frail wispy trees that you've drawn, and those extra stones situated to the right hand side of the main complex; well, I believe, that this confirms the identity of the site as that of the

The Rollright Stones

Rollright Stones!"

A rush of adrenaline raced rapidly around my body, as my eyes took note and carefully tried to evaluate the series of photographs that lay before me. It was quite evident to us all, that the sketches which I had handed to Dave, represented an accurate, and convincing representation of the Rollright Stones; a Bronze Age circle of some seventy stones, situated on the A34 between the Oxfordshire villages of Long Compton and Chipping Norton.

So it appeared that the sketch which I had intuitively drawn, during the visualisation of Friday, 7th January, '94, was in fact an actual ancient site. But what of the Golden Arrow of Sabrina? Would it be reasonable therefore, to assume that likewise, it existed in some form or another?

Tuesday, 5th April, 94. Dave had organised a meeting with local amateur archaeologist and namesake, Mike Smith, along with his good friend Joyce Newley. The purpose of the meeting that evening, was the pending plight of Baydon Hill and its associated area. Dave felt confident that both Mike and Joyce would be more than interested in our thoughts pertaining to Baydon Hill, and could even perhaps, offer us help in clarifying some of the more elusive aspects of our quest.

It was 7.30pm. The initial introductions were over, and the evening discussion was about to begin. Mike instantly took up the lead, enquiring as to what our thoughts were regarding the ancient hill-fort.

"Mike, why don't you tell them of our pursuit so far?" Dave remarked, handing me my jumbled collection of notes. "I'm sure they'd find some of our ideas interesting, if nothing else!" he concluded. A look of intrigue covered Joyce's face as she willingly waited for my response. Finally, and after some deliberation, I eventually began, being quick to notice that Mike was showing more than just passing interest in the material which I presented to them, particularly the assortment of information which we had amassed, that focused itself around the holy well dedicated to St Kenelm.

"Do you mind if we go over your ideas regarding Baydon Hill?" he politely enquired. Once again I informed them of our beliefs, explaining how we had come to arrive at these assertions.

The Sun & The Moon, The Hill & The Well

Nodding in approval, it was obvious to me that Mike agreed in principle with at least some of our ideas, in particular, our thoughts suggesting that the Celtic Sky God Luga, was once connected with Baydon Hill.

Mike pondered our suggestions, pointing out that at the base of Baydon Hill, the remnants of an alleged ancient bridge had been discovered, a crossing which by all accounts, just happened to have the uncanny name of Ludd attached to it - no doubt derived from the Celtic name Lugh/Luga. Mike's suggestion regarding Ludd's bridge, represented an intriguing link that neither Dave nor myself had expected, and needless to say, certainly helped confirm a major part of the psychic material.

Joyce interjected, intrigued by the inclusion of Mean Hill - a prehistoric hill, which we had subsequently identified as Meon Hill. Suddenly, she began to explain a peculiar correlation which she had also shared with the hill. According to Joyce, she had stumbled upon Meon Hill some ten years earlier, while involved with American-Indian support work. Joyce went on to explain that during the course of her work, she had instigated a possible American/British twining, and had selected Baydon Hill as the centre for the British wing of the proposed collaboration.

Reputedly, Joyce, having put forward a map that featured the Heart of England as the British phase of the proposed twin-up, befriended a Colombian Indian, who, subsequently, highlighted a partial circle or tepee upon her map. It would appear, that her Colombian friend chose to use Baydon Hill as the central axis for this imperfect circle, with the selection of lines which he had drawn, touching upon a host of hill-forts that were each relatively close to Baydon Hill. What's more, the most intriguing of these intuitive alignments, was a particular line which had been attributed to Meon Hill, being positioned in such a way as to indicate a straight line between Baydon Hill and Meon Hill. As a final note, Joyce's Indian friend added, that as far as he was concerned, Baydon Hill was an important sacred centre, an omphalos, which in many respects, could even be considered as the hallowed Heart of England.

Armed with a supply of tea, coffee and biscuits, Mike walked through into his lounge and settled himself down. Joyce was ready to continue.

"It's odd you know," she explained, "but during the early eighties, I attended a fascinating lecture hosted by Graham Phillips - you know, the author of that paranormal classic, *The Green Stone*."

My ears pricked up as Joyce continued.

"Well, during the lunchtime break," added Joyce. "I managed to talk to him, particularly as he'd mentioned something, which to this day, I still consider to be an incredible idea."

I listened with added interest.

"Having told him that I lived quite close to Baydon Hill," she explained. "He looked me straight in the face, and announced that it was his belief that Gwevaraugh, the purported name behind King Arthur's Guinevere, was buried somewhere beneath the Palace of Minos."[1]

Gwevaraugh, according to authors Andrew Collins and Graham Phillips, was said to be a descendant of the exiled 18th dynasty Egyptian Pharaoh, Akhenaten, believed by many to be the possible father of Tutankhamen.[2]

History portrays Akhenaten as a complete and total tragedy for ancient Egypt. As a young king, he took control of a kingdom, which, in reality, sought a military and/or political leader. Yet Akhenaten is said to have possessed none of these special talents, but instead, decided to concentrate all his efforts towards the construction of a system of spiritual dominance, with the introduction of his monotheistic principles, as seen in his worship of the Aten.

Collins and Phillips postulate, that after the untimely death of Akhenaten, a group of his closest followers began an exodus, journeying out across Europe, and eventually landing upon the shores of ancient Britain, arriving sometime during the Middle Bronze Age period.[3]

After settling in Britain, Collins and Phillips suggested that the monotheistic belief of the Aten flourished, centring itself around a growing culture, which according to the authors research, was allegedly based in what is now know as Staffordshire. They proposed that a powerful warrior Queen, with the help of twelve others, took control of the developing community. Authors Collins and Phillips, then proposed that the

The Sun & The Moon, The Hill & The Well

success of this Queen, ultimately created the basis for a fascinating collection of myths and legends, which would eventually mould themselves into what is now commonly perceived as the Arthurian Romances.

This conjecture proved particularly interesting, especially as the supposed Baydon/Gwevaraugh link, had never been included in the remarkable book, *The Green Stone*, or in fact, in any of Phillips or Collins subsequent publications. A logical query instantly arose. Was Joyce correct with her assertions? Did Graham Phillips *seriously* imply that a correlation between Gwevaraugh and Baydon Hill had once existed? Assuming that perhaps her information was correct, could it be that this material had forged the fountainhead for the eventual emergence of the local Arthur/Baydon conjunction?

A further point that I had certainly found most perplexing, was the apparent connection that Joyce had inferred regarding her Colombian-Indian friend. Taking this material on face value, was I to assume that my data relating to 'crossed Indian feathers', collected during my January meditation, was in some way linked with the crosses that had been highlighted on the map which Joyce had shown us. On her map, it clearly unveiled the apparent association that Baydon Hill shared with Meon Hill.

It all seemed just a little too coincidental, I thought, as I packed away my collection of notes and prepared to leave Mike's flat. Anyhow, no doubt all would be revealed on Sunday, I concluded, the day which Dave had planned for the group outing to the Rollright Stones.

Sunday, 10th April, 94. We were all ready to leave when Chris Wright pulled up outside the house. Trudie looked patiently down at her watch. It was 10.30am. From Dave's implications, I gauged that we would arrive at the Rollrights sometime around 11.30am. We just hoped that the rain, forecast for late morning, held off. Starting the engine, Chris gently pulled away from the house.

Stepping out from the warmth of the car, we were greeted by the cutting reminder that winter was still looming secretly in the background. In fact, I couldn't believe how cold it was, as I gasped for breath and quickly zipped up my jacket.

The walk around the ancient circle of stones, was certainly an

The Rollright Stones

interesting one, the Rollrights appearing just as I had perceived them during my earlier meditation. Accepting the possibility, that perhaps the Rollright Stones were in fact the circle of stones which had featured in my visualisation, it followed therefore, that there was obviously a motive for our presence here. But for what reason and why?

Leaving behind the constant chatter of the group, I cautiously made my way towards what I believed to be the furthest point within the ancient site. Suddenly, I sensed that I had to approach this point via the centre of the circle, and in so doing, realised that this would have to be accomplished in a particular way.

Beginning the slow, helical journey towards the central point of the ancient stone circle, I found myself suddenly overwhelmed by a curious sickly sensation, a nauseous feeling that welled up inside. Stirred by these anomalous sensations, I began to perceive a spiral of light, slowly rising up from within the central confines of the circle, and connecting each and every one of the ancient stones with its spidery fingers of white light.

My concentration began to wane, being drawn away towards one particular stone situated close to the far side of the circle. Focusing my thoughts, I began to sense a peculiar vibration, a pulsating sensation emanating from either within the stone, or from somewhere directly beneath it. I could feel it undulating as it emitted some kind of bluish silver light. I realised that I had to walk towards it.

The nauseous sensation that I had begun to experience only moments earlier, was getting progressively worse. Dave walked over towards me and asked if I was okay. Strangely though, as he, like myself, neared the central portion of the circle, he too began to experience the same unpleasant, sickly sensation. What was happening?

Kneeling down, I placed my hands on either side of the stone in an attempt to psychometrise it. Instantly, I was overcome by a sudden, sharp jolt, an electrical pulse that radiated violently across my body, forcing my consciousness to absorb the full impact of the electrical burst. Within my mind's eye, I could sense that I was encompassed amidst a dense, eerie blue light.

By touching the stone, I felt that something had evidently been 'clicked' into place, like a circuit being switched on, but for

The Sun & The Moon, The Hill & The Well

what possible use? And for what kind of purpose? Was I the one destined to trip the circuit?

Pulling away from the stone, the thoughts and impressions, which only moments earlier had run riot through my body and mind, slowly subsided. Normality had returned.

After a rather full and thorough investigation of the site, it was decided that the group should extend our stay, and visit the nearby village of Great Rollright. Dave decided that perhaps we would pick up further information. Chris checked on the map, and stumbled on the fact that we were only a short distance away from Meon Hill, the place that had featured in an earlier visualisation. Within minutes of this discovery, a prompt visit to the hill was hastily arranged.

Chapter 21

Meon Hill

The narrow country roads, which gradually guided both vehicles onwards towards the quaint Oxfordshire village of Lower Quinton, were certainly not short on surprises. Sharp left, hard right we turned, as the winding country roads progressively drew both cars into the darkened domain of Meon Hill. Ahead in the distance, watching over and towering high above the small rural village, stood the single, ambiguous prehistoric hill.

A peculiar sensation hung in the air as the hill drew us nearer; each of us believing that we could feel the attraction that the antiquated mound appeared to discharge. Focusing my thoughts once again, I looked down towards the map. We were about to make the final turn, which by all accounts, would guide us directly into the picturesque village of Lower Quinton.

A solitary, conical spire broke through the uncluttered sky line. Images of the meditation that had previously featured a church surmounted by a towering spire and a white gravel pathway, slowly began to intoxicate my thoughts - perhaps this was the church which I had visualised? Nearing the village centre and positioned immediately before us, stood the lone Christian edifice. A grey slate wall encased the perimeter of St Swithan's Church; its white gravel pathway, forming the only visible access route into the region and sanctuary of its wooden porch-way. Somehow, I simply knew that St Swithan's Church, was in fact the church that had featured within my Sabrina visualisation. What's more, it even matched the scribbled drawings that I had sketched during that same visualisation! Chris indicated, and eased his foot off the accelerator pedal. Slowly, the car drew to an eventual halt.

With each member of the group walking silently towards the

The Sun & The Moon, The Hill & The Well

church, it appeared that our adventure had finally begun. The group followed the gravel pathway, secretly hoping in many respects, to discover a pair of crossed Indian feathers as characterised within my earlier meditation. But then I was confident that the information which Joyce had kindly given me, regarding her Indian friend and the map which he had highlighted, more than adequately covered this aspect of the quest.

Walking quietly in through the entrance of the peaceful parish church, my attention was immediately drawn towards a specific tomb, a crumbling shrine that featured the immortalised carved image of a solitary knight in armour. Approaching it, I began to sense a peculiar presence, which appeared to radiate from within the centre of the archaic stone tomb. Sitting in silence, intoxicated amidst the serenity that the hallowed building discharged, I allowed my stilled thoughts to wander. I reached out and gently placed my hands on the cold stone statue, waiting, patiently hoping to make contact with the ethereal presence that surrounded the tomb. Almost at once, a male voice roared out.

"I am John," said the presence in a deep resounding tone.

"What is it that you so seek of me?" The entity proclaimed.

In silence, I informed John of the intent of our quest and the reasons for our brief visit to the church, his church.

Trudie appeared and quietly sat down beside me.

"Mike, I'm picking up on the name John," she said, breaking my concentration and diverting my thoughts. With a look of shock, I turned to acknowledge her.

"Who is John?" she curiously enquired.

I forced a smile, the whole episode was beginning to take on a peculiar twist, I concluded.

"I think that John is in some way intimately associated with the church," I casually replied. "In fact, I think we'll discover that he's some sort of custodian," I added.

A sonorous tone dispersed my thoughts.

"You seek the puzzle of Sabrina?" The male voice forcibly inquired. Answering it, I quickly affirmed that we did, and wondered if the 'spirit of John' could offer us his help.

The voice spoke out.

"A tie has been forged where the veil lies thin," the anomalous entity replied.

Meon Hill

"Your visit to the sacred stones has substantiated this bond - bringing forth the balance of the Lion with the Unicorn, the symmetry of the Sun and the Moon."

The communication abruptly ended. Silence remained. I was totally puzzled, but what did it mean?

Sitting quietly in a pew, contemplating the inspired words spoken by the memory of the dead knight, I hypothesised upon the vague possibility that somehow, a subtle link had been forged between Baydon Hill and the Rollright Stones - the Lion and the Unicorn, the positive with the negative. An intriguing notion flashed vividly across my thoughts. Surely, both of these sites represent male or solar locations, I inquisitively thought, as opposed to masculine and feminine sites as proposed by the dead knight.

Deciding that I would have to give this possibility a little more thought before I could support a suitable answer. I took the option of not troubling the rest of the group with the contents of my peculiar encounter. If necessary, that would come later.

Having spent more than enough time admiring the interior of the church, it was decided that we should each spend a few moments quietly relaxing; absorbing the tranquil pleasantries of St Swithan's Church. Anyway, I thought, who knows, one of us might pick-up further information apropos to the Lion and the Unicorn.

With the brief meditation completed, and no subsequent results obtained, the group headed outside. From the rear of the church, Meon Hill dominated the horizon. There it stood, dominant, motionless, standing like a quiescent guardian that watched over the village, while its covert sense of unease, radiated chaotically across the open landscape.

Dave looked out towards the hill, realising that by this stage, a walk on top of Meon Hill would have to wait until such time as a secondary visit to the village could be organised. It was getting late, and the spring daylight was fading quickly.

Tuesday, 12th April, 94. Sam barked as the postman delivered our perpetual quota of morning mail. Kneeling down to pickup the usual assortment of letters, bills, leaflets and other junk mail, I

The Sun & The Moon, The Hill & The Well

was somewhat surprised to open up a letter from my namesake, Mike Smith. After reading his letter, it was obvious that he had undertaken a large amount of research in respect of the known history of Meon Hill, believing that perhaps his findings would possibly be of some use to Trudie, myself, and the quest for the Sun and the Moon, the Hill and the Well.

Mike had discovered that Meon Hill was an Iron Age hill-fort, a fort that appeared to exhibit many similarities to Baydon Hill, in as much as Meon Hill was of a similar size, and age to Baydon Hill. What's more, according to Mike, it appeared that both hills also shared in a rather bizarre assortment of conjectural links. Firstly, they had both featured ritualistic style murders, which had been attributed initially, to a possible Witchcraft/Occult connection, and with both slayings seemingly occurring sometime during the late thirties/early forties - perhaps even the same year!

It was St Valentine's Day, when the brutally murdered body of local villager, Charles Walton, was discovered lying upon the grassy slopes of Meon Hill. Reports from the scene, suggest that Walton was found with his own pitchfork thrust into his neck, and that some form of cross had been carved upon his chest. The obvious ritualistic implications of the murder, along with a rather bizarre collection of other anomalous happenings within Lower Quinton, suggested the probable involvement of some form of debased witchcraft or occult involvement. In charge of the Meon Hill murder hunt was the famous Inspector Fabian of Scotland Yard. But even so, after extensive investigations by Fabian and his team, the case of Warwickshire villager, Charles Walton, was eventually left unsolved.[1]

The Baydon Hill link in the Meon murder investigation, occurred as an alleged MI6 agent disappeared while investigating the Walton murder case during a visit to Lower Quinton and Meon Hill. No trace of the missing agent was discovered until the mid-fifties, when apparently, her carious remains were evidently discovered hidden inside a hollow tree, a tree locally known as the Witches' Elm, and situated in Woodleigh Woods, set in the Heart of England. Interestingly however, was that the tree, immortalised in the case of the missing agent, was sited extremely close to Baydon Hill, and under the protective custody and estates of Baydon Manor.[2]

Meon Hill

But there was more to this fascinating correlation. It seemed that Mike had clearly noted, that curiously, both sites were situated adjacent to the River Stour, and even more astonishing was the fact that Meon Hill and Baydon Hill, were both positioned in close proximity to a place named Quinton.

Taking a final mouthful of coffee, I re-read Mike's letter, allowing the Meon/Baydon conjunction to flow freely across my thoughts. I pondered his comments, wondering if it was conceivable that the purported Golden Arrow of Sabrina, related in some strange way to an ancient energy configuration which had once connected together both sites?

Continuing with the conjecture, was it just possible in some fantastical way, that the group visit to the Rollrights, along with the subsequent touching of one of the stones and the later visit to Lower Quinton and Meon Hill, had, in some unexplainable way, resurrected some form of antiquated reciprocity between both sites?

Hypothesising, I proposed that once the group had re-dressed the energy balance at St Kenelm's Holy Well, and conducted a similar procedure at Baydon Hill, then perhaps a current of subtle energy would be released across the open landscape, inevitably joining together Baydon Hill and Meon Hill.

Placing Mike's letter back in its envelope, another thought radiated across my cognisant mind. What exactly was the Golden Arrow of Sabrina?

Chapter 22
The Hill & The Well

Sunday, 17th April, 1994. The shrill pitch and the sudden burst of the radio alarm, shattered the serenity which had filled Dave Taylor's darkened bedroom. Rubbing his tired, bloodshot eyes, he finally managed to lift up his pounding head. Once again, those familiar sinus pains radiated violently across his ailing, pounding forehead. He propped himself up, attempting to focus his tiresome eyes upon the impious hour displayed upon the face of his radio alarm clock. It was 5.15am.

Succumbing to the undeniable fact that it was unfortunately time to get up, Dave reluctantly left the warm comforts of his inviting bed. Hastily dressing, he proceeded downstairs. With the advent of consciousness, he found himself gripped amidst an air of excitement as he recalled the purpose as to his early rising. It was the day which had been set aside for the clandestine induction of both the Solar and Lunar talismans, in preparation for the fast approaching Beltane Ritual.

A cool April breeze embraced him as he opened his car and quietly climbed inside. Briefly focusing his thoughts, he began to recollect the bizarre sequence of events, which had seemingly culminated in this, his early morning appointment at the two antiquated sites. Looking out onto the quiet country road that lay before him, a solitary beam of radiant sunlight, unexpectedly ruptured the soft blanket of low level cloud.

"If nothing else," he muttered, "at least the weather should hold out until I get back home."

Approaching the first of the two ancient sites, Dave Taylor indicated, and pulled up onto the small grassy lay-by that stood at the base of Baydon Hill. Relaxing his mind in preparation for the forthcoming task, Dave opened up his rucksack and removed the

The Hill & The Well

obligatory talisman. He stepped out of his car and reluctantly began the steep and enduring walk that was to lead him to his ultimate goal - the summit of the antiquated hill-fort.

Arriving at the pinnacle of the hill, with the new-born sun bursting high up over the adjacent tree line, Dave initiated a brief walk around the boundaries of the sacred site, hoping to discover an apt location for the concealment of the Lunar disc. Realising that this task might pose a problem, Dave had selected early morning as the best time in which to discover a befitting locality for the installation, and subsequent embodiment of the talisman, as planned during the final Beltane rite.

It was so peaceful on top of the old hill, he thought, as a refreshing spring breeze blew delicately through the bud-laden branches of the surrounding trees. A vivid recollection of the November meditations, gently caressed his thoughts. He had reached the old yew tree. Stopping briefly, he smiled, allowing his tired mind to soak up and recall the sequence of events, which had seemingly caused him to be walking around the perimeter of the ancient hill.

With the shadow of the folly looming behind him, Dave continued his search. As he carefully climbed the frail wooden gate that overlooked the sanctuary of lower fields, suddenly, Dave began to feel relaxed. An incredible warmth radiated throughout his body. It emerged that he had found his chosen location, that ideal haven for the concealment of the disc. Directly before him, standing in the grassy fields below, stood a large solitary tree, an ageing tree growing besides a stream of fresh water which had emerged from inside the hill. This was the spot that he had been searching for, he concluded, as he focussed his thoughts upon the tree.

He began the slow descent, heading through the unkempt muddy field, attempting to make his way towards the solitary tree. Before him stood two large horses, one black and the other one white, barring his way.

"This is the place all right," Dave said, speaking aloud and gazing towards the two horses which acted as sentinels, guarding the portal to a magical kingdom.

Dave approached the solitary tree. He stopped fleetingly to check behind him. Clearing his thoughts, he bent down and began

The Sun & The Moon, The Hill & The Well

to pull up clump after clump of moist grass. It was 6.55am by the time he had successfully removed enough turf, enabling him to loosen the compacted earth from beneath the roots of the old tree. Scooping out a small quantity of soil, the covert spot for the first talisman was ready, set to enshroud the simple artefact.

Standing in silence, Dave carefully removed the Lunar symbol from the safety of his draw string bag. He lowered his head and commenced with the interment of the Lunar disc. The ritual began by conducting a simple visualisation; a cleansing ritual designed to consecrate the site, and to temporarily associate the disc in its covert abode. Gently placing the artefact under the protection and sanctuary of the solitary tree. Dave began to replace the loose clumps of grass. He stood up. It was time to initiate the conclusive phase of the visualisation. It was time for Dave to seal his intent.

With each aspect of the ritual successfully completed, Dave zipped up his hold-all and headed back down the hill. He was ready to partake in the ritual placement of the second artefact.

Leaving the hill-fort behind, Dave drove out towards the nearby village of Clent. As he arrived at St Kenelm's Church, he realised that an early morning service was still in progress. Locking his car, he cautiously made his way across the small churchyard, heading towards the region of the holy well. Silently standing, Dave realised how different the well now looked. The birds were singing and the buds on the trees were ready to burst; waiting to herald a full stock of leaves.

Intuitively, Dave decided that the best location for the concealment of the Solar disc, would presumably be inside the remnants of the holy well. Bending down to examine the area immediately surrounding the well, his hand stumbled upon a selection of loose stones that formed the rear wall of the small sacred well. Carefully, Dave removed a handful of stones; he opened up the second of his draw string bags and cautiously removed the tiny Solar talisman.

Exonerating his mind, Dave initiated the second cleansing rite, he spoke the words of the rubric, ceremoniously securing the Solar emblem amidst its ephemeral location. Scrupulously, he slid the circular talisman neatly out of sight, and picked up the pieces of loose stone, and returned them to their rightful positions.

The Hill & The Well

Standing up, he collected his thoughts and continued with the completion of the second ritual; the two artefacts were successfully in place.

After concealing the second talisman, Dave decided that a visit to the *other* 'well' was definitely in order. Once there, he began to experience an overwhelming sensation, a strange feeling urging him to conduct a simple meditation, believing that it would lock his mind onto the subtle energies, which as a group, we believed surrounded the sacred pool.

Walking warringly across the rurid muddy fields that steered him towards the 'other' well, Dave stood still and looked out upon the two pools which lay directly ahead. Instantly, he perceived that this was where he had to be. This was the site of the real holy well.

In silence, standing by the larger of the two murky pools, Dave closed his eyes and gently opened his inner eye; preparing himself in readiness to receive any visual or audible imagery, thought forms that might present themselves to him. Almost immediately, a highly detailed, moonlit image, gradually began to form within his mind's eye. Before him, standing close to the well, stood a small group of women, each dressed in simple clothing, peasants cloths. One of the women, being much younger than the others, looked upon Dave and slowly approached him. To Dave's clairaudiant perception, she introduced herself as Sara.

Slowly the images changed. A new picture began to form, a likeness that resembled a form of baptism - a consecration of moonlight. Calling out to Sara, Dave pleaded with her, requesting to be told more. But unfortunately, she could offer him no more; her time in his sphere had ended. The spectral image slowly faded.

Chapter 23
The Puzzle of Sabrina

The peculiar reference to the Golden Arrow of Sabrina, had posed us with a number of notable problems. For instance, it appeared that the only reference which I had been able to locate, apropos to an acceptable definition of Sabrina, was that the River Severn had derived its name from a rather corrupt variant of the term Sabren, or Sabrina. With a view to this incredulous link, I decided that a series of more thorough investigations concerning the origins of this association, should duly occur.

Looking up at the small wall-mounted clock, which clanked away in the background, I realised that I had been sitting within the confines of the town library for well over two hours! I had been sitting there, peering though countless books, each purporting to the numerous myths and legends associated with Great Britain. The problem was, however, that while most of them gave a brief exposition of the legend of Sabrina, not one of the references that I had painstakingly perused, offered me anything more conclusive.

Picking up the last two editions that stood amongst the cluttered shelves, each claiming to deal with the notable aspects of British Folklore, I was pleasantry presented with what appeared to be a promising conclusion to our curious situation.

Written by Geoffrey Ashe, *The Mythologies of Great Britain*, provided a detailed insight into the reputed legend of Sabrina. The fifteenth chapter of his fascinating book, put forward the tale of Gwendolen, which, as I quickly discovered, offered a comprehensive expose' of the popular myth embodied within the River Severn. The legend of the Severn, according to Ashe, proposed that in the 23rd year after the mythical arrival of the Trojans to Great Britain, Locrinus, Kamber and Albanactus - the

The Puzzle of Sabrina

alleged sons of Brutus, ruled Britain. Ashe proposed that Locrinus ruled England - Loegria, Kamber reigned over Wales - Cambria, and Albanactus was said to have resided over Scotland - Albany.

According to the legend, Ashe informs us that Albanactus was killed whilst fighting in a fierce battle, defending his territory against the invading Huns. Locrinus, with the assistance of Kamber, defeated his brother's adversaries in the northern province of his own kingdom, drowning their chief - Humber, in the river known to us by his name. Amongst the prisoners captured after the lengthy battle had taken place, was a German girl, Estrildis. Locrinus, fraught with burning passion, wanted her as his wife, but was promised in marriage to Gwendolen, the daughter of his late father's second in command, Corineus.

The story continues, informing us of how Locrinus was persuaded to honour his word with Gwendolen, and how at the same time, he also kept Estrildis as his mistress, housing her in a covert, hidden dwelling. The anecdote then explains how Locrinus secretly visited Estrildis, courting her for a period of some seven years, and during which time, she bore him a daughter, Habren.

After the death of Corineus - Gwendolen's father, Locrinus is reputed to have deserted Gwendolen in favour of his mistress, Estrildis, whom he then made his Queen. But Gwendolen, in a fit of burning rage, secretly prepared an army, engaging Locrinus in a raging bloody battle situated close to the River Stour; where it is written that he was killed by a single arrow. Upon the death of her unfaithful husband, Gwendolen, free to reign in her own right, ordered the immediate deaths of Estrildis - the wife of Locrinus, and Habren - his daughter, by drowning. What is interesting however, is that while putting them to death, the legend purports that Gwendolen decided to commemorate the daughter of Locrinus, and ordained that the river - the place of their drowning, should be endowed with the title Habren: a name which became Sabrina in Latin, and Severn in English.

The mythical legend of Sabrina, certainly held true to many aspects of the meditational material, which we had collected, in particular, the vivid imagery of a pool featuring a leaning tree, where I proposed that a young girl had drowned. Was it just possible that this imagery was acting as an allusion towards Sabrina? After consultation with the other Mike Smith, a further twist to the correlation occurred. Thankfully, Mike was able to confirm my thoughts concerning the River Stour, in particular, the belief that the Stour had originated from the primitive spring, or holy well, situated at Kenelmstow, and had then eventually joined up with the River Severn.

With regards to the 'Golden Arrow' scenario, we were still unsure as to its actual relevance to the quest. Initial thoughts inaugurated the opinion, that this could in fact be a direct referral to the arrow, as embodied within the legend? Nevertheless, I quickly realised that mention of the Golden Arrow, could in some respects, relate possibly to another more important aspect of our investigation. It was evident furthermore, that we needed to analyse the relevance of its symbolic imagery in greater detail.

Research revealed that the attribution of the arrow, personified the masculine principle; i.e. lightening, fecundity, virility, and power. The arrow, as with both the lance and the sword, were perceived as representations of the Solar symbol, and with the embodiment of the 'golden' aspect of the tale, portraying a direct association with the Sun, illumination, sacredness, incorruptibility, wisdom, equilibrium, and honour.[1] Interestingly however, was the intriguing fact that the arrow also heralded symbolic allusions pertaining to the ancient tradition of Shamanic flight.[2]

Intuitively, this last point led me to conclude that we were possibly dealing with some form of golden/sacred energy line, a divine line which, owing to an energy imbalance on Baydon Hill, had lay quiescent for many years. Furthermore, by re-dressing the subtle energy matrix at both Baydon Hill and St Kenelm's, it seemed plausible that the group could re-vitalise and re-establish this sacred ley-line, a golden arrow which perhaps had travelled between Baydon Hill and Meon Hill; rejuvenating the localised energy matrix, and in so doing, nourishing the indigenous landscape as a whole.

Generically, the phenomenon of shamanism evolved out of the depths of animism - the attribution of a living soul to plants, inanimate objects and natural phenomena, and totemism - a doctrine conferring an alliance that correlates specific animals to the needs of a particular clan. The shaman - the tribal priest/witchdoctor, with his or her ability to enter into trance and/or altered states of consciousness, was thought to act as an intermediary between both the spirit world and the natural world in which we live.[3]

Popular belief suggests, that during their astral journeys, the shaman could assume the magical guise of either an animal or a bird, in order to assist him on his magical flight. This particular custom is said to exist at the heart of most world mythologies, for instance, the Celtic Sun God, Luga, is alleged to have changed into an eagle.

We can see from the comprehensive research of author, Paul Devereux, that the familiar symbol of the 'arrow' was used extensively as an attribute pertaining to shamanic flight. Devereux proposes that the straightness of an alleged Ley-line, seemingly arose from the belief that shamanic flight *is* the straight way across the landscape, hence, 'as straight as the crow flies', and 'as straight as an arrow'.

As an interesting conclusion to the extraordinary puzzle surrounding the analysis of Sabrina and her golden arrow, I was presented with two remarkable allegories. Firstly, I discovered an intriguing myth relating to a springtime ritual, an ancient practice which emphasised allegiances towards pre-Christian Solar veneration. This antiquated custom, was commonly known as 'Seeking The Golden Arrow', and was discovered lying amongst authors, Janet and Colin Bord, superb publication, *Earth Rites*. After reading through the anecdote, I believed that the myth, in many respects, echoed aspects of the beliefs which we had regarding the inclusion of the mythical golden arrow.

As late as the 19th century, large crowds of people allegedly gathered on the summit of Pontesford Hill, a popular landmark situated off the A488, close to Pontesbury in Shropshire. The annual hill-top gathering, occurred as local people tried to locate the mythical golden arrow, as embodied within the Pontesford myth. There are countless explanations pertaining to the mythical artefact, which includes stories of defrauded heirs, and of fairy curses being relinquished. But surely, these are nothing more than later accretions, myths based upon a collection of ancient rituals designed to 'welcome in the rising Sun'. Therefore, would we be correct to suggest that the Golden Arrow of Sabrina, was perhaps the first shaft of light seen from the rising Sun on a particular festival date?

The Sun & The Moon, The Hill & The Well

The second piece of information, referred directly to the legendary King Arthur and his battle, 'Mons Badonicus' - translated as the hill of fresh water. This remarkable account featured in a local archaeological report written by Graham Georgiadis, and implying that 'Mons Badonicus' was situated in an imperious position. From his extensive research into the origins of 'Mons Badonicus', Georgiadis was able to offer us the following statement: *'qui prope sobrinium ostium hobilur,'* which, when interpreted, reads: That at the mouth of, or the crossroads of, or the meeting place of the Sabrina, there is the habitation of Badon.

Georgiadis carries on to informs us, that the only implication that can be derived from this statement, is that at the mouth of the Severn, or the crossroads of the Severn, or the meeting place of the roads across the Severn, nearby is Badon. In his report, Georgiadis states that this can only be a location which commands the Roman roads and the crossing of the Severn between Redstone and Blackstone. As the report states, it would appear, or so Georgiadis believes, that only one place has this command. Baydon Hill.

Placing the report down momentarily, I reflected upon the information that we now possessed. It appeared that in one sense, we had seemingly found Sabrina and the basis of her Golden Arrow. All that remained for us now, was to instigate the final preparations for the forthcoming Beltane ritual; preparing ourselves mentally, in order that the task of re-dressing the energies at both Baydon Hill and St Kenelm's, could be accomplished effectively and successfully.

Chapter 24

Final Preparations

In the days that passed following the ritual concealment of the Sun and Moon talismans, the team continued on with my required vigil of daily meditations, believing that in so doing, the consecrated discs would attract subtle energies appropriate to the inherent structure and harmony of each concealed talisman. Dave unfortunately, had agreed to take on the irksome task of designing and modelling each emblem; constructing them so as to retain within each symbol, a subtle charge suitable for the re-harmonisation and protection of each sacred site.

With less than a week before the final re-balancing act was to occur, I had found it increasingly more difficult to comply with the requirements of the daily meditations. In particular, the early morning adorations in honour of the Solar amulet, concealed at St Kenelm's Holy Well. Every morning without fail, and as the youthful spring sun was re-born into the eastern skies, Trudie and I crawled reluctantly out of bed, in readiness to begin the thankfully short period of dawn homage! At the opposite end of the scale, the conclusive aspects to each daily meditation, culminated in a closing visualisation, a process that was designed to both link and perpetuate the inherent charge of the Lunar disc - aligning it with the negative energy matrix, which had engulfed Baydon Hill.

Wednesday, 26th April, 1994. Dave Taylor had decided to leave work slightly earlier than usual. It was 3.30pm. Throughout the day, Dave had been experiencing the growing pressure of an approaching stress headache, and had realised that his only sensible option, was to leave work and go home to bed. Hoping to surpass the busy rush hour traffic, Dave began his journey home.

The Sun & The Moon, The Hill & The Well

He found himself patiently waiting for the traffic lights to change, as his pounding headache slowly grew in pitch. Heavy traffic spilled onto the congested carriageway, as Dave reflected upon the bizarre sequence of events of the past six months, and realised that in just a matter of days, the quest of the Sun and the Moon would hopefully reach its zenith.

Dave, like myself, had begun to experience a series of peculiar feelings during the course of the previous week, a disturbing sequence of sensations that equated in one sense, to a gradual build up of energy at each of the two sites. He could feel the forces growing, straining against each other, and empowering the talismans as each disc absorbed the required ancestry of subtle energy, channelled from each sacred site.

Lightly tapping the steering wheel, and still waiting for the traffic lights to change, Dave considered the possibility that perhaps the build up of energy at both sites, was in fact, the source of his growing discomfort. The lights turned green and he finally pulled away, realising however, that he would have to engage upon another detailed visualisation.

Indicating and quietly pulling up outside his house, Dave stepped out of the car and allowed the cool afternoon breeze to gently envelope him. The tense headache that had risen to a peak, only moments earlier, had thankfully subsided. He had left the trivial pressures of day-to-day work, well behind.

Reaching across to his hi-fi, Dave picked up a bundle of compact discs, scouring the contents of each disc. The distinctive sounds of 'Chopin' radiated softly amongst the book-filled walls of his incandescent room. Dave sat down and silently began to prepare himself for the forthcoming meditation.

Deep within his mind's eye, the circle of protection gained momentum. Shrouded imagery, thoughts that had clawed their way into his normal conscious mind, suddenly flashed into focus. A sense of purpose had returned.

Finding himself poised at the base of Baydon Hill, Dave realised that he was not alone. Something, or someone, was trying to communicate with him. But why? Standing before him were the decaying remnants of an old wooden fence. A curious figure, small and brown with tiny pointed ears, sat motionless upon the gateway to the lower field. The entity spoke, announcing himself

Final Preparations

as Oghma the shinning one - an ancient Celtic Solar deity, who had allegedly resided upon the hill long before man.

"The combined meditations are working," announced the Sun god, in a deep sonorous voice.

"The Lunar energies, which have so drained my master's hill, are being absorbed into the structure of your talisman," the entity proclaimed.

"But the harmony of the hill is unbalanced," the guide added, "the hill remains vulnerable."

Thanking Oghma for his kind information, Dave continued his climb towards the summit of the ancient hill. But as he slowly ascended the sacred hill, he became distinctly aware of an anxious feeling clawing at his stomach, a sensation indicative of a raging storm, a feeling that centred itself around the field which temporarily housed the Lunar talisman.

Reaching the outskirts of the grassy field, and beginning the gradual descent, heading towards the solitary tree which concealed the talismatic disc, a raven-headed woman, dressed in dark blue robes appeared before him, her arms raised uppermost. But the ethereal icon was rapidly replaced by the image of an old hag. He turned to face the woman, realising that, even though our intentions were true to heart - good and right, the goddess was fighting back as the Lunar talisman absorbed the female essence which had so wrongly governed the sacred hill.

The spectral forms slowly faded. A sudden, sharp jolt, brought the rush of life back in to Dave Taylor's tranquil body. His encounter had ended, but the contents of his experience still flooded his thoughts.[1]

Chapter 25

The Guardian

Saturday, 30th April, 1994. Traditionally, the month of May is dedicated to the Virgin Mary and the Roman Goddess Flora. May Eve was also recognised as Walpurgis Night, so named after the Saxon Goddess Walpurga. The Celtic title attributed to this important festival date, is Beltane, an annual event which begins directly after sunset on May Eve, and concludes at sunset on May Day. Research attests, that the origins of Beltane can be traced back to the god 'Bel' - Belinus an ancient Celtic Sun God, equating with the Latin Bellus, meaning beautiful, and an earlier correlation with the Babylonian Earth-God, each forming an attribution of the Sumerian Belili - the Great Mother Goddess.[1] With regards to the remaining portion of the word, it would appear that 'Tan' or 'Tine', suggests an apparent derivation from a Cornish/Gaelic expression, which when defined, signifies the notion of 'Fire'.

The festival of Beltane, represents one of two major events within the Celtic calendar year, and highlights the division of the year into two equal halves - winter and summer, Samhain and Beltane. These particular pre-Christian celebrations, are also considered to be the best times in which to communicate with the 'other-worlds', as it is said that the veil between the two kingdoms is at its thinnest - the doors of the Sidhe are believed to be open.

As far as I was concerned, it was apparent that the celebration of Beltane, represented the ideal time when the group could re-dress the problems inherent at Baydon Hill and St Kenelm's. Not only did the festival feature male related energies, Solar in origin, but from the course of my research, it transpired that certain aspects pertaining to a feminine energy current, could also be

The Guardian

ascribed to the ancient May Day celebration. This, I realised, was exactly what we needed, a festival date that would allow us to utilise both male and female currents, calling upon them, as a means of re-establishing the correct energy polarity, so required at each of the two sacred sites.

Rubbing the sleep from her tired weary eyes, Trudie carefully knelt down and gathered together the assortment of morning post, which lay strewn across the porch carpet. A small white envelope innocently fell to the ground as she stood up. Retrieving it, Trudie opened the package and found enclosed, an intriguing letter from the other Mike Smith. His correspondence outlined an enticing local legend, an anecdote that he believed, heralded some significance in our interest concerning St Kenelm's Holy Well.

The allegory to which he had referred, was an ancient myth, encapsulated within the curious title of 'The Legend of St Kenelm's Furrow'. Apparently, the alleged furrow, which was probably an Iron age, or early Saxon boundary ditch, was evidently created by a runaway yoke of oxen belonging to an old lady. The legend stated that the old woman in defiance of local law, had persisted in ploughing her land on St Kenelm's Day, 17th July. As a direct result of this sacrilegious act, the oxen, disgusted at such sacrilege, disappeared up the legendary hill dragging their plough behind them, and so, the legend of St Kenelm's Furrow was created. Reputedly, the purported oxen disappeared, and the old woman was struck blind for her blasphemy.

After reading through Mike's account, and then considering the embodiment of both the old lady and the reference to cow symbolism, it became obvious to me, that concealed within the boundaries of this curious myth, was the distinct possibility of an allusion attesting to the immortalised presence of a pre-Christian goddess.

In his letter, Mike had expressed the hope that perhaps we would find some use in the peculiar legend which he had written out. He was most certainly correct in his assumptions, I concluded.

As the dying sun retreated into the ever-open arms of the western skies, I prepared myself psychologically, in readiness for the onset

The Sun & The Moon, The Hill & The Well

of our covert adventure. It was 8.15pm, and there was no time for second thoughts. The hill was awake, and the ritual of the Sun and the Moon had already begun.

Carefully packing away the three swords into the protective sanctuary of Simon's green fishing hold-all, neatly coincided with the planned arrival of the group. It was 8.45pm. The arrangement was that the group would meet up with Dave inside the Rookwood Arms at around nine-thirty. Dave, like myself, believed that a final briefing regarding the proposed proceedings, should occur prior to the teams actual entry into either of the two sacred sites.

Picking up the swords and my trusty black hold-all, we left the safety of the house in readiness for the commencement of the first leg of our covert operation. Sitting quietly in the front of Chris's car, a nervous tension descended upon me, an awning realisation endorsing the fact that there was no turning back. It was too late. We had crossed the point of no return, beyond the threshold of the arcane. Starting the engine, Chris gently pulled away from the protection of the house. At last we were reaching the denouement of our quest.

As the car approached the Rookwood Arms, Simon called out. He had spotted Dave standing in the car park, awaiting our arrival. Armed with my bag, packed with a varied collection of incenses and other magical paraphernalia, I followed the team into the homely warmth of the public lounge. Simon slowly made his way towards the lounge bar and ordered the first round of drinks. However, it certainly didn't help knowing that 'Cokes' were the strongest drinks that we were allowing ourselves, yet it was paramount that we maintained a clear, and focused approach to the forthcoming clandestine events.

I handed a copy of the planned re-balancing rite onto each member of the team, thereby ensuring that the group was fully conversant with each and every aspect of the proposed ceremony. Both Dave and myself, had gone to great lengths to explain in detail, each and every parameter, including a synopsis of all symbolic, and/or physical actions which constituted the healing ritual of the Sun and the Moon.

Gathering together his assortment of notes, Dave decided to refresh the group of the more important aspects of the quest to

The Guardian

date. Sipping a mouthful of iced 'Coke', he quietly began.

"After Chris and I have retrieved the charged talismans," he quietly announced, "we'll rejoin you, back here in the lounge."

A rowdy cheer from a crowd of boisterous youths seated at the opposite table, swamped Dave's whispered words. Unflustered, he simply cleared his throat and sipped a further mouthful of his drink.

"Shall we try again?" he calmly announced, a faint hint of sarcasm shaping his words. Picking up his collection of notes, he continued.

"Once we've collected the talismans, we'll meet up here in the lounge," he announced, as the noisy group at the opposite table, finally arose and walked past us as they left the confines of the bustling public lounge. Dave resumed his briefing, explaining how the team would be split into three smaller groups, with the idea being, that one person from each team would represent the Solar, or masculine aspect of the ritual, whilst the other remaining member, would personify the Lunar, or feminine aspect of the affair.

With regards to the symbolic/physical inclusion of the three swords during the final healing ceremony, the concept was that their use equated in one sense, with the Qabalistic notion relating to the symbolic use of the number three, i.e. creative power, growth, forward movement, the triangle, the belief that an idea had become fertilised - from which a child could issue, and the power of the mind. Furthermore, their main function equated with the idea that each weapon could be symbolically 'charged up', and therefore used to retain either a Solar/positive, or Lunar/negative energy field.

To accomplish this rather immense task, the group were set to embark upon a lavish combination of creative/ritual visualisation, with the belief being, that this 'invoked energy' could be directed towards, and then suitably retained within the structure of each of the three swords.

With the weapons ceremoniously empowered, the theory was that the appropriate talisman, would then be ritualistically planted within the boundaries of each site, thereby, allowing its accumulated charge to slowly dissipate and begin the gradual process of energy replenishment. As an aid to this esoteric style practice, the 'charged' swords were to be thrust into the ground at specific locations; positions laid out forming the geometrical pattern of a triangle. It was at this stage that each weapon would then 'down-load' its stored energy field, thereby replenishing the localised energy matrix, and invigorating the effects of each talisman.

To seal our intent at each of the two sites, a simple Earth Shrine was to be left in situ. A procedure that involved the planting of a seed, shrub, plant or tree, with the intention being that the shrine symbolically represented the living polarity of the site.

Quietly speaking to the group, Dave outlined the procedure for the forthcoming ceremony. Suddenly, the significance of the nightmare that I had recently experienced, which had featured the three swords and the old hag, came into perspective.

The dream had cast allusions towards the meditation which had occurred during the Winter Solstice, 21st December, 1993. It was during that particular visualisation, that the group had invoked the inherent power of the holy well, believing that the latent energy embodied within the legend, would suitably charge up each of the three swords. Upon reflection, however, it seemed evident that from our actions, all we had in fact accomplished, was the purification and subsequent consecration of each weapon; the swords were most certainly not charged up, that would have to occur at the other well. Furthermore, it seemed apparent to me, that the purification of each sword during the Winter Solstice mediation, was a necessary prerequisite to any future magical involvement with the swords. They had certainly come a long way from that shop window in Tintagel, I concluded, as I sipped a further mouthful of my ice cold drink. But the reason for their purchase was now clear, and it was time for them to play their part. The circle was finally complete.

Chris and Dave stood up. It was 9.45pm, and time for the pair of them to leave the rowdy atmosphere of the Rookwood Arms, in readiness to prepare themselves in order to successfully locate, and retrieve, the charged amulets. They left the busy lounge.

Unlocking the car, a host of fleeting images flashed radiantly across their heightened consciousness, ethereal forms, mental

The Guardian

apparitions, each governed and coloured by this, the first stage of the final ritual.

Dave opened the passenger door and Chris stepped in. For a while they merely sat in the car, clearing their thoughts, preparing themselves for the onerous task ahead.

The car jolted into life, as the first stage of the ritual of the Sun and the Moon began. Approaching Baydon, Chris remained silent as he sat in the passenger seat reminiscing on his involvement in the sequence of peculiar events, which, if all went according to plan, would conclude later that night the ancient festival of Beltane, May Day. A stirring sense of poise slowly enveloped him, as he slowly began to realise the significance of his role in the quest. He was now ready to retrieve the Lunar talisman.

"Are you ready Chris?" Dave enquired, breaking his train of thought, as the car came slowly to a halt at the base of the darkened hill. Looking up, Chris cast his thoughts out beyond the choking blackness that lay ahead. He had visited the site countless times before, he thought, but this time things felt so very different. Tension circulated across his face as Dave's question was met with silence.

Removing the keys from the ignition, Dave enquired once again. Silence.

"Shall we conduct a simple protection rite before going up?" Dave announced, desperately trying to gain his attention. Chris remained motionless.

Again he repeated his request, urging Chris to let go of the negative thoughts which had seemingly invaded his troubled mind. As the pair of them sat quietly in the unnerving darkness of Dave Taylor's stationary car, eventually, Chris managed to pull himself together, and agreed that under the present circumstances, yes; they should initiate some form of mental protection.

The dazzling headlights from a passing car, illuminated the darkened interior of their protective sanctuary. Anomalous shapes, lifeless abominations reached out to them, as Dave called upon the protection of the familiar Qabalistic Cross. Almost immediately, Chris began to feel invigorated, focused, and more intuitive, as growing quantities of adrenaline were released into his body. Feeling strangely safe, he knew that he was now ready

The Sun & The Moon, The Hill & The Well

to continue.

Walking cautiously, silently, nervously along the single dirt track, which snaked obliquely round the darkened caliginous hillfort, a reassuring impression of calm, gradually descended upon the two adventurers. Chris broke the serenity.

"Where did you put it, Dave?" he queried. "Are we nearly there yet?"

"Just another couple of minutes," Dave replied. "Don't worry, its not far now," he concluded.

Reaching the pinnacle of the hill, Dave pointed towards what he believed formed the entrance into the lower field.

"The field where the talisman is hidden, is over there," he said. With Dave taking the lead, the two adventurers headed off, knowing that they were only moments away from retrieving the fully charged Lunar talisman.

Climbing over the rickety wooden stile, which overlooked and guarded the lower fields of Baydon Hill, Chris hurried down towards the old tree where the concealed amulet was said to reside. Standing in silence, he cleared his thoughts and approached the single tree. It was his task to represent an incarnate personification of the Lunar energies, which had so wrongly invaded the hill.

With a radiant image of the full moon flooding his every thought, Chris carefully knelt down. Placing his cold, numbing hands against the damp, exposed roots of the old tree, he directed his thoughts towards the covert talisman. Guiding his fingers cautiously amongst the moist clumps of grass, which lay at the footing of the old tree, slowly, Chris began to remove a small area of grass from around its roots. Sliding his hands into the dank cold earth, he began his search, desperately trying to feel for the location of the hidden Lunar disc.

Five minutes passed by and still the talisman eluded him. Turning towards Dave, he shouted out.

"Dave! I can't find the disc!" he called out, "Its not here, I can't find it." Dave quickly knelt down as Chris continued searching.

"It must be here somewhere," Dave insisted, as he directed the beam from Chris's torch towards the base of the tree. "I put it there," he added, "just keep trying, it's got to be there."

The Guardian

But it was nowhere to be found.

Frantically continuing with the search, Chris turned slightly to his right. Fumbling in the dark, his hand fell upon a slightly raised area of earth. Pulling recklessly at the wispy blades of sodden grass, he finally managed to slide his fingers into the moist earth that lay beneath it. Instantly, his fingers came to rest upon a solid item buried within the soil. Easing the compacted earth from around the object, he gently released the alien article from its shroud of roral earth. Picking up the torch, Chris confirmed the identity of their find. They had recovered the Lunar talisman.

As last orders were finally called in the Rookwood Arms, we sat patiently at our table fully aware of the fact, that Chris and Dave's return was long overdue. Where were they? I thought, as an anxious sensation welled up in the base of my stomach. Surely they must be on their way back to the pub by now?

Gently braking and slowly easing the car onto the small parking lot, which lay adjacent to St Kenelm's Church, Dave brought the car to a gradual halt. It was his turn to retrieve the second of the two concealed artefacts. Like Chris, who, only moments earlier had retrieved the Lunar symbol from Baydon Hill, it was now Dave's task to assume the role of custodian of the Solar amulet, and thereby initiating its removal from the confines of the old pagan well.

Quietly opening the side gate that led onto the hallowed grounds of the soundless church, the two adventurers walked quietly past the Norman oratory; slowly making their way down towards the domain of the old pagan well. An eerie aberrant sound, suddenly caught Dave's attention. He turned around, straining his eyes against the darkness which engulfed them.

"Did you hear that?" he nervously announced, "I'm sure we're not alone." Chris stood still; listening to the silence emanating from within the churchyard. He responded.

"Sorry Dave, but I can't hear anything," remarked Chris, "perhaps it was just the wind blowing through the trees?"

But whatever it was, Dave felt certain that he had definitely heard something, and had not merely imagined it. Chris continued to forge his way down towards the well. Dave, still feeling

The Sun & The Moon, The Hill & The Well

nervous, followed some distance behind. They had to retrieve the Solar talisman at any cost.

Suddenly, Chris heard a strange noise emanating from somewhere close by. Puzzled by the bizarre sequence of sounds, he turned to acknowledge Dave, realising that the anomaly which they were both now hearing, was in fact the same sound that Dave had heard only moments earlier.

Concerned by the audible anomaly, they both remained perfectly still, listening and watching, hoping to trace the source of this unusual noise. Five minutes of agonising silence elapsed, and they both moved forward. Deciding that it was safe, they cautiously approached the well.

As they entered the sanctuary of the old pagan well, Dave felt swamped by a disturbing sense of unease. He realised that something was wrong. Something or someone was trying to warn him, protect him, and possibly prepare him for what lay ahead. His heart began to pound violently, beating faster, as a loud sickly buzzing noise, filled his anxious thoughts. He felt sick, drained of his life force; something was definitely amiss.

Kneeling down, he cautiously leaned forward. Just a few more inches, he thought, trying to keep calm as he reached out into the abyss of unholy darkness, and then we can leave this place. Adrenaline raced uncontrollably around his nervous aching body. His intuition desperately fought to warn him; preparing him for the impending danger.

He stretched out his right hand, probing the blackness. His fingers came to rest on top of the sand stone perimeter of the small holy well. Dave's trembling fingers entered the cold water, clumsily caressing the ageing stone, which protected the fully charged talisman. Slowly, Dave carefully lifted up the protective stone. Contact with the talisman had been made.

"Chris, I've found it!" he nervously exclaimed.

Dave moved forwards, sliding his hand into the darkened waters of the well; painstakingly trying to grip the disc before he lost all sensation in his prying fingers. He took hold of the amulet and slowly began to ease it from its resting-place. It slipped; again he had lost contact with the Solar talisman. A sudden noise caught his attention, louder than before and appearing from all directions. He turned, desperately trying to discover the source of the

The Guardian

peculiar sound, and knowing that this time Chris had also heard it.

"Come on Dave, hurry up!" Chris announced, speaking in an agitated manner.

Reaching for the well, once again Dave's clammy fingers came to rest upon the water's edge. Dipping into the fresh, cold spring water, his heart began to pound violently A tense headache radiated painfully across his forehead. He knew that he was only moments away from retrieving the talisman. It would soon be in his hand.

Taking a deep breath, he reached further into the well, searching, scouring, and trying to make contact. Surprised, he looked up; something had distracted him. He tried to re-focus his thoughts; he had to collect the charged amulet at all costs. Straining his eyes amidst the dense blackness, Dave realised that something had invaded the serenity of the well. Whatever it was, appeared to be emanating from somewhere along the old pilgrim path. Frantically, Dave continued his search; trying to feel for the ledge which concealed the tiny talisman.

Contact was made. He had found the sandstone ledge and could feel the ensnared disc. Gently tugging at the amulet, his numbing fingers slowly eased it out of its secret chamber, removing it from the sanctuary of the well. Dave turned; he could sense something watching him as he knelt by the well. Once again he looked out into the pitch-blackness that surrounded them. Nothing. He returned his attention to the well. Suddenly, he sensed a hostile feeling, a hideous unholy blackness, spilling and tumbling, violently along the old pilgrim pathway and heading directly towards them.

"Chris! Watch out!" Dave anxiously shouted, as the unholy abomination surged towards them.

"Look out! There's something coming towards us"

The sphere of undulating blackness engulfed them, choked them, grappled at them, as a hideous, malevolent, blood-curdling scream, shattered the tense silence which had surrounded the sanctity of the sacred well.

Dave reeled backwards, sliding and losing his footing, his face ashen.

"Come on Chris, lets get the hell out of here!" he shouted, his thoughts filled with panic and the painful memory of the

The Sun & The Moon, The Hill & The Well

screaming banshee. Without hesitation, the pair of them scrambled up the muddy embankment that led on into the churchyard. Breathless and shaken; hoping that whatever had attacked them down at the well had not followed them, Chris spoke out.

"What the hell happened to us down there?" he anxiously remarked. Catching his breath, Dave responded.

"Chris, I've absolutely no idea," he said, "but I certainly know one thing, no animal could ever make a noise like that!"

Opening his moist, shaking hand, Dave checked that the Solar talisman was still intact, and placed it safely in the shielded custody of his pull-string bag.

Reaching the car, a welcome sense of relief flooded through their veins. The whole episode was something that they both could have done without, but equally, something that they would have to share with the rest of the group.

Sitting quietly in the car, desperately trying to calm down and come to terms with their encounter, Chris suggested that maybe they should only inform Mike of their unwelcome visitor. There seemed no point in unduly worrying the rest of the group at this late stage in the quest, he concluded. Nevertheless, they both agreed that it was undoubtedly the worst experience that either of them had ever encountered.

Chapter 26

Healing The Land

11.15pm, May Eve, 1994. "Ladies and gentlemen, can we have your glasses please," the barman politely remarked, his words parting the rolling veil of cigarette smoke which filled the busy lounge of the Rookwood Arms. Apprehensively, I looked across the crowded, smoke-filled lounge, hoping to see Chris and Dave re-entering the pub. Turning around momentarily, I noticed a nervous expression emanating from Tracey. She, like the rest of us, was obviously quite worried; they had been gone far too long, and they should have been back well before now. Nevertheless, all we could do was patiently sit and wait.

Suddenly, Simon piped up. Chris had walked into the lounge. Leaving the table, I walked towards him, sensing that something was obviously wrong. A blank expression radiated painfully across his ashen face.

"What is it Chris?" I queried.

He looked cautiously towards Tracey and then the rest of the group. "We've got a problem," he nervously muttered. "Dave will explain later. He's sitting in his car waiting for you."

An unnerving shudder ran the length of my spine. He continued.

"Listen, we'll meet up with you and Dave at the base of the hill," said Chris, trying to reassure me, and at the same time, not alarm the rest of the team. "Hopefully by that time," he whispered, "Dave should have filled you in."

Approaching the car, it was difficult not to notice the look of utter concern painted across Dave Taylor's troubled brow. What had happened? What was wrong with them? I had to find out.

Dave remained silent as we pulled away from the Rookwood Arms Car Park, failing to answer the barrage of prying questions which I directed towards him. However, it was obvious that something was bothering him, but what? Eventually, and after much persuasion, he finally conceded to my constant bout of nagging.

Pulling up at the base of the hill-fort, Dave reluctantly began recounting the relative ease by which the Lunar talisman - concealed at Baydon, had been ritualistically recovered. Following on from this, he conveyed a detailed account of the appalling assault which they had both experienced during their clandestine visit to St Kenelm's Holy Well, in search of the concealed Solar talisman.

With Dave's uncomfortable words still fresh at the forefront of my troubled mind, an intuitive thought penetrated my anxious mind. The dreadful occurrence which they had both experienced down at the well, had a ring of familiarity about it. But exactly what, I couldn't be sure.

Sitting in the quiet of the car, waiting for the others to arrive. Dave expressed his obvious concern for the safety of the group. Neither of them it seemed could offer an acceptable or logical explanation as to the origins of their unpleasant encounter.

A sudden disjointed image flashed radiantly across my thoughts. Instantly, I recalled how Trudie, some months earlier, had experienced a nightmarish vision, a premonition which had featured the young Kenelm and some form of Guardian or Black Knight. Interestingly however, was the fact that the anomalous Black Knight had suddenly 'homed in' on the young Kenelm; travelling from that very same spot where Chris and Dave had encountered their malevolent, bloodcurdling scream. What's more, the odd thing was, that while Trudie had relayed her experience onto me, she had most certainly not mentioned it to the rest of the team.

"So what do think?" said Dave, as my thoughts flitted between Trudie's premonition and the gruesome experience that Chris and Dave had evidently encountered down at the well.

"Do we carry on with the quest and perform the healing ritual?" Dave enquired.

Waiting for the rest of the group to arrive, I pondered his remarks, fully aware of the severity of the situation, but equally unsure of what to do. A fresh current of insight flooded my

Healing The Land

innermost thoughts, reaffirming the belief that abandoning the final stage of the quest in favour of opting for the easy way out, was, in my opinion, an unfavourable option. As far as I was concerned, it was too late, it was out of our hands and we had no choice but to continue.

"Mike, there's one other thing," Dave concluded. "I don't think it's a particularly good idea for us to discuss our experience with the others," he nervously announced. "Do you?"

Nodding in approval, I felt that I had to agree with his decision. The glaring, dazzling beams of a fast approaching vehicle, illuminated the darkened interior of Dave Taylor's stationary car. It was 11.40pm. Breaking suddenly, the approaching car dimmed its lights, turned and pulled sharply onto the grassy verge which lay hidden at the base of the solitary prehistoric hill-fort. The passenger door slowly opened and Simon got out of the car.

"Well, were here at last!" he exclaimed, as one after another of the team clambered quietly out of the car and onto the dank, lifeless grassy verge, ready to begin. Dave got out of his car. He looked at his watch. We only had twenty minutes left before midnight - May Day, and we still had to climb the hill, unpack the equipment, and then finally set the scene for the first stage of the forthcoming re-balancing ritual.

One by one, each member of the team climbed precariously over the wooden stile, heralding a pathway that eventually led up onto the summit of the ancient hill. Adrenaline began to pump violently around my body, as a loud sickly buzzing noise infiltrated my already anxious thoughts. I fought to keep calm. I had to keep control.

Suddenly the noise grew louder, much louder. Anomalous images flashed spontaneously across my heightened consciousness. I felt alone. The familiar and friendly sounds of the group quickly receded. A new image had began to form. I found myself walking through the boundaries of an ancient settlement camp. Smoke billowed haphazardly in and around the collection of primitive huts that adorned the slopes of the ancient hill. A raging fire, a beacon pyre, illuminated the darkened starlit skyline. Three warriors stood in silhouette, highlighted against the torrid flames of the raging fire, marking the pinnacle of the

The Sun & The Moon, The Hill & The Well

ancient hilltop.

"Mike! Are you okay?" Shouted Dave, desperately trying to attract my attention, and realising that perhaps I was experiencing something untoward.

Silence.

He tried again, still nothing.

"Mike! Speak to me!" He nervously exclaimed, as the vivid images of the Celtic settlement quickly subsided.

Chris interjected.

"Are you okay," he said. "What's happened?"

Turning slightly to look out upon the hill, I informed the group of the imagery that I had received, in particular, that relating to the ancient settlement and the silhouette of the three tribal warriors. The group continued the gradual climb towards the summit of the hill; the air around us feeling distinctly electric.

Before us stood the Georgian folly, it looked so elegant, so radiant, so totally out of place. The group moved forward, heading onwards towards the protective sanctuary of the wire fencing, which surrounded the crumbling monolith.

As the team reached the outer perimeter fence, I began to find myself being mentally drawn towards the folly, and yet at the same time, being led out across the open landscape. Luga, the Celtic Sun God, was beginning to call upon us, we could each feel his warming presence as he desperately awaited his release.

Climbing over the barbed wire fencing, which surrounded the crumbling shrine, the group approached the Georgian folly. I looked up. The sky was ablaze amidst an impermeable blanket of flickering stars. It was 11.55pm.

A sudden breeze rustled malevolently through the sanctuary of the surrounding trees, the festival of Beltane was about to begin. An unusual tingling sensation slowly engulfed my body. Something had began to stir. The dormant ancestral spirit of the ancient hill was alive. I could feel its growing presence spiralling, undulating, twisting and twirling, spilling up from the heart of the ancient hill.

Dave called the group together. May Day was just moments away. Hastily, we arranged the equipment, forming a central point into which our working energy could eventually be channelled. Chris placed a terracotta dish filled with incense at each of the cardinal points. Kneeling down, Simon ignited the four saltpetre blocks. Pungent spirals of acrid incense wafted aimlessly, chaotically, in and around our makeshift magical circle. Beltane had arrived.

The group huddled together and formed a circle, ready to tap into the subtle current of energy which alluded to the ancient festival of Beltane - May Day. Stilling our minds, we each drifted deeper and deeper into an ever-unfolding state of sentience, becoming one with the hill.

Dave stood up, shattering the tense silence, as he initiated a simple invocation in honour of the festival of Beltane, and the Celtic Sun God, Luga.

One by one, each member the group called upon the guardians of the four quarters, beginning with the invocation of Air, positioned in the East and under the presidency of Domnu. Turning to face due South, the group reverently called upon Belonus, the all-powerful, all-seeing, great god of fire. Morgan, beholder of the mighty waters and ruler of the West was next to be called upon, followed by Cerenos, the ruler of the element of Earth and the guardian of the North.

An immense sensation of well being rushed spiritedly around the confines of our protective circle; empowering it, charging our cone of power and endowing the whole group with great strength of mind. At each of the four cardinal points, stood colossal representations of the guardians of each elemental station. A host of vivid colours flashed vibrantly before our eyes, as we each perceived detailed images pertaining to the elemental watchtowers.

The three sword holders stepped forward and moved into the centre of the circle. We stood in silence, ready to 'charge up' each weapon in readiness for the release of Luga and the subsequent re-balancing ceremony. In front of us stood a vast temple, a six-sided holy edifice with lions guarding the entrance into its sacred chamber. Inside the holy structure, the six walls of the hexagonal temple were ablaze amidst the hues of golden light. I walked towards the sacred shrine and requested admittance. Instantly my request was granted and I ventured cautiously into the palace of golden light. The shimmering walls of the temple were adorned with Solar deities, religious icons that appeared to watch my every move.

The Sun & The Moon, The Hill & The Well

Placed centrally within the confines of the holy oratory, stood a golden altar, a sacred tabernacle raised upon a golden hexagonal platform. A radiant image of a holy child stood before me. I approached the hexagonal rostrum and climbed the six rows of steps, which led up to the sacred altar. From within the holy tabernacle, I could feel the resplendent power of the sun, its rays of golden light bathing me in its protective, purifying light. I raised the sword and plunged it into the vast current of brilliance. An immense veil of light descended from above; consecrating light, purifying light that ebbed amidst the heart of the temple of light.

A subtle tingling sensation raced around my elated body, I could feel the sword absorbing the golden light, consecrating it and charging it in readiness for the release of the Sun God, Luga. My hands began to tremble, the sword began to glow as an electrical current suddenly rushed along the hilt of the weapon. Gently removing the sword from the veil of angelic light, I knew that my task was complete; the sword was fully charged.

The temple of light faded as we prepared ourselves for the symbolic release of the Sun God. The three sword holders approached the central sector of the circle. We raised the weapons and plunged them deep into the heart of sacred hill. Slowly, the hill began to take on an inner glow, a feeling that passed through the three sword holders and the rest of the group, and then finally out into the surrounding ritual landscape.

Dave knelt down in silence, and inserted the Solar talisman deep into the earth. Six beams of replenishing light radiated out across the sacred hill, bringing life, light, and a growing sense of harmony back into the holy hill. An intense swirling wind arose, engulfing the three sword holders and whistling violently around the summit of the hill. The successful release of Luga had begun. All that remained now, was the initiation and concealment of our Celtic Earth Shrine.

It was 1.30am by the time the two cars came to an eventual halt on the white gravel lay-by, situated to the side of St Kenelm's Church. Ethereal fingers of silvery light burst silently, unexpectedly, out through the sparse scattering of low-level cloud, forming a protective mantle over the tiny Romsley village.

Healing The Land

The outer hedgerow of the tiny Norman chapel, heralded our pathway forward, leading the group into the stygian world of awning blackness, that boundless abyss of the unknown. Ahead of us lay our final destination, the two pools, the dwelling of the goddess, the real holy well.

Crossing the solitary wooden stile, which led the group forwards into the hallowed sanctuary of the two murky pools. I caught a fleeting glimmer of the larger pool; its stagnant waters invigorated amidst the lustre and splendour of the glorious full moon.

From within the depths of my anxious mind, an image began to form, an unholy semblance pertaining to the bizarre sequence of events that Chris and Dave had encountered down at the other well. My attention slowly began to wane; something lying in the writhing mask of irreverent darkness stirred my attention. My heart began to pound. Something was out there.

Silently probing the uneasy blackness which had surrounded us, I desperately tried to focus my tired eyes onto anything that moved. Nothing. Again I probed the darkness, still nothing.

Tracey squinted, her eyes and looked straight ahead. Something had disturbed her. She stopped dead in her tracks, straining her eyes against the enveloping mantle of darkness, hoping to find what had troubled her.

Nothing.

She turned her head, half expecting to tune into the source of the peculiar sound, desperate to settle her anxious mind. Silence. A momentary break in the light covering of cloud allowed the full moon to rise up over the darkened tree line, illuminating the field ahead, reflecting off the larger pool.

The two pools of water drew nearer; the sacred well was in sight. A sense of urgency accompanied the group as we finally left the boundary field and entered the domain of the sacred well. Suddenly, an intense feeling of unease radiated rapidly amongst the group, the final phase of the ritual of the Sun and the Moon was about to begin.

The still waters of the larger pool stood before us. Each member of the group approached the pond and stood in silence. Clearing our thoughts, we focussed our minds firmly on the body of still water - the true holy well.

The Sun & The Moon, The Hill & The Well

I looked out across the pool, a reflection of the full moon rebounded off its soundless, tranquil surface. I began to drift off into the imagery that surrounded us, drawing on the subtle currents of the new-born full moon.

Chris knelt down. A sudden burst of phosphorescence briefly illuminated the darkened sanctuary of the well before it faded and rapidly died. He struck a second match, only this time the saltpetre block spluttered and sparked violently into life. One by one, Chris ignited the remaining three blocks, placing a terracotta burner at each of the four cardinal points.

Unpacking the three broadswords, Simon carefully placed each weapon down upon the dank uncut grass, laying them out in the form of an equilateral triangle. Dave assembled the group; the ritual was about to begin. Closing our tired eyes, we allowed our minds to absorb the subtle essences of the sacred site. The ritual had begun.

Calling reverently upon the four guardians, so as to watch over and protect our sacred ceremony, Dave mentally constructed the circle of protection. Round and round the brilliant white current of primeval energy spiralled, absorbing, protecting, consecrating the team; spilling up into a vast funnel of energy - a protective cone of power.

The three sword holders each stepped forward, ready to invoke the primordial current of the full moon, beckoning the subsequent charging of the three ritualistic weapons. Chris slowly raised his sword, before him stood a holy temple, a nine-sided translucent structure summoned in reverence to the Moon. The walls of his ennead house of worship, pulsated, vibrating in ever-changing hues of violet and silver. He approached the entrance of his sacred shrine. Two magical unicorns guarded its sacred gateway. Calling upon the Dianic power which encircled the holy edifice, Chris was granted access into the temple of the silver goddess.

The translucent walls of his temple of light, were lined with the rays of the seven planets, and of the head and tail of the Dragon of the Moon. A host of Lunar deities, goddesses in honour of the midnight sun, adorned the ceiling of this most sacred place. Positioned before him, placed high up upon a nine-sided rostrum, stood a crescent shaped altar, the symbol of the Moon. Chris approached the holy table and carefully climbed its rows of shimmering steps. Before him stood the silvery crescent altar, its rays of intense silver and violet light, flooding his elated consciousness. He raised the weapon above his head, and a lustrous shower of silver light descended from the vitreous ceiling, bathing him, purifying him, and initiating him in the knowledge and power of the Moon. Chris plunged the sword down deep into the heart of the crescent shaped altar. The pulsating power of the temple of the Moon, entered the sword, rushing up through its hilt as he watched in awe. Slowly the weapon began to glow, empowered by the light of the full Moon. A sudden vibratory sensation overtook his elated body, Chris could both feel, and hear, a peculiar resonating effect rushing uncontrollably through his body. He lifted the vibrating sword from the light of the altar. It was complete. The sword was now charged.

I looked across towards Chris and the other two sword holders, I could see the three swords pulsating, as coloured flashes of light radiated chaotically along the blades of each weapon. Around our sacred circle, the atmosphere was to changing, a build up of static charge was beginning to invigorate the air.

Dave summoned the sword holders to the centre of the circle, it was time once more to download the charge from each weapon. The three sword holders approached the central sector of our magical cone of power, as one by one each sword was plunged into the moist earth surrounding the sacred pool. Silver arms of light radiated out into the landscape, replenishing the site, pouring Lunar energies in to the area of the two pools, and releasing the ensnared goddess. Dave knelt down and ritualistically concealed the Lunar disc deep into the silt which surrounded the sacred pool. I looked towards Dave, he, like myself, sincerely hoped that by downloading the charge attributed to each of the three swords, we would in effect, 'kick- start' the Lunar disc into life, and thereby help dissipate its accumulated energy throughout the localised energy matrix.

Chris walked over to the pool; he raised his arms in reverence to the Lunar deity and stood in silence. In his mind, he began summoning the goddess as he silently knelt down and planted our Earth Shrine. His task was complete.

The Sun & The Moon, The Hill & The Well

As the healing ritual drew to its inevitable close, a low-pitched humming sound undulated suddenly throughout the hill. Chris and Dave moved into the centre of the circle, ready to initiate the final stage of our quest - the symbolic exchange, the passing over of the Solar and Lunar energies, the final re-balancing factor.

Before us stood the semblance of two vast angelic figures each moving elegantly across the open landscape. I could see the colossal image of the Sun God, Luga, as he approached his kingdom, his sacred holy hill. Behind me, walking slowly towards the larger pool, was the graceful image of the Lunar goddess, her silvery mantle flashing vibrantly as she approached the domain of the holy well. I looked out across the pool, the full moon reflecting angelically across its tranquil surface. An overwhelming sensation of repose gently enveloped me, radiating throughout my consciousness, and leaving me totally at one with the pool. I gazed knowingly towards the team, I closed my eyes; we had completed our task and our quest was at an end.

Notes & Bibliography

The Awakening
1. The events surrounding this particular experience, only came into perspective during the final writing stages of this book. After reading through our original notes taken during the quest, a sudden and unprompted act of synchronicity, caused me to peruse through the vast collection of notes and micro-cassette tapes, which we had amassed earlier that year. Upon stumbling upon this particular experience, I felt that the whole encounter formed an interesting prophetic prologue to the story. But it must be remembered, these events occurred many months before our first visit to Baydon Hill and the inevitable formation of the group.

Chapter 1 - Three Swords
1. For a detailed account of the tale of Uther Pendragon's deception of Ygerna, see *Folklore Myths & Legends of Britain*. Readers Digest 1973, page 144, and Phillips & Keatman, *King Arthur – The True Story*. Arrow Books 1992, page 13.
2. Source material taken from: *Folklore Myths & Legends of Britain*. Readers Digest, page 144.
3. See Collins, Andrew *The Seventh Sword*. Century 1991 page 299.
4. For a full account of the discovery of the sword, see Collins, Andrew *The Seventh Sword*. Century 1991. Phillips, Graham & Keatman, Martin *The Green Stone*. Neville Spearman Ltd.
5. See 'King Arthur's Great Hall of Chivalry' free guide, facing page.
6. Ibid. facing page.

Chapter 2 - First Stirrings
1. Selected pseudonym incorporated to conceal the true identity of Baydon Hill.
2. Ibid.

Chapter 3 - Initial Contact
1. Most of the visualisation material presented within this account, will be granted a line space so as to isolate this material from the rest of the account.
2. Taken from Trudie's original hand written account of her peculiar experience. No micro cassette was used at this stage.
3. For a detailed account of the interaction of psychics around archaeological digs, please read Goodman, Jeffrey *Psychic Archaeology* Granada Books 1979.

Chapter 4 - The Magic of Baydon
1. Please refer to the original article which appeared in *Moonshine* magazine 1993, for a full account of the mysteries of Baydon Hill.
2. Selected pseudonym due to association with Baydon.
3. Ibid.
4. Please refer to original and full account featured in *Moonshine* magazine 1993.

Chapter 5 - The Lady In White
1. See Collins, Andrew *The Seventh Sword* Century 1991 'What is Psychic Questing?'
2. For a full explanation of the Questing phenomenon, see Collins, Andrew *The Seventh Sword* Century 1991.
3. Ibid.
4. Taken from a fascinating paper written by Dave Taylor.
5. See Collins, Andrew *The Seventh Sword* Century 1991 'What is Psychic Questing?'
6. For a full account of this extraordinary factual story, read Collins, Andrew *The Seventh Sword* Century 1991 and Phillips and Keatman *The Green Stone*.
7. Please note: for convenience, all dream-type experiences will be shown in Italics so as to separate them from all visual encounters.

Chapter 7 - The Holy Qabalah
1. For a superb introduction to the Qabalistic belief, please read: Andrews, Ted *Simplified Magic* Llewellyn Publications 1989, and Regardie, Israel, *A Garden Of Pomegranates* Llewellyn Publications, Second Edition 1970.
2. For a detailed investigation of the Qabalistic doctrines, see Regardie, Israel *The Golden Dawn* Llewellyn Publications, Sixth Edition, 1989.

Notes & Bibliography

Chapter 8 - The Serpent and 1947
1. See: Zalewski, Pat *Kabbalah of the Golden Dawn* Llewellyn Publications, page 10.
2. Please refer to Cooper, J.C. *An Illustrated Encyclopaedia Of Traditional Symbols* page 55-56 for a more detailed expose of the Dragon & the Serpent.

Chapter 10 - The Hilltop Meditations
1. After considering Simon's information during the final stages of this publication, I suddenly realised that his reference to Dionysus, could be considered as the bringer of balance. Dionysus is positioned at the sixth station of the Tree of Life, the balance point of the Tree.
2. Here again I realised whilst compiling the final manuscript, that this information formed a direct allusion to the Qabalistic concept of both the Sun (6) & the Moon (9).
3. At this point during our involvement with Baydon Hill, I can assure you that I had no prior knowledge of the pending development plan.

Chapter 11 - The Plot Thickens
1. Please refer to Collins, Andrew *The Black Alchemist* ABC Books 1988, for more detailed information relating to this notion.
2. Ibid. page 399.
3. Ibid. page 133, and Collins, Andrew *Alien Energy* ABC Books 1994 page 100.
4. Ibid.

Chapter 12 - In The Sanctuary of The Well
1. For More information concerning the 'dagger' please refer to the Postscript.

Chapter 14 - The Legend of St Kenelm
1. The whole account can be read in its entirety as featured within the *Douce Manuscript*. I have simply incorporated the more important aspects of this tale necessary for our story.
2. Taken from an article printed in *Mercian Mysteries* February 1994 written by Dave Taylor and myself.
3. Please refer to Bord, Janet & Colin *Sacred Waters* Granada Publishing 1985 chapter 3.
4. Ibid. Chapter 3.
5. Ibid.

Chapter 15 - The Crone
1. For a complete rendition of this ritual, please refer to Regardie, Israel *The Middle Pillar* Llewellyn Publications, seventh edition 1991.

Chapter 16 – The Winter Solstice
1. Zalewski, Pat *The Equinox & Solstice Ceremonies of the Golden Dawn* Llewellyn Publications 1992 pages 19 - 47.
2. Ibid.

Chapter 17 - The Golden Arrow of Sabrina
1. For a full explanation of the Cone of Power, please refer to Collins, Andrew *Alien Energy* ABC Books 1994 page 101.
2. It would appear that the bent pin is still in the hands of local authorities, except our research revealed that the alleged 'pin' appears to have been mislaid.

Chapter 20 - The Rollright Stones
1. Unfortunately, I have not been able to confirm or dismiss this suggestion of Joyce Newly.
2. Read Collins, Andrew *The Sword And The Stone* ABC Books 1982 page 15.
3. Ibid.

Chapter 21 - Meon Hill
1. Read Collins, Andrew *The Sword And The Stone* ABC Books 1982 page 43.
2. Ibid. page 44.

Chapter 23 - The Puzzle of Sabrina
1. See: Devereux, Paul *Shamanism And The Mystery Lines* Quantum Books 1992. Cooper, J.C. *An Illustrated Encyclopaedia Of Traditional Symbols* Thames & Hudson 1978.
2. Devereux, Paul *Shamanism And The Mystery Lines* Quantum Books 1992.
3. Ibid. chapter 4/5.

Chapter 24 - Final Preparations
1. This account was suitably constructed from a detailed report which Dave Taylor handed to me.

Chapter 25 - The Guardian
1. Please refer to King, John *The Celtic Druids' Year* Blandford 1994, page 137-8.

Recommended Reading List

Psychic Questing

Phillips, Graham & Keatman, Martin *The Green Stone.* Granada Publishing Ltd, London 1984.
Phillips, Graham & Keatman, Martin *The Eye Of Fire.* Grafton Books, London 1988.
Collins, Andrew *The Sword & The Stone.* ABC Books, Leigh-on-Sea, 1982.
Collins, Andrew *The Black Alchemist.* ABC Books, Leigh-on-Sea, 1988.
Collins, Andrew *The Seventh Sword.* Century Ltd. 1991.
Collins, Andrew *The Second Coming.* Century Ltd. 1993.
Andrews, Ted *How to Work With Spirit Guides.* Llewellyn Publications, 1992.
Collins, Andrew *Alien Energy.* ABC Books, Leigh-on- Sea, 1991.

Earth Mysteries & Folklore

Bord, Janet & Colin *A Guide To Ancient Sites In Britain,* Latimer New Dimensions Ltd, 1978.
Bord, Janet & Colin *Earth Rites* Granada Publications, 1982.
Bord, Janet & Colin *Sacred Waters* Granada Publications, 1985.
Bord, Janet & Colin *Ancient Mysteries of Britain,* Grafton Books, 1986.
Readers Digest, Folklore, *Myths & Legends of Britain,* The Readers Digest Association Ltd. 1973.
Richardson, Alan *Earth God Rising* Llewellyn Publications 1990.
Ashe, Geoffrey *The Mythologies of Great Britain.*

The Sun & The Moon, The Hill & The Well

Symbolism & Qabalah

Frazier, James *The Golden Bough,* Macmillan & Co ltd. 1922.
Fontana, David *Secret Language of Symbolism,* Pavilion Books, 1993.
Cooper, J. C. *Illustrated Encyclopaedia of Traditional Symbols,* Thames & Hudson Ltd, 1978.
Zalewski, Pat *Kabbalah of The Golden Dawn,* Llewellyn Publications 1993.
Fortune, Dion *The Mystical Qabalah* Aquarian Press 1987.
Crowley, Aleister *777 & Other Qabalistic Writings,* Samuel Weiser Inc. 1973.
Achad, Frater *Q.B.L.* Samuel Weiser Inc. 1922.
Regardie, Israel *A Garden of Pomegranates,* Llewellyn Publications, Second Edition 1970.
Regardie, Israel *The Middle Pillar,* Llewellyn Publications, Second Edition 1970.
Javane, Faith & Bunker, Dusty *Numerology & The Divine Triangle,* Para-research Inc, 1980.
Barrett, Clive *Egyptian Gods & Goddesses,* Aquarian Press 1992.
Crowley, Aleister *The Book Of Thoth,* Weiser Inc. 1974.
King, John *The Celtic Druid Year,* Blandford Books London 1994.

Occult Studies

Barrett, Francis *The Magus* Carol Publishing 1989.
Agrippa, Henry Cornelius *Three Books Of Occult Philosophy* edited Donald Tyson Llewellyn Publications 1993.
Conway, D.J. *Celtic Magic* Llewellyn Publications 1990.
Zalewski, Pat & Chris *The Equinox & Solstice Ceremonies of The Golden Dawn,* Llewellyn Publications 1992.
Andrews, Ted *Simplified Magic* Llewellyn Publications 1989.
Regardie, Israel *The Complete System Of Golden Dawn Magic* New Falcon Publications 1984.

Post Script '97

Having read *The Sun & The Moon, The Hill & The Well*, I accept that certain sections of this story require elaboration, in particular, the objective reality of this account. No doubt, the first thing that many readers will question having read this story, is whether or not the authenticity of the account warrants an accurate portrayal of the truth. My answer to this natural query is simple, yes; the story is an accurate representation of the events described herein, being written as it actually occurred, as seen from my own personal perspective.

The Sun & The Moon, The Hill & The Well undoubtedly questions the very boundaries of our perception of the world we live in. Yet this 'questioning' approach, I believe, represents a healthy, and equally objective attitude to the type of occurrences such as those portrayed within this story. Equally, I also believe, that there are countless occasions when logical thinking should be temporarily cast aside in preference to the complex process of intuition.

Over the past three years, I have slowly come to realise that countless individuals, from all walks of life, continually experience whispers of information; anomalous events, perceived in the form of dreams, intuitive feelings, visual concurrence, and/or direct psychic events.

Whilst most people, it would appear, simply pass these day-to-day encounters off as acts of sheer fanciful coincidence, Trudie, myself, and the rest of the group, agreed - in response to the collective series of events surrounding this story that we should simply accept these experiences, following them through to a natural, yet seemingly magical conclusion. As a direct result of this alternative approach, I believe that the quest for *The Sun & The Moon, The Hill & The Well* was given an intuitive breath of life, a subtle current of energy, which allowed the quest to evolve.

The Sun & The Moon, The Hill & The Well

What is of interest, however, is that contra to what some people may believe, the questing phenomenon remains a reality; a growing presence, which continues despite our own preconceptions of the countless feats it can often display. Nevertheless, one thing is for sure; the questing phenomenon remains amongst us and is here to stay.

On a more physical level, and perhaps as a direct result of our involvement with the quest, it would appear that Trudie, myself, and the group as a whole, have each encountered a sequence of changes that have deeply affected and shaped our lives, in a totally positive, beneficial, and spiritual way.

It is also interesting to note, whether coincidental or not, that the intended redevelopment plan set to dramatically affect both the sanctity of Baydon Hill and the localised environment as a whole, was suddenly scrapped just days after the ritual of the Sun & the Moon had been completed.

As the quest of *The Sun & The Moon, The Hill & The Well* evolved, not all the material acquired during this adventure was actively involved within this account, for example, the purported Golden Dagger, allegedly displaying the head of a serpent.

As far back as early '94, the period surrounding the initial imagery of the dagger, I had come to believe that perhaps this object would appear to us in the form of an 'apport' - an artefact or object believed by many, to manifest itself due to some form of psychic or mystical intervention. As the quest progressed, Dave, Trudie, and myself, had come to presume that perhaps the Golden Serpent Dagger, would be given to us as an indication marking the end of the quest. But that was not to be the case, and as the ritual of the Sun & the Moon drew to its inevitable close, no such artefact appeared.

However, during the early months of '97, and as the final editing stages of this book were being completed, a succession of bizarre synchronicities occurred, incidents which culminated in the possession of an Egyptian styled golden dagger; a short sword featuring the headpiece of a sun god, and complete with the resultant serpent imagery.

As a result of these remarkable synchronicities, and after moving away from our Kidderminster home, both Trudie and I, found ourselves immersed amidst a fresh current of psychic

Post Script '97

information pertaining to our new locality, material which, I must add, includes some really enticing allusions towards Catherine of Aragon, the first wife of Henry VIII. So perhaps as this book quietly draws to its predestined close, then from the quality and quantity of new material that we are receiving, maybe we are being guided forwards towards a new and exciting mystical adventure.

Mike Smith
Oak-Apple Day 1997

PS

It is my intention to compile a series of short manuals explaining many of the techniques described within this book. So if you feel like joining us, and honing your intuitive potential, ready to embark upon a possible quest within your own area, then by all means please keep in touch. If you feel that you have any information that you believe may be of use to us, or would simply like to be put on my forthcoming mailing list, then please feel free to contact me at the PO Box number listed below.

House of Isis Publications
PO Box 64
Stourport on Severn
Worcestershire
DY13 OYR

The Sun & The Moon, The Hill & The Well

INDEX

A

Aghma 59, 150
Akhenaten 159
Akhma 59, 74, 150
Albanactus 172, 173
Albany 173
Allah 120
Amrog 93
Aphrodite 26, 52, 108, 144
Archangel Michael 120, 136, 141
Area Development Plan 76
Arthurian Romances
    Arthur 3
    Book Shop 5, 6
    Gorlois 2
    Great Hall of Chivalry 3
    King Arthur 2-8, 14, 24, 25, 176
    Merlin 2, 3, 7
    Merlin's Cave 2,3
    Myrddin 3
    Uther Pendragon 2
    Ygerna 2
Ashe, Geoffrey 172
Astrological Correspondence
    Cardinal 45
    Fixed 45
    Mutable 45
Astrological Correspondences
    Cardinal Points .. 38, 45, 194, 195, 198
Aten 151, 159
Avebury 61
Aztecs 120

B

Badon 176
Balance of the Lion/Unicorn 165
Baltic Coast 142
Baydon Hill 7-11, 13-19, 24-27
   30, 31, 49, 57, 59-62, 64, 66, 68, 70
   85, 86, 88, 90, 91, 93, 111, 116, 117
   118, 122-126, 136-138,140-144, 147
   151, 152, 157-160, 165-168
   174, 176- 178, 180, 186, 187
    Heart of England? 158
    Secondary Site 79
    Solar Link 139
    Site Guardian 86
    Symbol on the Hill 91
Baydon Hill Meditation 70

6/9 the Hoards 72
    Analysis of 80
    Astral Imbalance 80
    Balls of Light 71, 80
    Celtic Crosses 72
    Dionysus, the Bringer of Balance 72
    Electrical Spheres of Light 80
    Psychic Frenzy 80
    Sacrificial Altar 73
    Stone Altar 73
    Tribe of Warriors 73
Baydon Manor 141, 166
Baydon/Gwevaraugh Link 160
Beacon Site 62
Bel - Belinus 180
Belonus 195
Beltane Ritual 168
    Preperation of 176
Bent Pins 109
Blue Oyster Cult 139
Bord, Janet and Colin 175
British Museum 34, 35, 37, 42, 45, 54, 60
Broadswords
    With Quest 93
Bromsgrove 98
Bull 86, 137
    Symbolism 138

C

Cambria 173
Camelford 2
Celtic
    Cross 58
    Earth Shrine 184, 196
    Festival of Beltane 150
    Festival of Samhain 76
Celtic festival
    Beltane 152
    Luga - Lughnasadh 136
    Samhain 150
Celtic Field Systems 26
Celtic God
    Luga 135, 136
    Lugh 135
    Yuga 135
Celts 26, 135-137, 142, 143
Ceremonial Short Sword 30
Cerenos 195

Index

Celtic
   Earth Shrine 153
Chapel of Fierbois 29
Chipping Norton 157
Christ 108, 110, 120
Christ - Sacrificed Lamb 120
Christ Church, Canterbury 105
Circle of Protection 71
Clent 95, 110, 143
Clent Hills 25
Cole, Alan 138
Cole, Alan - Bull Imagery 87, 88
Collins 159
Collins, Andrew 28, 30, 32, 37, 159
Cone of Light 35, 127
Cone of Power 128, 198, 199
Circle of Power 38
Cone of Energy 38
Consecration of Moonlight
   Sara 171
Corineus 173
Cornovil 26
Crossed Indian Feathers
   St Swithans Church 164
Crowley, Aleister 46, 47, 48
   54, 55, 136

D

Dagda 149, 150
Dead Sea Scrolls 47
Deep Breathing Technique 37
Devereux, Paul 175
Devils Spade Fall 100
Domnu 195
Doric 26, 70
Dove
   Symbol of 110
Dowsers 22
Dragon 60, 61
Dragon Energy 61
Dragon of the Moon 198
Dream of Old Crone 113
Druidism
   Druids 26, 138, 144
Druids Grove 26
   Norbury Woods 26
Dudley 98

E

Eagle 137, 151
Earl of Cornwall 2

Earth Mother 106, 109
Earth Mysteries 81
Egfrith 104
Egypt 23, 159
Egyptian
   Anch - Symbol of Life 36
Egyptian festival of Isis
   / Sirus / Ursa Major 108
Egyptian gallery 22, 35
Egyptian Pantheon
   Amoun Ra 35
   Canopic Jars 45
   Goddess Sekhmet .. 35, 36, 37, 54, 136
   Hathor 108
   Horus 45, 108
   Isis/ Hathor 109
   Osiris 110
   Sun-God Ra 120
   Thoth 35
Egyptian Shop - London 34
Egyptian/Greek Galleries 37
Egyptian / Greek Rooms
   British Museum 34
Elementary Vocal Technique 38
Energy Balance
   Re-Dressing Problem 144
Energy Re-Dress 144
Entity
   Three Horned Deity 94
Estrildis 173
Excalibur 6

F

Falcon Headed Sun Deity
   Invocation 123
Female Lunar Devotion 107
Fertility God
   Cernunnos 142
   Freyr 106, 142, 143
   Green Man 142
   Horned God 142, 143
   Ing 143
   Luga 143
   St Kenelm 143
Festival of Beltane 180, 185, 194
Festival of Samhain 180
Fibonacei Series 106
Fire 151
Fraser-Clark, Simon 27, 28
   62-65, 69, 72, 74-78, 85, 90, 93, 94
   96, 97, 121, 124, 131, 132, 151, 182

The Sun & The Moon, The Hill & The Well

191, 193, 194, 198
Imagery of Turner's Hill 85
Frederick Thomas Glasscock 4
Frozen Hill................................59

G

Genius Loci 82
Geomythical/Totemic Entity 82
Georgiadis, Graham 25, 176
Georgian Folly 9-11
   15, 18, 20, 58, 59, 72-75, 78, 79, 84
   86, 89, 92, 94, 123, 148, 169
   194
Georgian Folly Meditation
   Aghma 74
   Celtic Crosses 75
   Dark Entity 75
   Geomantic Landscape 75
   Image of a Henge 75
   Sacrificial Altar 75
   Small Henge 76
   Three Druid Figures 76
Germanic Ingnaeones 142
Goddess's
   Cybele 140
   Flora 140
   Isis 140
   Juno 140
   Hecate 140
   Here 140
   Demeter 140
   Frigga 140
   Walpurga 180
Golden Dawn...............................48
Golden Fleece - Jason.....................20
Golden Monarch - Discovery of 148
Great Rollright..........................162
Greco-Roman Entity 92
Greco-Roman God-form 92
Guardian of the Well 122
Guardian Spirit/Genius Loci 82
Guardian Spirits..........................81
Guardian/Black Knight 192
Guided Visualisation 35
Guinevere................................159
Gwendolen 172, 173
Gwevaraugh........................159, 160

H

Habren 173
Hallowed Heart of England................158
Hallowed Well..................122, 129
Hasbury Grove....................9
Hathor 107
Hephaestion 26
Hephaestus / son of Zeus 26
Hercules.......................150
Hereford and Worcester.........25
Holy Well......................109
Holy Well - Origin of Fertility 109
Holy Well Lore 110
Horned God...................120
Horrigan, John 31
Humber 173

I

Identity of Emblem 139
Inca's 120
Incense
   Mercury 82
   Saturn 70
Induction of The Talismans...168
Ing 142
   Cult of 142
   Identity of 142
   Possible Link With Kenelm 142
   Symbolic Meaning 142
Ing/Freyer
   Uniting Link 142
Ingon 83
Ingthon......................83
Inspector Fabian 166
Iron Age hill-fort..........7, 166
Irvine, Tracey 62, 65, 84, 85, 93
   117, 131, 144, 191, 197
Irvine, Tracey - Imagery of the Aten ..84
   Large Horns/Bull Horns 85
   Restore the Aten 84
Isis of Nature...............107
Isle of Purbeck..............31

J

Joan of Arc 29

K

Kamber 172, 173
Kenelmstow..................174
Kidderminster 7, 9, 27, 30, 40
King Arthur's Car Park 5, 7
King Arthur's Great Hall 3, 4

Index

L

Lancelot 6
Leo 136, 151
Leo/Baydon Link................................136
Lleu 136, 137
Localised Ancestral Spirit 81
Localised Energy Matrix................79, 81
Locrinus......................................172, 173
Loegria...173
London 28, 136
Long Compton....................................157
Lower Quinton 163, 166, 167
Ludd...158
Luga 141, 144, 149, 151, 152, 158
  175, 194, 195, 196
Luga/Mercury 142
Lugh/Luga 158
Luminifrous Ether 50
Lunar Cult 107, 134, 143
Lunar Talisman 186, 187

M

Magical Guided Tour 35
Marah...145
Marsham Lane...................................9, 11
Mary Queen of Scots 30
Mary/Marah Link 145
May Day 18, 151, 152, 180, 181, 185
  193, 194, 195
Mean Hill 118, 158
Meon Hill 158, 160, 162, 163, 165
  166, 167, 174
  Links With Baydon 166
Meon Murder Investigation................166
Meon/Baydon Hill
  Witchcraft/Occult Connection........166
Mercury 141
Merlin - Sword 6
Mickleton...26
Minotaur 138
Monolith 14, 15, 31, 59, 69, 72, 73
  74, 76, 78, 93, 123, 144, 194
  Symbol of The Sun 138
Monolith- Solar Worship.....................79
Mons Badonicus 25, 176
Moon 108, 141
Morgan...195
Mormons
  Mormon & Moroni 29
  Golden Texts 29
  Nephites...29

Smith, Joseph 29
Mother Goddess 109
Museum Street......................................34

N

Newley, Joyce 25, 157, 158,
  159, 160, 164
Numerical Sequence
  1947 _ 36, 42, 43, 44, 45, 46, 47, 48
  49, 54, 57, 60, 61, 136

O

Offa 104
Ogham Script......................................150
Oghma 148, 149, 150, 151, 178, 179
Old Crone 117, 118, 121, 123, 124
Old Norman Church 83
Old Post Office 3
Old Yew Tree..93

P

Palace of Minos 26, 70, 72, 138, 159
Paranormal
  Artefact Retrieval 32
Parapsychology 21, 22
Path of Leo 54
Pentagram of Fire 92
Perranporth 2
Phillips, Graham 28, 30, 159, 160
Place of the Dragon 58, 60, 61
Place Psychometry 78
Planet
  Mercury 82
  Saturn 139
Pontesbury 175
Pontesford Hill 175
Pope Leo III..105
Port-Issac 2
Prehistoric Energy Matrix 15
Protective Amulet 58
Psychic Abilities 28
Psychic Cleansing of Ritual Sites 32
Psychic Imbalance
  Baydon Hill 140
Psychic Phenomena..............................30
Psychic Phenomena - Study of 21
Psychic Questing.....................28, 29, 30
Psychic Questing Conference 28, 57
Psychic Questing Fraternity 81
Psychometry 22, 23, 64
Psycho-Spiritual Exercises 51

The Sun & The Moon, The Hill & The Well

Pythagoreans 45, 108

Q
Qabalistic Doctrines
   777 55
   Aimah 140
   Ain Soph Aur 50
   Aleph 56
   Amoun 53
   Angelic Beings 51
   Animals 51
   Astral Plane 52
   Astrological Correspondeces 51
   Binah................52, 139, 140, 141, 145
   Chesed..............................52, 53, 54
   Chokmah 52
   Colour Scales 51
   Daleth 46, 53
   Elemental Sphere 52
   Etz Chim 50
   Geburah 52, 54
   Hebrew Alphabet...............................51
   Hebrew Mystical Knowledge 50
   Hebrew Qabalah 46
   Hebrew root QBL 50
   Hod 52
   Holy Sephiroth 50, 107
   Jupiter 52, 53, 107
   Kether 51, 52
   Luna - Moon 107
   Macrocosm 50
   Malkuth 53
   Mars 52, 107
   Mercury...52, 107
   Moon 107, 108
   Netzach 52, 107, 108
   Perfumes 51
   Planetary names 51
   Poseidon 53
   Qabalah.........................46, 48, 49, 50
   Sephiroth........................50, 51, 52
   Sol - Sun 107
   Tarot 48, 51, 56
   Tav 56
   The Tree of Life 50
   Tiphareth 52
   Tith 55, 56, 60
   Tree of Life 139
   Venus...52, 107
   Western Magic 46
   Yesod..52, 107

Yod 56
Queen of Paradise 120

R
Reginald of Cornwall 3
Richard - Son of Henry 111 3
Ritual
   Qabalistic Cross 116, 185
   The Sun & The Moon............152, 197
River Stour
   Links With Baydon/Meon..............167
   Origin of 174
Rollright Stones.........156, 157, 160 - 165
   Group Visit 161
   Method of Entering Circle 161
   Presence of Eerie Blue Light 162
Roman Sky God 137
Romans 143
Romsley...196
Rookwood Arms Public House 66, 68,
   69, 73, 182, 184, 187, 191
Rosicrucians 63
Ruskin Hotel............32, 34, 67, 116, 117

S
Sabrina
   Allegories of 175
   Circle of Ancient Stones 128
   Construction of Circle...................127
   Crossed Indian Feather 129
   Devotional Pins 129
   Golden Arrow of....................131, 134
   156, 157, 167, 172, 176
   Golden Serpent Dagger...................90
   Location of 176
   Location of Bent Pin.....................134
   Sabren 172
   Seeking The Golden Arrow 175
   The Old Tree 130
   The Puzzle of 164
   The River Severn...........................172
   Two Pools 130, 131, 132
   Two Pools of Water.......................132
Sacred Pit...58
Sara 171
Satan - Adversary of God 60
Saturn Emblem 140, 141
Saxon Goddess Walpurga 180
Scale of Seven 107
Serpent 55, 60, 61
Serpent & Dragon 60

Index

Serpent Energy 144
Serpent Power 61
Serpentine Avenues 61
Severn/Trent Valley 25
Shamanic Flight................................174
Sidhe 180
Sidhs 149
Sign of Leo 54
Site Guardian......................................82
Site Guardian of Baydon Hill........76, 81
  85, 86, 91
Site Guardian of Hill.........................117
Sky Gods 137
Smith, Daniella............2, 6, 9, 10, 11, 41
  42, 99, 133
Smith, Hollie 2, 6, 10, 11, 41, 42, 99
Smith, Joseph 29
Smith, Mike 8, 11, 41, 47
  63, 64, 69, 76, 131, 134, 149, 157
  158, 164, 166, 190, 193, 194
Smith, Mike - imagery of Guardian 86
Smith, Mike - The Other One....157, 158
  160, 166, 167, 174, 181
Smith, Trudie 2, 4-6, 8-11, 13-20
  27, 32, 34, 40-42, 44, 47, 57-59, 62
  64-69, 73 75, 76-77, 78, 82-84, 86, 88
  90, 95-99 111, 112, 114, 124, 125
  127, 130-132, 134-136, 142, 146,
  148, 149 150, 153-155, 160, 164
  166, 177 181, 192
  Confirmation of The Church............95
  Guardian/Black Knight 154
  Nightmare 153
  Imagery of Church 84
  Wheelbarrow 84
  Wooden Lych-Gate 84
Solar King 123
Solar Talisman...................187, 188, 190
Son of Light 120
Sons of Brutus...................................172
Sphere of Light 82
Sphere of Orange Yellow Light..........116
Spirit Guide
  Marianne..............67, 72, 91, 118, 126
  128, 129, 130, 145
  Marianne - Analysis of Name........145
St Catherine..29
St George..60
St Kenelm
  Allusion To The Legend of............138
  Analysis of 142

Apparent age 104, 107
Askobert 101, 102
Baydon/Kenelm Link 138
Brakspear, Harold 97
Burenhilda..............................101, 104
Church 88, 90, 95, 96, 97, 115, 125
  131, 144, 153, 187
Cow-Vale...102
Douce Manuscript...........................100
Expansion of Analysis 144
Feast Day..108
Gargoyles..98
Holy Kenelm 102
Holy Well 89, 98, 109, 114, 115
  125, 129, 130, 144, 157, 167, 181
Holy Well - Swords........................117
Hypothesis..143
Induction of The Talisman 170
Kenelm...........................101-105, 154
Kenelmstow 98, 105, 143, 153
Kenulph..........................101, 104, 105
Legend of St Kenelm's Furrow......181
Link with Seven 144
Location/Description of Church 97
Oswald..99
Pass 88
Pope Leo Junior 103
Possible Baydon Link 142
Quendryda.....................101, 102, 104
Red Cow Inn 98, 105
Ritual Sacrifice 107, 111
Sacred Spring 98
Sacred Well 153
Sandstone figure 98
Sandstone Tympanum 97
Solar King.....................106, 110, 111
Kenelm's Day 98
The Legend of.................................101
Tudor Porch Way 97
Village of Romsley 88, 97
White Dove 103
Wlfwin..99
Wlwene..101
Wooden Lych-Gate 97
Saturn; symbol 141
St Leonard 60
St Materiana's Church.........................3
St Michael 136
St Peter's Church..............................104
St Swithan's Church 163, 165
  The Entity - John 164

215

Stella Maris 144
Stone Altar.....................................92, 148
Sumerian Belili 180
Sun and the Moon 38, 84, 123, 151
    155, 165, 166, 178, 182, 185
Sun-face 18, 148, 150, 151
Symbolism of the Dragon 60
Symbols of Cernunnos
    Bull 142
    Horned Viper................................142
    Link With Solar God.....................142
    Ram 142
    Stag 142

T

Talisman..152
Taylor, Dave............63- 66, 68-71, 73-78
    81, 83, 85-88, 92-96, 99, 104, 113
    114, 121-125, 130-132, 134, 138
    146, 148, 149, 150-152, 155-158
    160-162, 165, 168-171, 177-179
    182-189, 191-200
    Imagery of an Old Church 86
    Imagery of the Woman in Black......92
    Three Keys of Equilibrium 93
    Temple of Light. 39, 196
    Temple of the Holy Ghost...................53
Tetractys...45
Thought Forms/Elemental Forms 82
Three Broadswords............6, 16, 89, 198
Three Horned Deity............................140
Three Swords.......................................183
    Dream of Triangle 93
    Ritual Charging 121
    Suggestion of Ritual Charging 93
Tintagel 2, 3, 4, 5, 7, 8, 10, 34, 184
Trevena 2
Tuatha 149
Turner's Hill 85, 90, 91, 131
Tutankhamen 159

U

Urban Shamanism 30
Ursa Major...108

V

Village of Clent 86
Visual Imagery
    Ancient Stone Circle 156
    Visualisation to Seek Identity of
    Guardian 146

Visualisation/Meditation 66
    alien-like qualities 21
    Angelic Form 33
    Concentric wheels of light 15
    Dream-like Experience 34
    Eight Tentacles of Light 15, 210
    External intelligence............20, 29, 30
    Golden Crucible 37
    Greek Temple 37
    Guardian Intelligences 32
    Museum - Visualisation 42
    Orange Ball of Light........................67
    Orange sphere of vibrant light 14
    Pools of murky water 17
    Psychic information 19, 21, 28, 118
    Spoken Visualisation 35

W

Waldron, Ian 30, 32, 34, 35
Walpurgis Night..................................180
Walton, Charles 166
Ward, Richard 31
Web of Ancient Power Sites 32
West Midlands...............................25, 40
Whale, Chris.................... 4-10, 136, 137
Wheel..151
Wilfred..103
Winchcombe Abbey 103, 105
Winchcombe Parish Church 105
Winter Solstice 120
    Meditation..............117, 124, 125, 184
Woodleigh 9, 66
Woodleigh Estates 26
Woodleigh Woods 166
Worcestershire village of Woodleigh 6
Wright, Chris 65, 68, 69, 71, 75
    77, 85, 96, 98, 114, 115, 121, 122
    124, 131-133, 160, 162, 163, 182
    184-189, 190, 191, 198, 199

Y

Yew Tree Meditation
Ball of Blue Light 78
Balls of Blue/White Energy 78
Flying Sensation 78
Protection Ceremony...........................78
Yew Trees 25, 94
Yngoi 142
Yugar 59
Yule 120